MW00572159

PRAISE
FOR THE MINDS AND WILLS OF MEN

"Jeff Lanier brilliantly evokes the energy and excitement of the New York art world in this Cold War thriller with an artistic twist. Along the way he gives us fascinating insights into Abstract Expressionism and the power of art to communicate values and ideas."
—Ross King, *New York Times* bestselling, award-winning author of
The Judgment of Paris, Brunelleschi's Dome, and
Michelangelo and the Pope's Ceiling

"Lanier intelligently limns not only the American obsession with Communist infiltration in the wake of World War II, but also the emergence of abstract expressionism in the U.S. This is an exceedingly intelligent and unpredictable story, one that astutely combines a love of art with an exciting tale of intrigue. A mesmerizing spy thriller, thoughtful and dramatic."
—*Kirkus Reviews*

"Truth can be stranger than fiction, it's true—but great fiction can also be inspired by true events. In this must-be-read-to-be-believed book, Lanier brings the real story of art as a key player in mid-century American politics and international relations. Sweetened with romance, intrigue, and historical knowledge, this book is a fun romp for readers of all stripes."
—Jennifer Dasal, author of *ArtCurious: Stories of the Unexpected,
Slightly Odd, and Strangely Wonderful in Art History*

"*For the Minds and Wills of Men* is a captivating tour through the art world of postwar New York City, blended with an enthralling whodunit that leaves you guessing until the end."
—*Glasstire Magazine*

"Jeff Lanier's terrific *For the Minds and Wills of Men* sweeps readers into 1950s New York City where abstract art is thought to contain messages to help enemies destroy democracy in America. Lanier skillfully and effortlessly captures the era, but his outstanding talents are his vivid descriptions of paintings and his keen understanding of the avant-garde art world. A fresh voice and exciting storyteller, Lanier's 'who-stole-it' mystery is of the highest order."

—Ann Weisgarber, award-winning author of
The Glovemaker and *The Promise*

"Jeff Lanier has written a true unicorn of a novel. Taken as historical fiction, *For The Minds and Wills of Men* works on a fantastically authentic level, as its setting—1950s New York City, amid the Cold War milieu of paranoia, post-war patriotism, and the rise of abstract expressionism—is rendered utterly convincingly."

—Tyler Stoddard Smith, author of *Whore Stories*

"Author Jeff Lanier's easy-to-read writing style urges the reader on while authentically replicating the chaotic feeding-frenzy feel of the times... The story is filled with memorable characters, both fictional and historical figures... With its '50s-noir flavor, engaging down-to-earth characters, and enticing art world plot, *For the Minds and Wills of Men* is highly recommended for readers of mystery fiction, historical fiction, or political thrillers, and especially those readers interested in American modern art and abstract expressionism."

—*Lone Star Literary Life*

"Finding a historical mystery novel that utilizes history as a central mechanism of its dramatic impetus is a rare delight indeed, and Jeff Lanier achieves this beautifully through his thrilling novel where art meets espionage. The description of each person, time, and place is second to none, with vivid descriptions that bring the world around Will and Liz to life as vividly as the art which surrounds them. I found the work educational as well in terms of art history and the cultural and social impacts that the fear of Communism had in the 1950s the world over. This was also wonderfully displayed in the timely, well-penned dialogue and narration. *For the Minds and Wills of Men* is a superb read that I would certainly recommend to fans of sophisticated mysteries with plenty of atmospheric and accurate historical detail that only enhances the storyline."

—*Reader's Favorite*

FOR THE
MINDS
AND WILLS
OF
MEN

A NOVEL

JEFF LANIER

Boyle
&
Dalton

Book Design & Production:
Boyle & Dalton
www.BoyleandDalton.com

Hardback ISBN: 978-1-63337-609-0
Paperback ISBN: 978-1-63337-610-6
E-Book ISBN: 978-1-63337-611-3

Printed in the United States of America
1 3 5 7 9 10 8 6 4 2

For my wife, Erin, and kids,
Henry, Georgia, and Charlie.

OUR AIM IN THE COLD WAR is not conquering of territory or subjugation by force. Our aim is more subtle, more pervasive, more complete. We are trying to get the world, by peaceful means, to believe the truth. That truth is that Americans want a world at peace, a world in which all people shall have opportunity for maximum individual development. The means we shall employ to spread this truth are often called "psychological." Don't be afraid of that term just because it's a five-dollar, five-syllable word. "Psychological warfare" is the struggle for the minds and wills of men.

—*President Dwight D. Eisenhower*

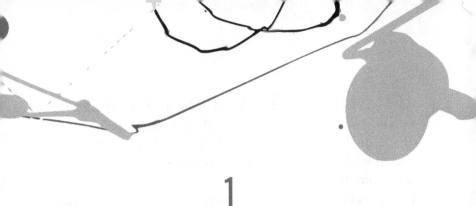

1

MARCH 1953

WILL OXLEY had questioned his decision at times. Why not sell cars? Work for Chevrolet? Everyone bought cars after the war. That's where the money was. Chrome, billet grilles, and radios. Mercury. Lincoln. Studebaker. The Ford Crestline Victoria. But instead, he had started his one-man art division at All American Insurance to protect paintings.

He sat back on the vinyl seat as his cab sped toward the Third Avenue elevated, the last iron relic of the steam-powered trains that threaded through Manhattan like a soot-stained ribbon, winding through the Bowery and up Third Avenue to Harlem. He hadn't expected a stolen painting from the Stable Gallery. Unlike the galleries selling Monets and Picassos on Sixth Avenue, where sales had doubled since the war, the Stable Gallery was new and on the fringe, showing modern, avant-garde artists, nothing like his other clients. The green iron girders of the el loomed over the avenue as he passed under. The jostling of the cab only worsened as it ran along the cobblestone streets of the Village and did not let up until they reached the newly paved Second Avenue with its fourth-floor walk-ups built after Will had returned from the war, when the paintings began to mean something to him.

Will bounced on the seat as the cab careened up FDR Drive and along the murky-green East River. The stench of truck diesel mixed with fresh fish and sour trash floated in through the cracked window. Dockhands pushed dollies along the pier, the same pier he had waited on to board the battleship convoy to Liverpool. The memories were fresh, as if eight years hadn't passed. He had packed weeks in advance, eagerly waiting to receive his deployment date. Then there was the farewell dinner with his dad at the Lexington Diner, a year of basic training, the staging in England, and on to Omaha Beach as an infantry replacement—twenty-nine days after Normandy.

Today, on the dock, workers cleaned and restocked a freighter tied down by rope woven thicker than his leg. As FDR curved around the wharf, the newly developed Stuyvesant apartment complex towered before him; a thousand windows textured the buildings with uniformed consistency, punctuated here and there with tattered white curtains. Will's cab sped past the United Nations, which rose from the bedrock like a green glass curtain, then lurched left and carried him into Midtown, past the Waldorf Astoria, MoMA, and the Stork Club, before tossing him out at the Stable Gallery on Fifty-Seventh Street.

Elaine Carter stood in front of the gray stone building. Her straight, coffee-black hair gave her an arresting appearance, framing a face some men would describe as unattractive, long with sunken eyes.

"Will Oxley!" she said as he stepped from the cab. "Thank God you've come. You're absolutely the best." Will had learned that Elaine shrewdly overcame her odd looks with profuse flattery. She told everyone they were absolutely the best before turning to the next fabulous person. She dusted her hands on the back of her jeans, wrapped her arms around his chest, and gave him a hug with great animation.

When she released him, Will smiled at her. Slightly crooked, his smile turned the corner of his mouth up on the right side as if he were in the middle of a wink, often giving the impression the conversation was more intimate than he intended, yet he always gave the smile with sincerity. It made his square face, one that might otherwise get lost in the crowd, rather pleasant and memorable. His saddle-brown hair was cut short like most men's, and he wore a modest suit with a handkerchief in his back pocket.

"Why don't you show me where they broke in," he said.

Elaine took hold of his arm, intertwining hers with his. "Can you believe it? My preview for the MoMA exhibit opens in four days, and here I am dealing with this."

She led him along the large-cut gray stone wall of the gallery, which had served as a livery for horses back when commercial stables extended the length of Manhattan. After horse and carriage transportation waned, the building was converted to a short-lived mannequin warehouse. Then it languished for years, empty until Elaine fashioned the space into an art gallery.

"It's dreadful what's happened," Elaine said. Then, feigning an urgent whisper, she leaned in for emphasis. "I've told no one, Will. A gallery must uphold its reputation. Where would I be without my reputation?" She stopped mid-thought, pursed her lips together, and then added, "Well, I did call the police, but they were completely incompetent. Can you imagine?"

Will could. After six years in the business, he knew that art thefts were eccentric cases. And unless the investigator was good, unless he cared, there was little chance for recovery and almost no chance of catching the thief, a fact that provided little motivation for the police. But Elaine had done what he had told her to; she would need the police report for the insurance claim.

"What did they say?" he asked, expecting little.

"Nothing. Absolutely nothing." Elaine waved dismissively. "They came out and asked questions, took some photographs, and had me fill out ungodly amounts of paperwork. Just look at my hand." She unrolled her hand in display as evidence of her torture.

"All they did was log it in," he said, obliging Elaine's dramatics with a concerned glance. "Now they'll sit on the report and wait for a lead to fall on their desk. This is an ordinary robbery to them, like a stolen car. They see it as a victimless crime, so they won't waste much energy trying to solve it."

Elaine groaned and rolled her eyes, placing two fingers on her temple. "They had no idea what they were doing. They took up half my morning. But I know you can fix this. They say this is what you're good at."

And he was, but success hadn't come easy. For seven months after starting the art insurance division at All American Insurance, he'd stared out of his office window twenty-three floors above Broadway and Wall Street with nothing to show for his time and effort. No clients, no calls. He'd persevered because of what paintings had come to mean to him.

After returning from the war, he would walk along the streets of Manhattan, trying to clear his head of the images that flashed before him without warning, and he often found himself in a museum, away from the noises of the crowded city. He would sit in front of one small Monet and study the tiny, broken brushstrokes that created a soft impression of a sunrise over a misty maritime scene. A blood-orange early morning sun cast its warm glow over a blue-gray harbor as two black fishing boats floated on the tranquil bay, their shadows dotting the water. Will imagined himself standing at the harbor's edge alone, gazing out over the sea, not a sound in the air but the soft wind rolling over the water. When he lost himself in those moments, the memories of the hedgerows and the sound of bullets and tanks would fade, the darkness of the war would lift, and his mind would clear, if only for an hour.

He had fought his boss, Lou Pritchett, for a year to let him start the art division. He did not mention the war or the nightmares or the need to protect the moments of peace that kept these memories at bay. That pain he kept to himself, burying the hurt deep in the darker corners of his mind. Rather, he discussed rising art prices and the growing market.

The fact that Will had to recover the paintings made Pritchett dislike the idea. Why do you have to play *art detective?* Pritchett would say with a sarcastic tone. Will's answer was always the same. Unlike other insured valuables, when a painting was stolen, there was no replacement. There is only one *Woman with a Hat* by Matisse. There is only one *Impression, Sunrise* by Monet. Therefore, he had to recover the original. There was no one else. The police wouldn't bother themselves with a stolen painting, and if Will wanted to continue having clients, to insure works of art, to protect them, he had to recover the paintings. A thief's goal was to sell the painting back into the market for quick cash; and Will needed to find it before the canvas changed hands, or the picture could disappear, hidden away in a warehouse or a brownstone, only resurfacing years later when everyone had stopped searching for it.

Eventually, after determining the business made financial sense, Pritchett let him make sales calls. But not until Christie's auction house sold a painting for a record three hundred thousand dollars did collectors take notice of their art's value. A month later, Will recovered a Renoir oil sketch that had been stolen from a wealthy collector's home. By posing as a buyer, Will helped the police make a dramatic arrest at the maître d' stand of Le Coq Rouge. After a splash about the recovery in the newspaper, people began to call, and Will began to insure their art. Since then, he had built a good book of clients—galleries, museums, wives of Wall Street bankers, and collectors with family money.

When he and Elaine reached the far end of the warehouse, she pointed to a service door.

"They came through the storage entrance. It was wide open this morning."

Will ran his hand along the thin edge of the door, his thin fingers sliding down the smooth, dark wood coated thick with lacquer. At first, nothing struck him as out of place—no signs of a break-in, no splintered wood, no evidence of forced entry. He bent down on one knee and angled his head, peering at the face of the lock.

"What is it?" Elaine asked.

Will pointed to a clean drill hole in the lock. "They drilled straight through the teeth of the cylinder. Not too fancy, but it required the right tools. This theft took some planning."

Will rose and glanced back down the building's facade. The scene did not make sense. Something didn't feel right, like when you walk into a familiar room and something is out of place, but you can't put your finger on what. To Will, the building resembled a fortress more than an art gallery. The heavy stone facade had few windows at street level and two heavy bay doors, unlike the high-end galleries on Sixth Avenue, which had large windows that would be easy to break. Those galleries were where a thief could make money.

Will pushed open the door and stepped into the large, cold storage room. The rawness of the space did not surprise him, but its neatness did. He had expected a mess from the break-in, debris thrown across the concrete floor or broken shelving, but none of those signs were evident.

Will surveyed the room, trying to put the scene together, and Elaine followed his gaze. A floor-to-ceiling rack, divided like a grid, stood against the exposed brick wall. The open slots were empty since the paintings were out in the gallery. Opposite the rack stood two large metal shelving units with sculptures not currently on display. On the floor in front of the shelves sat a large wooden rolling drum. And in the center of the room stood six wooden crates, each the size of a door but almost a foot wide. The storage room revealed nothing Will had expected, no broken frames, no empty spaces on the walls, no overturned shelves.

He pulled a crumpled pack of cigarettes from his suit jacket, tapped one out, and lit it. The familiar sting of smoke rushed through his nostrils as he exhaled.

"Is this how you found it?" he asked. "Did you clean up?"

"God, no. I haven't had time. I've been dealing with the police and trying to prepare for the exhibit."

"But I don't understand. Where's the mess? What's been stolen?"

"This way." Elaine led him across the floor until the second row of crates came into view. One crate lay on its side, pried open at the top, its interior straw packing spewed out onto the floor. A few feet away, the missing painting's stretcher boards had been discarded, snapped and splintered.

Will turned to study the rest of the storage room. "None of the other crates were opened? Was nothing from the racks or shelves touched?" he asked, surprised. He could not imagine why a thief would bother with the crates. Breaking into one would take too much time.

"Just the Jackson Pollock, thank God. The warehouse next door receives shipments at four in the morning. The noise from the delivery trucks must have startled them."

"Maybe." But Will considered the answer too convenient.

Jackson Pollock had hit the cover of *Life* magazine a few years before and had created several significant pieces, but Will hadn't heard much of him since. Other paintings, many of which were more expensive, leaned against the painting racks out in the open and hung on the walls in the exhibition space, making them much easier to take.

"These are storage crates, right?" he asked, searching for a starting point.

"Shipping. We leave the paintings in the crates until we hang them in the gallery."

"And the big drum?"

"That's how Pollock transports his larger paintings. They come in the drums, and we stretch them onto the frames. It's half a day's work, depending on the number of paintings."

"But the stolen Pollock came from a crate?"

Elaine nodded. "It was an earlier work, not one of the large ones. Maybe six feet by three."

"Less prominent?"

"Yes, but still beautiful, mostly black and white with an undercoat of yellow and gray, some muted blue-green."

"Do you have a photograph?"

"In the back. The Bowers loaned the piece for the exhibit."

Will took pause. He recollected what he knew of the Bower name from the occasional article in the *Wall Street Journal*. Frank Bower headed Bower Manufacturing, which bought cotton and wool from textile mills and developed fabrics that it sold to clothing producers. They were the biggest fabric producer in the country. Elizabeth Bower, his daughter, had started the Bower Foundation a few years ago to promote the arts and provide financial support to exhibits like Elaine's. They had supported several MoMA exhibits over the last couple of years.

Will pulled the gallery's file from his satchel and flipped the pages, searching for the value of the painting. He flipped through once, then again, but didn't find the Pollock. "When did it come in?" he asked.

"Four days ago."

Will considered what he knew of the painting—small, relative to other paintings in the gallery; modern, not an impressionist or American realist. People paid money for those types of paintings, a picture with a subject matter, a frame they could hang on their living room wall. But this odd collection of New York painters was barely recognized in the art world, much less outside it. "Just based on size and type, I would value it at approximately six hundred and fifty dollars."

"That sounds right."

"Not a bad score for someone who probably makes twelve hundred a year. It's quick cash." Most paintings could be fenced within a few weeks. But still, more expensive paintings hung out in the open, untouched.

"The larger Pollock in the gallery space is valued at three thousand, wouldn't you say?" he asked.

"Absolutely."

"So why leave them alone?" he said, almost to himself. As soon as he asked the question though, he knew the answer; the other paintings were gigantic. But before he could answer aloud, Elaine had already turned toward the main gallery.

She pushed through a wide door at the front of the storage room and led him into the back of the gallery. The familiar smell of fresh oil paint, chalky concrete floors, and gray cigarette smoke surrounded Will. The whitewashed brick columns broke the space into three large open bays, each the size of a small gallery.

Massive unframed canvases stretched across the walls of the gallery. The images painted on them were impulsive and disturbingly flat, smeared and scratched across the stark surfaces. The vibrant colors of some fought with the monochromatic black and white of others. Paint had been dripped, splashed, or splattered onto the surfaces with abandon. Will absorbed the images, overwhelmed by their aggressiveness and size. Most spanned from floor to ceiling. They were the wildest paintings he had ever seen.

Elaine led him to the back of the gallery and stopped in front of a canvas that swallowed the entire wall. The enormity of it overtook Will—almost seventeen feet wide and half as high.

Will had never bothered to study a Pollock up close. Jarring and discordant, the paintings did not calm the mind like his Monet. Splatters of paint. Black and white with red and yellow. An impulsive and knotted mess. He did not see the attraction. Most people didn't. To Will, the sinewy paint appeared to have been flung on the canvas with no thought at all, as if it were the drop cloth of another painting. Something a nine-year old could do. The pooled paint seemed to have been poured right out of the can in certain spots, requiring no talent at all. The image contained no more than wild lines and whips of paint. Complete randomness. Not the type of painting Will would expect to be stolen.

"You can't tuck that under your coat," he said.

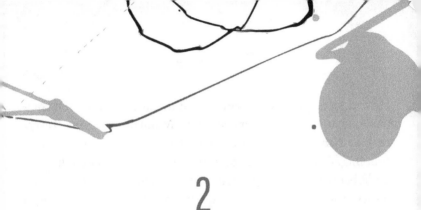

2

IRA FENTON paced the alley outside the Artist Equity Union in Hell's Kitchen, pulling on his third cigarette. The tip glowed in the darkness that persisted despite the two electric lights hanging from the fire escape. The stench of onion and stale beer did not bother him as much as the filth that walked in and out of the strip bars a few blocks away.

He checked his watch again. Twelve past ten, three minutes later than last time he had checked. Shit. He had been on eight raids since he had started with the private investigative firm ALERT, and the damned FBI contact arrived late every time. This was a situation for which he had no patience. There was no reason they should not already be inside. Waiting out in the open made them too easy to notice.

A high-pitched sizzle of a dying light bulb fought through the thick night air. Ira looked up at the streetlight above his men across the alley and watched the bulb flicker then go out with a sharp pop. The two men paced back and forth with their hands shoved deep into their coat pockets. They both had joined ALERT with Ira after he lost the union election at New York Steam. The union newsletter called his loss a humiliating defeat given Ira's years with the steam service company.

But losing the election made it easy to leave and join ALERT. Ira would never work for a company with a commie-run union.

He had spent thirty years with New York Steam, one of two companies that brought steam power to Manhattan—from Battery Park to Ninety-Sixth Street, Grand Central to the Empire State Building. A hundred miles of steam pipe now penetrated the city's underbelly, making it possible to press clothes, clean restaurant dishes, and sterilize hospital equipment. It was a perfect target for the Russians, a core of the city's infrastructure as important as the water systems. No one had questioned why the city required loyalty oaths from fishermen at the city's reservoirs. What if they were Commies trying to poison the drinking water while pretending to fish for brown trout? Ira had no intention of helping the Commies taking control of the city's steam power. He had worked his way up from a pipe fitter and given it everything he had, including late nights away from his family. By the end, Ira supervised the main station at Kips Bay, along the East River, and that bullshit article on his defeat was the thanks he got.

The unions were riddled with Communists, even if no one would admit it. The Russians were infiltrating the unions to cripple the country with riots and strikes and rate increases. They wanted to overthrow the government and ruin the country. They had to be stopped. After they announced the election results, when Ira stood up and yelled, "Damn Commies," the room went silent. He told his boss the same when he quit the next day, though spilling the coffee cup when he shoved the desk was an accident. His boss had stood there staring at him, not saying a word in response, and in Ira's mind, his silence sharpened his guilt. Communists were inside New York Steam. They had taken control of the union, and his boss was too scared to act.

Now Ira, standing underneath a fire escape, was a part of the solution, working to eradicate the vermin. He had brought his tools and could go inside the building on his own. But he risked getting pulled off the job, and he could not let that happen again.

At the sharp clack of a man's heels echoing in the street, Ira looked up to see a slim man dressed in a charcoal suit approaching from Broadway. When he reached them, Ira flicked his cigarette to the curb, almost hitting the man's shoe.

"You're late." Ira's voice was tight with impatience.

The man shrugged.

"We could handle this ourselves," Ira continued.

"You know how it goes. The boss says one of us has to be on every black bag job."

Black bag job. That was what they called it. But they were illegal break-ins, Ira knew that much—gathering information on subversive targets. The team worked at night, which Ira didn't mind. He had spent most of his early years as a pipe fitter down in the manholes, working with his blowtorch underneath the city in the dark. Besides, the night work left him his days to listen to the HUAC trials on his Firestone radio, hour by hour. These trials fortified his resolve. He relished listening to the committee members' speeches and the pathetic mumbling of the guilty on trial, sitting there on the stand trying to hide their secrets.

"Then why does Hoover bother to hire us?" Ira asked.

"Hey!" The man shot up a quick hand. "No one said the name Hoover. And I'm not here. You're not here. Got it? Private investigation means you don't exist. Not to us, anyway."

Ira rolled his eyes. J. Edgar Hoover's men acted like Ira's team was incompetent every time, but the FBI hired ALERT as contractors anyway because they didn't want to dirty their own hands. ALERT left no trail back to the FBI, and as a result, the FBI came across as clean and respectable. Private blacklisters were what the FBI called them. The notion that the FBI was uninvolved was bullshit. But what did Ira care? As long as they were rooting out the communists.

"Are you going to do this, or am I?" Ira asked.

The man brushed past Ira and stepped to a gray metal delivery door. While he worked the lock, Ira searched the street for movement, ready to alert the others if someone started down the alley.

Hoover's man turned and laughed. "Relax, Ira. No one walking through Hell's Kitchen cares enough to pay attention to what we're doing."

A minute later, the lock clicked open, and the four men stepped inside. The heavy door slammed shut behind them, and Ira started breathing again. From here, he expected the job to be easy like the others. Names. Associations. Anything that showed the artists having worked on projects with Communist propaganda. And they didn't even need that much. All they needed was something to create guilt by association. Finding that association was a matter of splitting up, searching the premises, and diving into their records.

Ira switched on his flashlight, which revealed a small kitchenette with a refrigerator and two hot plates sitting on a counter. He pushed past his men and stepped through the kitchen into the Artist Equity Union's main office.

Long and thin, the office opened to his left, with the front door and three storefront windows punctuating the street-facing wall. Small wooden desks crowded the main room, each revealing the personality of its daytime occupant—a stack of papers neatly aligned along one desk edge, an empty coffee cup to be filled in the morning, high-heeled shoes tucked underneath.

Directly in front of him, a wooden staircase led up to an open loft. Ira had no doubt that if incriminating evidence were found, it would be in the file cabinets upstairs. He waved his men onward, and as they climbed, he crossed to the first desk on the main floor. When he yanked on the handle, the side drawer held firm. With his interest piqued, Ira pulled out a small pocketknife, went down on his knee, and twisted the blade into the keyhole.

The latch clicked, and he threw open the drawer. Inside, several rows of manila folders hung on metal slides, each carefully labeled. He fingered across the folders, finding nothing more than empty envelopes and bills containing account numbers he didn't need. He slammed the drawer shut and glanced up at his men.

As they worked through the file cabinets, their flashlights flickered and flashed like lightning bugs caught in a glass jar. He turned to the front windows and then looked back to the balcony. In a quiet voice, he told them to keep their lights down so as not to be seen from the street. They could not afford to be caught. And if they were, the government man would leave them out to dry. Ira knew that for sure. His men pulled drawers open and threw papers on the floor; they always left a mess. Raids were common now, which meant they never bothered to tidy up. But targets never dared speak of a raid the next morning, because no one wanted it known they had been the target of an investigation.

The younger one, Sam Rainey, shouted over the balcony. "Found something!"

But before Sam could explain, a heavy metallic knock on the front window silenced him. Ira turned toward the front. At the window, he could make out a silver badge and tie clasp, a cop pressing against the glass with his hands cupped around his eyes, struggling to peer into the dark room. Heat radiated across Ira's face, and he whipped back toward his men.

"Turn 'em off," he said in a harsh whisper. He dropped to the floor and ducked down behind the desk. "Get down."

Hoover's man disappeared into the kitchenette. Sam and Milton dropped prostrate on the loft floor without a word. Nobody made a sound. With the air-conditioning off for the night, Ira could hear nothing more than his own breath. He pressed his back against the desk and closed his eyes tight. He couldn't let this fail. His outburst in front of union leaders, the lost election, the article, his humiliation—all came flooding into his head. He wanted to get back at the Communist rats who took away his job, his life, everything he had worked hard to achieve. A successful raid would give him that. He would be respected again.

When the cop rapped on the window, Ira froze and held his breath. His men lay in position on the loft, waiting for whatever would happen next. Ira gathered his nerves and peered around the desk to get a position on the policeman. The cop was pressing his flashlight against the glass, and a hazy stream of light pushed inside, trying to wade into the darkness as he searched the walls. At the sound of keys slipping into the lock, Ira mentally cycled through his options. He could fight, but that would bring him more trouble. He could run and humiliate himself. Or he could wait. It seemed like a poor set of choices. He was not the type of man to run, and he could not risk fighting a cop.

But before Ira could set out a plan, the policeman swung the front door open and entered. The light of his flashlight darted around, searching for intruders. Ira took another chance to peek around the desk, hoping to decipher how determined the policeman might be, whether he might search further into the office. Ira decided if the cop began to move inward toward him, he would shift around the desk to remain unseen. But when he turned to steal a glimpse, Ira found himself staring straight into the flashlight beam. Panicked, he pulled back, his limited options racing through his head. Then, before he could second-guess himself, he stood up and faced the policeman directly. They both stood stock-still. Ira straightened himself to appear official, hoping he had made the right decision. Then the government man stepped out from around the kitchen door, barely noticeable in the dark. The policeman shined his light directly on the government man, then back to Ira. He moved the beam around the room and up to the loft, where Ira assumed the open file cabinets and papers strewn on the floor would clarify the situation for the cop. He shined the light back on Ira, then on the government man, and held it there a beat. Ira studied the policeman's face and discerned a barely noticeable supporting smirk. Then the cop switched off his flashlight, turned, and walked out, locking the door behind him.

"Jesus," Ira said to himself. His heart hammered against his chest, and he concentrated to slow his breathing.

"What's going on down there?" Sam whispered over the balcony.

"Nothing. It's over."

"Thank God. That could have gone the other way. You never know if they're on our side. Let's get out of here."

"What did you find?" Ira said, not about to quit.

"Exactly what we're looking for. A list of artists. Maybe two hundred of them. All members of the Artists' Congress."

Sam dropped the list over the loft railing. Held together by a single corner staple, the papers flipped and butterflied as they fell and landed flat on the desk in front of Ira.

He picked up the list and scanned the last names. Albro, Dehn, Gottlieb, Soyer, Roschin. Each page listed members of the defunct Artist's Congress, a group known to operate as an offshoot of the Communist Party in the late thirties, specifically formed to create propagandist art in America. ALERT suspected a silent emergence had occurred, and this list was all they needed as proof of Communist subversion. Ira smiled and tucked the papers into his coat pocket.

Back in the alley, Sam and Milton moved down the narrow street toward Ninth Avenue, and Ira scanned the list of two hundred names again. His men had done all the work—they always did—but in the end, he would give the list to Hoover's man. He had to admit the FBI knew how to get the damn information into the right hands. Legal or not, Hoover had every congressman in his pocket.

"It should be enough," Ira said, handing the list to the government man. "Two hundred artists."

Hoover's man took the list. "It's a start. Collateral. We'll get it into the papers and see who gets skittish. Try to flush out the lead. There's always one."

Ira buttoned his coat. Then the two men turned from each other and walked in opposite directions down the avenue.

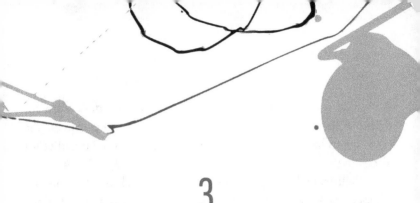

3

ALTHOUGH IT WAS SMALLER than the rest of the space All American Insurance occupied, Will's office on the twenty-third floor of 80 Broadway overlooked the gothic spires of Trinity Church. In the mornings, fractured sunlight filtered through the window frames, laying geometric patterns across stacks of old newspapers and against shelving piled with insurance contracts, notarized appraisals, *ARTnews* magazines, and stills of old paintings. Several open-topped cardboard boxes filled with police reports and auction records sat on the floor. The books, stacked in piles next to the cardboard boxes, were organized by research topic, allowing Will to reach similar books at the same time.

Will tolerated the mess because his boss, Pritchett, would not allow him more shelving. To Pritchett, every insurance company in the world needed to reduce expenses. He would not pay for paint either, so a faded yellow covered the four walls, which, in contrast to the shelving, were bare other than a small landscape of Catskill Creek. Will had found the painting in a shop in the West Village—a calming picture of a stream winding through sycamore trees then dropping over a cliff down into a sun-kissed valley.

Will pulled the Pollock file out of his leather satchel and dropped it on the double desk. Made of dark mahogany, the oversized partner desk had cupboards and drawers on both sides and a single phone set in the middle. When he'd first joined All

American out of college, Will had sat across the desk from his dad and listened to him describe the contracts and explain the coverage to his clients over the phone. They'd worked together for almost a year until Will left for basic training.

Will tacked the small photo of the Pollock on the wall and stepped back. What he found interesting was that the Pollock painting had been stolen right before going on public display, and no other pieces had been disturbed. Why? There had to be relevance. He pulled out a file he had started on Bower Manufacturing and wrote *MoMA preview* at the top.

Then he settled into his seat and picked up the phone to call the police. If he requested the police report today, he might receive it within four weeks, which was later than he needed but the best they would do. When the operator came on the line, Will asked for the New York Police, and after a few seconds and several mechanical clicks, the switchboard operator made the line connection.

"No lead detective on something like that," the policeman said after Will asked about the Stable Gallery theft. "Mick O'Connor filled out the paperwork. He's out on patrol. I can have him call you back."

Will placed the phone back on its cradle, knowing Mick would never call.

Next, he punched the value of the Pollock into his Comptometer by pressing the small, round, numbered keys—six, five, zero—which appeared in the dials at the bottom. Each key had two sets of numbers, larger numbers for addition and multiplication, smaller numbers for subtraction and division. He then calculated the reward amount, multiplying by the recovery percentage, which gave him $97.50.

Like in other cases, Will would work with the newspapers and offer a reward for information that led to the recovery of the stolen Pollock: information from a neighbor, an accomplice, or a relative. At the same time, he would pressure the paper to publish an article on the difficulty of selling the Pollock back into the market. True or not, it didn't matter. When the thief believed he could not sell the painting, he would be more inclined to return the Pollock to Will and receive the reward.

Will picked up the phone to call the newspaper just as his office partner, Charlie Beam, strolled into the office, the fresh smell of coffee floating in with him.

"I heard you lost a painting?" Charlie said, letting out a booming laugh, the kind that draws you in and makes you smile when hearing it. And you could always find him laughing. Will sometimes thought Charlie told jokes just to hear himself laugh. He threw his coat over the Royal Deluxe typewriter and slid his tall frame into his desk chair opposite Will. At six foot three, Charlie had large hands and long arms but was too gangly for athletics, so he resorted to humor. On occasion, Will thought the daily banter between them may have been the single reason Charlie came to work.

"Stolen, Charlie, not lost," Will said, placing the phone back on its cradle.

"Man, Pritchett's going to be pissed. He hates when you play detective. And the Bowers, of all people," Charlie continued with a hearty chuckle. "They might as well be the Rockefellers. And you're going to have all these people tied up with a stolen painting. I mean, Jesus Christ. We're in the goddamn insurance business, for Christ's sake. But you sure as hell wouldn't know it. An art cop." At that, Charlie dropped his head back and let out a booming laugh.

Will had met Charlie at All American during the summer after college, before Charlie married a girl from Poughkeepsie and started riding the Metro-North commuter an hour and forty minutes into the city every day. He and Charlie became close friends hoofing the streets of Manhattan, getting rejected as they went door to door. Unlike Will's dad, Charlie's father owned a dry cleaner in upstate New York, so Will's dad had trained them both. Eventually, they figured out their sales pitch and their tag-team approach.

But Charlie's draft number had come up, and the army sent him to Fort Meade. Six weeks in, they disqualified his conscription because of his flat feet. They classified him 4-F, physically unable to serve, which devastated him. To be useful, Charlie signed on to build the M1 Garand semiautomatic rifle at the Springfield Armory. He spent a year at the end of an assembly line, stamping the manufacturing initials *SA* on the rifle's barrel and hammer.

Will had deployed two months after Charlie. He took the ten-hour bus ride down to Camp Butner for basic training, and after an hour's sleep, inhaled some breakfast then huffed it down to building twenty-two for clothing issue. He stood in line in his undershorts and white undershirt waiting to be handed his greens, a helmet, and dog tags inscribed with his name, army serial number, religion, and next of kin. The helmet liners were made of plastic and fiber, which they told him was better than the older tin helmets because they provided cushion and did not heat up in the sun. All Will wanted to know was if the helmet would stop a bullet.

"What's next?" Charlie asked from across the double desk.

"The usual drill. Newspapers, reward, talk to the employees."

"Don't forget the owner," Charlie said. "Remember Willington?"

"Insurance fraud?" Will shook his head. "I doubt it."

The Willington case from two years ago was different. Will always felt sorry for whoever married the daughter. Mrs. Willington lived in an expensive three-story brownstone on the West Side with her daughter and an inherited Bierstadt painting. In her case, several expensive items were taken from her brownstone, including the painting, but no family heirlooms and nothing of sentimental value. Will had never met a thoughtful thief before, which, combined with the fact that the front window had been broken from the inside, made the daughter his top suspect. After he spent a week pressuring her with questions, she broke. Turns out the two of them had faked the robbery in hopes of receiving enough insurance money to last them until the daughter got married. Then their secret debt would be resolved with the husband's money.

Will shook his head at the notion. "Wrong profile." He flipped through the pages he had collected on the Bowers, most of the information well known from the occasional newspaper article. "Frank Bower, fifty-nine years old," he read aloud to Charlie. "Acquired three cotton manufacturing companies in the thirties. All three were shutting down and laying off men: Carson Cotton Manufacturing in Georgia, Dodson Trading in Chattahoochee Valley, and Arlington Manufacturing in Virginia. The acquisitions expanded his company beyond the tri-state area. A year later, he consolidated the companies into Bower Manufacturing, and now he's one of the larger textiles manufactures in the country.

"This is the interesting part," he said before resuming his reading. "During the war, the US military awarded him contracts to produce camouflage nets, uniforms, and gas masks. Now the government is one of the company's largest contracts."

"Military contracts," Charlie said, pulling out his account book. "I guess that's as good a way to make money as any. Nice to have connections in Washington." Then, with pen in hand, he began notating which customers he needed to collect monthly insurance payments from that day. Pritchett favored Charlie's diligence in collecting his monthly premiums. Charlie had even called on clients the day before he left for the Springfield Armory.

While Charlie had spent his time building rifles, Will spent a year in basic training, then joined the other sixteen thousand young men on three transport ships that steamed out of New York Harbor. He held the same excitement as the other soldiers, all hanging over the boat railing in their olive uniforms, waving to their relatives on the dock. The following five weeks of special training, then the two hours staging outside London before departure, could not have passed quickly enough. All the training, running, and drills led up to the moment they would cross the channel to join the fight. The letters he wrote to his dad could not capture the excitement on paper. Eager and anxious, no one in his regiment slept an hour the night before they crossed the channel. How could they? He laid on his cot, his heart beating rapidly with excitement, then panic would rush through his body. He focused on his kit, the one thing he could control. Had he packed his ammunition pouches, his spade? Had he grabbed his tinned rations? He wanted to get across the water and fight. He wanted to be in the action. And, at the same time, the rumors of the number of men who had died, pinned down by enemy fire during the Normandy invasion, tempered his excitement.

Finally the next morning, on July 5, they loaded into the landing crafts and crossed the channel, one hundred and fifty miles across the choppy waters. The day was calm, with a cloudless sky of a light cotton-candy blue. Will wondered if the sky was the same on the beach on the other side of the channel. What did the sky look like over war? When they arrived, Will waded onto shore after the Higgins boat's bow ramp had dropped, alarmed by the broken-down trucks and tanks and debris covering the sandy beach, pocked by twenty-foot-deep bomb craters. The sky hadn't changed, but the air had. He covered his nose with the crook of his arm to avoid the smell of wet canvas, truck diesel, and char. From all directions, soldiers were loading trucks and moving supplies, with the sound of gunfire popping off in the distance. Columns of gray smoke rose along the horizon. Morbidly, but unable to keep himself from doing so, Will scrutinized the wreckage for bodies. At first no one spoke, shocked by the scene swirling around them. The pit of his stomach felt hollow, but the energy on the beach, the jeep horns blaring, the soldiers yelling as they stacked ammunition boxes, fortified him. He and the other soldiers stepped carefully in single file around the white tape outlines of the minefields that had not been cleared, and the men began to whisper amongst themselves. The one thought pounding in Will's mind had been, how did anyone make it?

Will shook off the memory and reached for the phone to call the newspapers as his boss, Lou Pritchett, stepped into the office and dropped the morning's *Hearst Daily* flat on Will's desk.

"Jesus, Will. What does all this mean?" he said, pointing to the fifth page. With his squat frame and his nose protruding almost as far as his belly, Pritchett resembled an old gnome with thinning white hair.

Will dropped the receiver back on its cradle and quickly scanned the paper. A bold headline read, "200 Artists Exposed as Communists." The article identified paintings and wall-sized murals as Communist propaganda and referred to Artists' Congress memberships and Communist Party affiliations.

The fact that people were finding themselves on lists was no secret. Newspapers would report people's subversive activities daily: math professors, screenwriters, and even bellhops. Soon after the war, Will had noticed the change little by little, until one morning he woke up and a House Un-American Activities Committee was holding trials at an unapologetic pace.

"The firm can't be associated with any of this, Will. If any of these artists are in your clients' galleries…" Pritchett shook his head and skipped to his point. "We can't have Communist propaganda on walls the firm is insuring."

"Lou, this is a list of people I have nothing to do with." Will tossed the paper aside.

"You know as well as I do what's going on, Will. We have to be real goddamn careful. Association alone could put us in the crosshairs."

Will did not know which artists were included on the two-hundred-person list. Names were not listed. Thousands of artists lived in New York, all of them different. Most of them had been members of some association at some time, especially during the depression when food and jobs were scarce. Admittedly, the Stable Gallery was on the fringe. Elaine focused on modern and avant-garde art.

"You've got nothing to worry about, Lou," Will said, confident that none of his clients would be on the list. He could not put his finger on why, but he trusted his instinct.

"I better not. We write insurance here. It's pretty straightforward, plain vanilla stuff. People pay us for a promise to pay them money when something is damaged so they can buy a new one. That's our business. But now you've got me making promises to people like the Bowers on a bunch of stolen paint that's supposedly irreplaceable when the whole goddamn country's up in arms about these painters."

He paused a moment, then continued more calmly. "I don't mind you playing detective, Will, but I don't need bad press." Pritchett moved away from the door and then turned. "None of this better come back to the firm. The risk isn't worth it. My God, no one will even remember Pollock's name two years from now."

As Pritchett walked down the hall, Will picked up the *Hearst Daily* again. The accompanying photograph showed a multi-panel mural reflecting scenes of New York history, of gaunt farmers holding sickles in a wheat field and union workers rallying together, all by an artist named Andrei Roschin. The panels were in yellows, browns, and grays punctuated by strong reds. The photo resembled none of his clients' paintings. He dropped the paper in the waste bin, reached into his desk drawer for his pack of cigarettes, and then picked up the phone to call his contact at the newspaper.

4

THE THREE BAYS of the Stable Gallery were crowded with people moving in small groups of three and four from painting to painting, pointing and talking and drinking as they shifted into open spaces like water seeping into empty crevices. The groups never stayed together long, forming and reforming as naturally as if the crowd had performed the same choreography at different gallery openings on other Friday nights.

Will crossed the concrete floor, slipping between the clusters of black turtlenecks and jeans, and grabbed a paper cup off the folding table topped with jugs of red wine. He filled it to the top. A young artist next to him passed drinks back to others. The cacophony of voices that filled the gallery sounded like birds squawking at the water's edge.

The paintings hanging throughout the gallery were gigantic, aggressive, and overwhelming. Images erupted from the canvases with vibrant energy. Some paintings consisted of amorphic shapes and vertical black bars, while others displayed large fields of flat, solid color spread across the canvas that blurred together at their edges. Indian yellow, scarlet red, cerulean blue, and rose pink. Black, brown, and maroon. Bright orange. The colors were jarring. Could they have been mistakes, Will thought? Did the artists have any sense of color at all? Pritchett was right. Most of the country did not consider New York's painters artists, not even Pollock. "Garbage and drool" was how they described the paintings. The joke was that Pollock drank paint and then pissed all over the canvas.

At the far side of the gallery, Elaine stood with two other women, her fantastically wild bird-shaped earrings dangling as she laughed and touched the woman's forearm. Will didn't suspect her, not in earnest. She had sacrificed years of hard work and built a reputation around her gallery. She wouldn't ruin that. She had dropped out of Hunter College at eighteen and immersed herself with the artists of lower Manhattan, attended their gallery openings, hung around Washington Square at night talking with the artists. She would drop in on their studios and listen to them pick apart their paintings, encouraging different aspects of their style, wanting to shape a movement. Eventually, she bought the old livery stable and converted the space into an art gallery. Nothing good would come to her from stealing a painting out of the Stable, especially one owned by a client of such prominence as Frank Bower.

When Elaine noticed Will from across the gallery, her eyes widened with alarm. She dismissed herself from the women with whom she was talking and crossed the floor, skillfully addressing small clusters of guests as she navigated the crowd. When she reached Will, she took hold of his arm with a tight squeeze. "You're not going to arrest someone in the middle of my party, are you?" She forced a nervous laugh, but the crease at her brow betrayed her concern.

"Just snooping around," Will said, flashing his disarming smile. "You'd be amazed at what you can learn when people have a drink in them."

Elaine pulled him close. "Can't it wait until after? No one here knows anything. I want to solve this as badly as you, but not tonight. A gallery must uphold its reputation."

Will remained silent, reluctant to commit himself either way, and Elaine continued, flitting to a different topic as if she'd never asked the question. "Did you read the *Hearst Daily* article on the two hundred?" she said. "It's absolutely ruining my evening." She angled her body inward, protecting her words from eavesdroppers. "I want to completely ignore the whole ugly mess tonight, but everyone is making it so dreadfully impossible. It's completely absurd. There are rumors, of course, gossip. I heard the Met was sent the list of the two hundred artists and threatened with action if they don't remove paintings from the museum. All of this is going to be dreadful for the gallery, and for MoMA." She made a point to add MoMA, as if the association protected her as well.

Before Will could respond, a woman in a black turtleneck grabbed Elaine's arm and pulled them both into her threesome of ladies. "My goodness, Elaine, aren't you frightened? Do you think they'll shut you down?"

"Don't be ridiculous," Elaine said. "It's a list, nothing more. And if they shut me down, they'd have to shut down MoMA. This whole exhibit is for the museum."

"I heard the two hundred were being blacklisted," the woman said as if divulging late-breaking information.

"It's frightening, that's for sure," one of the other ladies added. "They're accusing people they don't know. I can't imagine it's legal."

"Look at what happened to the Rosenbergs," said the third woman. "My god! They've been two years in Sing prison and now they're to be executed in June. Actual spies. Sending nuclear secrets from their apartment."

"Yes, but making bombs is different from making paintings. What does the government expect, an overthrow of the White House by a bunch of painters?"

They all laughed, and Elaine gave a dismissive wave.

"Ladies, if you continue with this gossip, you'll absolutely ruin my evening. All this talk of lists is so dreadfully dull. We're supposed to be having fun." Elaine took a large sip of her wine.

"The war is over, and art is exploding in New York. It's all so fabulously exciting, don't you think? One party after another, one opening after another. Please forget about this nonsense and have a drink, for God's sake."

She excused herself from the group, hurrying Will along and sidestepping the need to introduce him. "As if the Bower's stolen Pollock wasn't enough to deal with," she said once they were far enough away from the women.

"Is he here tonight?"

"Who? Pollock? God, no. He's dreadful at these events. I keep him out of the gallery as much as I can. The last time he showed was a disaster. Complete disaster. He crashed over the bar table and yelled at everyone for being frauds."

"I meant Frank Bower," Will said.

Elaine laughed at the misunderstanding and gave him a playful slap on his forearm. "Look at you, always on point. I already told you to stop," she said, but then whispered, "His daughter is here somewhere. But please don't make a scene."

Will shook his head, reassuring her. He wouldn't, but he would mix into the crowd and listen. Elaine's was a small circle, and he would learn something if he paid enough attention. "Can I get a list of visitors to the gallery from the past several weeks?" Will asked.

"That will be difficult. People come and go like through a revolving door. Sometimes I think they sleep here. But it's basically a small circle of friends that attend each other's gallery openings. It's a bit incestuous that way, but I doubt that it will lead you anywhere."

Elaine pulled him through the gallery, pointing at different pieces and artists. At the Stable Gallery, younger artists could exhibit alongside more established ones, many of whom had been around for ten or fifteen years. Most of the younger artists didn't have enough paintings for one-man shows. They were still working out their craft and trying to define their statements. An artist could be talented, but without a statement no one cared. Elaine let artists come and go. The Stable was as much of a studio as it was a gallery.

"And a list of the artists showing tonight?" Will asked, thinking how many different artists there must be. "With any notes you can make, maybe who sells the most or if there is a rivalry?"

Elaine pouted at the question. "I doubt you'll find anything there either, but yes, that should be easy. We have thirty-four artists in all, different in every way, but all modern. There's nothing else worth painting in my opinion, even though the newspapers and politicians disagree." She gave a dismissive flip of her hand. "But what do they know? Roy Newell, Robert Motherwell, Philip Guston—anyone who's modern is here. There's a whole series of black paintings down in the basement. And a bicycle wheel a young kid named Rauschenberg put down there. Isn't that fantastic? A bicycle wheel with the spokes cut out. I have no idea what it means, but I love the wildest ideas."

She gestured toward two artists laughing together in the far corner. "That's Willem de Kooning and Franz Kline in front of Kline's painting. Most of the younger artists see those two as the leaders of the group, although they wouldn't consider themselves leaders. They refuse to be called a group, and certainly not a movement."

The two artists stood in front of a large black-and-white canvas almost ten feet wide. Both appeared slightly disheveled, as if they had stepped away from a bar fight, picked up their crumpled suits off the closet floor, and shown up. With full glasses of bourbon in hand, which Will guessed they'd smuggled in, the two stood laughing together, isolated from the rest of the crowd.

Kline's painting appeared as defiant as the artists themselves. Five gigantic black brushstrokes in a quasi-triangular form loomed dramatically on the canvas, contrasting against the white background. The paint was cheap and rough, like house paint scraped on with a wide brush. Thin, short drips came down from each stroke as if Kline had slapped the paint onto the canvas spontaneously, directly from the can. No discernable image presented itself, maybe sections of an iron bridge or railroad ties, but it was hard even to make that connection. One fact was certain: the sheer size of the canvas engulfed him. He felt like a small boy standing in front of a motion-picture screen.

Will considered the other paintings. All of them were massive, more than ten times the size he typically insured, and certainly not the kind you hung neatly on your living room wall in a quaint wooden frame. Even the smaller paintings were much too large for two women to hang.

"It's you and Miss Curry, right? No other employees?" Will asked.

"Yes, the two of us."

"And what does Miss Curry do?" he asked, making mental notes in his head.

"Everything. She manages the collection in the gallery, the invoices, and all the paperwork. She handles the temporary staff who clean and set up."

"So she has access to the records and knows the value of the paintings, the dates they are in the gallery, and when they're going out on the floor?"

"Yes, of course. But she's been with me since I started. She wants this to be her career. She wouldn't ruin that. Anyway, she has a key. Why on earth would she break in?"

To make it appear like a break-in, Will thought to himself. "Did you and Charlene hang all these paintings?"

"God, no. She's paper-thin and can barely lift her purse. And I certainly wouldn't be caught dead hanging a sixteen-foot canvas myself. I'd look absolutely ridiculous. I use Schneller & Schneller."

"What's that?"

"They. It's an art-hanging company on Riverside Drive. They handle all my large exhibits, plus the packing and the shipping. They hung the exhibit."

They passed another makeshift bar, and Elaine grabbed a paper cup, filled it to the top, and took a large sip.

"My God, nobody had hangovers five years ago. Now we're all having such a wonderful time. Isn't it fantastic?"

After a while, Elaine abandoned Will for other guests, so he grabbed another cup of wine and drifted to the back of the gallery where the large Pollock hung on display. If he stared long enough at the painting, maybe he would understand it. He lit a cigarette, took a long pull, and exhaled, the smoke floating around him as he stood before the painting.

He peered deep into the knotted web of black and white paint splattered across the canvas, some strands thick, others thin. In certain areas the black paint lay dull and flat, sunken deep into the canvas, while in others the blackness glimmered on top like it was still wet. Delicate touches of tan and gray and a hint of sea-blue whirled against a dusty pink background. A sense of controlled chaos emanated from the canvas as Will stared. Then as if from out of nowhere, a voice startled him from behind.

"What do you think of it?"

Will turned, surprised to find a slender woman standing behind him. "I could take it or leave it, I guess," he said. "It looks like a tangled mess of hair, though. I kind of want to comb it all out, you know?" He laughed. "Or we could shave it!"

He glanced at her for a reaction and saw that she was tightening the corners of her mouth, trying to hold back a smile. "Sorry," he said with amusement and smiled, the right side of his face turning up in a pleasant wink. "I should take it more seriously."

The woman let a slight smile turn. "I'd be lying if I didn't admit I found your joke a bit amusing. It was certainly more clever than the patent answers I hear from this crowd. But you don't like the painting?"

"The jury is still out, I guess. It's a bit muddled. I'm trying to understand if there is any meaning to it. Do you see it?"

"I hope so. I own one, or did." She gave him a sportive smile and turned toward the painting. "He lays the canvas on the floor and throws paint on it with a thick brush or a stick. He paints on the floor to get closer to the work. They're all trying to get closer to their work. It's what their pictures are about. During and after the war, after the two bombs, they couldn't make sense of painting flowers and nudes, so they turned inward, focusing on their experience with painting. Just them and their paintings."

Will turned to the painting and imagined a balding Pollock standing over the canvas, splattering paint, in a jean jacket with a cigarette hanging out of his mouth like a garage mechanic. Will stepped forward so his eyes were inches from the canvas, close enough to see the crisscross hash marks of the raw fabric underneath. On the surface of the painting, pressed into the paint and color, was the distinct impression of a work boot. Will could see the ridges of the sole. He could envision Pollock stepping into the painting, reaching to throw a viscous strand of paint.

Will turned back, and the woman offered her hand, looking directly into his eyes. "I'm Liz Bower. Frank's daughter."

Will shook her hand, feeling caught off guard. She was less of a socialite than he had expected. She had a well-educated demeanor, maybe Ivy League, someone who belonged in a leather chair at the Knickerbocker Club. Not because she was boyish. In fact, she held her paper cup with a feminine hand, but she held it with a confidence he hadn't expected.

Her long, brown hair was pinned back into a simple knot at the nape of her neck. A strand stuck out of the back as if she took no time to dress for the exhibit, preoccupied with more than looking pretty, though she'd accomplished that too. She wore a black sheath dress cut straight at the sides, but she seemed indifferent to her attire, a thoughtless yet perfect routine. To Will, the dress appeared to be a kind of uniform, the same black sheath dress for all engagements.

Her hand relaxed, and Will reluctantly let it slip from his fingers.

"Elaine said you're the art detective."

Will laughed. "Close enough. But don't tell my boss that. He hates it when I play detective."

"So what is it you can detect for us, Mr. Oxley?" she said lightly.

"I can find your painting. I can try at least. These cases are difficult and often go unrecovered."

"I suppose you've done this before?" She had a playfulness about her as though she were teasing him. Will heard the question, but the square-cut neckline of her dress pulled his attention to the soft curve of her collarbone and slight indention at the base of her neck.

"I've recovered the paintings we've lost." Will shook his head, correcting himself, surprised that the words came out the way they did, and tried to refocus. "Not lost, rather one's I've had stolen. I mean, not that I've had them stolen." Will stopped mid-sentence, embarrassed that he stumbled over his words. "Let me try again," he said in self-mockery. Will thought he saw another hidden smile behind the corners of her mouth.

Liz continued, "Follow the money? Isn't that what they say?"

Will stayed light. "Thieves usually steal for the money, yes. This case should be no different."

"I want to help how I can. Where do we start?" She asked the question as if they had become a partnership, a playful idea that Will admittedly found enticing.

"Answering questions, the usual. I hope to speak with your dad tonight," he said.

She threw him a judging eye. "My father runs Bower Manufacturing, Will." Then she intertwined their arms, laying a slight hand on his forearm. "I do hope 'Will' is okay, not 'Mr. Oxley.' I presume we don't have to be so formal." She smiled at him and continued without waiting for approval. "I deal with everything related to the Foundation—to the art—so you can ask me your questions."

Will's pulse quickened at her delicate touch. "Of course," he said as she began to lead him to the next painting. "We'll be a team."

She laughed. "You are quick, which will help you keep up." She patted his forearm and stopped at the next canvas.

Black lines crisscrossed the canvas like lightning streaks, and when the lines touched each other they resembled dancing torsos, creating a sort of structure that held pockets of blues and reds and yellows. Will reluctantly broke their embrace and bent down to read the artist's name: Willem de Kooning.

"The artists are all fighting for the top," Liz said, nodding back toward the main gallery. "To be the best American painter. After the war, when everyone fled Europe, the art scene shifted to New York, and the artists realize it's only a matter of time before one of them becomes the next Picasso."

"Is that what tonight and the upcoming MoMA exhibit are about?" Will said, wanting to demonstrate that he took her seriously.

"The Foundation and MoMA are calling it the *Twelve Modern American Painters* exhibit. It's the first show of exclusively abstract expressionist painters, and we're touring it through Europe."

"Is Pollock one of them?"

"Of course. Pollock. De Kooning. Many others." She motioned around the room. "Once we select the right pictures tonight, we'll ship them to Paris and then Berlin."

Will frowned. "Berlin seems like an odd choice."

"Does it? It's one of many cities on the tour. Paris, Zurich, Dusseldorf, Stockholm, Helsinki. We're particular in how we promote our paintings and artists."

"And you're paying for it?"

"The Bower Foundation and a few other foundations, yes."

"Why did you want the lesser, stolen Pollock in tonight's exhibit?" he said, hoping to steer the conversation to the case.

"The picture was created before he broke through, before his large murals. I wanted to show his progression as a way for people to appreciate his later work. No artist has accomplished what Pollock has. I believe the creative freedom he's shown should be shared with the rest of the world. Isn't that what our country is about?"

"But the painting wasn't expensive or sought after, not like a Monet?"

"No," she said, and then tilted her head in thought before adding, "But of course Pollock is taking off, if he hasn't already. He was on the cover of *Life*. And if the art world decides he's the greatest American painter, then I could see how an early work would be valuable."

"And he will, right? Take off? Your foundation supports him, MoMA has acquired one, and his work could become valuable. Isn't that how it works? Collectors buy a picture, then donate it to be placed in a museum, and the value increases."

"Yes. I guess so. But we don't buy pieces to make money. We buy paintings because they will make a place in history. There are many others—Kline and de Kooning. They're as good. They're right behind Pollock."

Will glanced back to where Kline and de Kooning had been standing, but they had disappeared into the crowd. When he turned back he was alone, Liz having sauntered off to the next painting. The blurred edges of red and yellow and ocher orange created fields of luminous color that seemed to hover on the canvas surface. She looked back at him with a smile, then nodded for him to join her.

Ira Fenton stepped off the curb and walked across the street to the Stable Gallery. The heavy door stood open as if mocking him, throwing the laughter and insidious conversations from inside in his face. He could see them all sipping wine and laughing and talking around the art. He ripped off the small poster nailed to the large wooden door, the edges crushing in his hand, and read it:

Exhibition of Modern Painting and Sculpture
MoMA Preview
Sunday, March 21, 1953
3:30 PM – 10:00 P.M.

Elaine Carter's
The Stable Gallery
Sponsored by the Bower Foundation

He crumpled the poster and stuffed it into his coat pocket. Closing the neck of his coat to protect himself from the cool wind blowing off the Hudson River and through the city's cavernous streets, he walked toward Broadway, huddling inward. At Broadway he cut the corner short, avoiding the muddy slosh in the street, remnants of the last spring snow. A white cloud of steam rose from a city manhole, a constant reminder of the engineering feats accomplished in Manhattan, a labyrinth of steam service pipes that had once been run by good union men like himself.

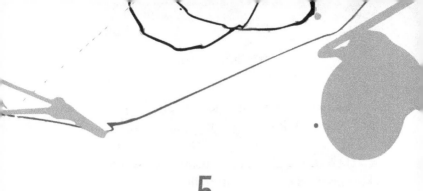

5

OF THE SIX ROOMS on the floor of the nondescript building on Forty-Fourth Street, ALERT occupied three; the others were empty. The cleaning crew rarely came, which meant Ira had to work in stale, dust-filled air that nestled into the cracks of the peeling olive-colored wallpaper. To make matters worse, the naked light bulbs from the drop ceiling bathed the office in a dim yellow glow.

Thomas Strout, head of ALERT, had chosen the office location for its proximity to the Astor Hotel, where he frequently lunched with the American Legion members. He often commented to Ira how the Legion had grown into such a strong, patriotic organization and how eager he was to hand off the information ALERT had collected on potential communists. The names of target individuals would typically pass from a congressman to a Legion member, then to Strout over lunch. Afterward, ALERT would investigate, collect information on the target, and hand over a comprehensive report, all for a fee. Ira could never tell for certain if the lists Strout brought back to the office came from the Legion or the FBI. Many Legion members had spent time in the FBI, if not still in their employ. But in Ira's mind, the two organizations were the same, one a stand-in for the other. And which one paid ALERT didn't matter to Ira. The groups collaborated, creating a web of information exchange that Ira found empowering.

Ira leaned back in the metal folding chair across the desk from Strout and listened to the small box radio sitting on the bookshelf.

"Here we go. The congressman's address is on," Strout said, cocking his good ear toward the radio. He'd lost the hearing in his left loading shells from inside a battery gun turret during the first years of the war. Congressman George Dondero's voice crackled through the felt screen, and Ira imagined the slender man with thinning gray hair sitting erect at a radio desk, speaking into a round microphone.

"Art is a weapon of Communism," preached the congressman, "and the artist its soldier! Modern art is Communist because it does not glorify our beautiful country and our cheerful and smiling people, but instead aims to destroy by disorder, by ridicule, by denial of reason." His voice rose in a crescendo.

With each word, anger raced through Ira's body. Commies could be anywhere, sabotaging anything. First they take over the unions, then they want to staff the education system with incompetent professors who brainwash the children. If they could spew out their propaganda on the radio and in the movies, nothing was safe. He turned to Strout, his fervor feeding off the address. "This country's being taken over. These Communist rats are in our malt shops. They're teaching in our schools and writing our movies. They're spouting lies and spinning Communist propaganda everywhere."

Strout took off his old military-issue glasses and leaned forward, placing his hands on his steel tanker desk. "God knows what messages they're sending through this art. Crisscrossed lines, paint splatters. You can't tell a goddamn thing from them." He picked up a brochure of a modern painting exhibit. "Could be maps for all I know. Secret messages revealing our defenses. Goddamn Rosenbergs all over again."

Ira shook his head in disgust. ALERT hadn't been involved, but any true American was proud someone had caught those snakes. Ethel Rosenberg and her husband Julius sent notes to the Soviets on the atomic bomb, military secrets, right out of their apartment. It made everyone realize even a neighbor could be one of these rats. The Commies were breeding spies.

Strout leaned back, placing his feet on his desk, and continued to listen to the congressman's address. He pulled at his collar to loosen its grip on his well-fed body, and the gray metal armchair creaked under the stress of his heavy frame.

Ira had met Strout at church the week after losing the union election. After the sermon, deflated from the week, Ira had walked to the common room and joined a small group of men from the community listening to Strout discuss the Communists. Spittle formed at the corners of Strout's mouth when he described rooting out the rats, telling the men this was no longer a political issue but one of law enforcement, which was where ALERT became important. Without question, Ira joined that day.

The sound of a fist banging against a table reverberated from the radio. Strout reached back and turned up the volume as Congressman Dondero continued his speech. "Today, I denounce institutions that support these subversive and demonic works, and I ask Congress to do the same." Dondero began to list each institution by name: The Metropolitan Museum of Art, The Fogg Museum, The Museum of Modern Art.

Ira stood and walked to the window. A cloudy grayness had settled over the city, and a light drizzle of rain began to fall. He had led a successful break-in, and because of his work the accusations were building. He could envision the path forward, like the cleansing of Hollywood. They would pressure the museums and other institutions, threaten them until they purged themselves of the evil filth. If they had to tap phone lines of museum leftists to rid America of these barbaric and dangerous images destroying the American fabric, Ira wanted to lead the charge. He would be the catalyst, a leader of the purge.

Strout slid his feet off the desk and onto the floor with a loud clap of his wooden heels. "They want more," he said. "We need to investigate everyone and everything."

Ira turned from the window. They. *They* could be anyone, he thought to himself. As a third-party contactor, ALERT sent its information on their targets to the Legion or Hoover's special FBI task force, part of the "Responsibilities Program," which was code for "secret investigations." But from there the information went into the hands of the House and Senate Investigative Committees without questions and, more often than not, straight to the target's employer. Sometimes, if they were high profile enough, the Commie rat stood in front of the House Un-American Activities Committee, but usually they were fired. *They*, the ones who wanted more, could be any one of the interested parties—Congress, FBI, an employer—which party it was didn't matter to Ira.

He reached into his pants pocket, pulled out the small poster that had been nailed to the door of the Stable Gallery, and began pressing out the creases with his hands. Art was a target of Congress. MoMA was on the congressman's list, and the Stable Gallery was as modern as you could get. He reread the poster, then dropped the paper on Strout's desk. "Take a look at this. It's the logical step given the Hollywood disaster."

Strout picked up the poster, peered at it, and then shot a wide grin at Ira. "You did good. Throw the net wide, Ira. Let's see who we catch."

Ira turned back to the window and gazed down Forty-Fourth Street. Outside, men like him hurried along the street under black umbrellas—good, hardworking men. Men who put dinner on the table for their families. God-fearing men with pride in their work and their country. Against the soft rain, Dondero's radio address continued, and the angry voices fortified Ira.

"Picasso was the first hero of all the crackpots in so-called modern art, but there are more who follow these art vermin:

Kandinsky, Motherwell, Jackson Pollock, artists and institutions selling the subversive doctrine of 'isms,' Communist-inspired and Communist-connected. The question is, what have the plain American people done to deserve this? And what are we going to do?"

Ira would start with the Stable Gallery and flush them all out.

6

WILL FLATTENED HIS BACK *against the hedgerow, trying to make himself paper-thin. He pressed his rifle against his chest, which heaved like it was going to explode. The mound of earth topped with brush and trees provided the only barrier against the German soldiers somewhere on the other side, hidden among the endless checkerboard of small fields. Two soldiers lay next to him dead, their legs bent in awkward positions from falling back on themselves. Blood in their hair and holes in their helmets.*

"Oxley, we've got to jump the hedgerow! We've got to go!" someone yelled.

He jumped. His boots sank in the mud, then it squished between his fingers as he fell forward into the trench on the other side. His helmet fell off. Mud and roots and rocks.

Then came the blood. The trench filled with crimson blood, and bodies lay everywhere, empty eyes open, staring at him. He climbed out of the trench on hands and knees. A sea of bodies covered the land. Some were naked, others half-covered by tattered olive uniforms. Many of the bodies clutched small white squares in their dead hands, photos of their wives and children. Photos floated in the rising smoke and char of the bodies. He was alone, the only soldier on the other side. On his knees. Alone with all the bodies. Nothing but dead bodies.

Will shot up in bed. Sweat covered the back of his shirt, and his heart beat against his chest at a rapid pace. The clock on the bedside table read 2:15 a.m.

Like every other time, he pushed the dream into the crevices of his mind, into the cracks he didn't talk about. By morning, the fragments would be hazy and dull, painful shadows of his memory. He stretched his neck to divert his thoughts, but his mind raced through the memories, replaying again and again. They had marched toward Saint-Lô along the narrow roads bordered by mounds of dirt, stones, and trees, under heavy machine-gun fire from the fortified pillboxes on the hill. Peering over the hedgerows, they could make out the top of a stone chateau and, beyond that, St. Gilles church with its eighteen-inch sandstone walls and fifty-foot bell tower. A sniper bullet caught the point man in the throat, and the whole line dove down, pressing themselves flat against the hedgerows for cover. Will had known the soldier for less than seventy-two hours—never even knew his name. They remained pinned against the hedgerow, stilled and staring, while the soldier bled out holding his own throat. Will had tried twice to crawl over and grab the soldier, but the bullets kept digging into the ground next to him. Only after they shot the sniper could he help the medic drag the soldier's body back to cover.

Will dropped his legs over the edge of the bed and curled his toes against the soft carpet, the short threads of brown fabric caressing his skin. He often wondered where the soldier would be today. Would he be married or have kids? Will reached for a cigarette off the bedside table. The light from his match danced in the dark for a moment, then the flame caught hold of the paper and tobacco shreds. He searched his bedroom for a distraction and focused on the details, the specifics, to bring him back to the moment. The water pipe in the corner of the room clanked as it heated. On the street below, a cab horn blew and a soft wind drifted past his apartment window. The city hummed quietly. He shut his eyes and pulled the smoke in hard to calm his nerves. He envisioned the Monet painting: the warm glow of the orange-red sunrise breaking the horizon, the calm blue-green sea. Boats rocking gently. He breathed out slowly and stilled his mind. He could see Monet standing before his easel at the water's edge, dabbing at the canvas in short, quick brushstrokes that captured the light of the moment as rays danced on top of the water. He pictured the thick pigment and heard the crunch of the bristles as Monet pressed the brush against the canvas.

The nightmares had come a month after returning from the war, like waves crashing over him, knocking him down over and again. At first, to avoid his thoughts, he tried picking up a book and flipping through the pages, but his eyes could never focus on the written words. They eluded him, crowded out by the noise in his head. Not until a year afterward did Will see the Monet at a Metropolitan Museum exhibit. The images of the small painting pulled him in and gave him a sense of calm, the distant town bathed in a purple-blue fog, the red-orange sun glistening on the water as a boatman navigated the sea. As time passed, the wave of nightmares lost their force, and instead of cresting over, they now lifted to a swell and passed through him. He longed for the day they would be but ripples at his feet.

When he opened his eyes, the blue glow of the night outside his window cast strange shadows into his apartment, and his cigarette smoke dissipated into the dark as he exhaled. He stood and approached the window cautiously, not sure what might lie outside or in which world he resided.

On the street below, a Checker cab rolled through the stoplight on Eighty-Fourth and Second as it turned yellow then red. Quiet. Peaceful. A ship horn moaned in the distance, somewhere on the East River. Will sat back on the edge of his bed and waited for morning. He needed to see the sun rise between the steel buildings and spread along the concrete avenues, miles away from the hedgerows.

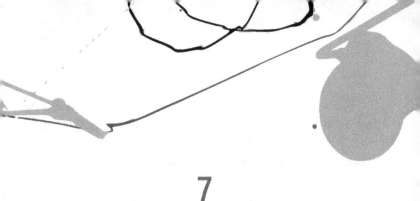

7

MOISE SCHNELLER looked as old as the art framing-warehouse itself and almost as dusty. Small and frail with a gaunt face, he shuffled away from the entry door of the nondescript red brick storage building and led Will into his office. Light trickled into the storage building through small windows yellowed with smoke and age. Empty frames of varied sizes lay against every wall of the framing shop. On the floor were stacks of newspapers and cardboard boxes. Inside, the shop was still and quiet.

"I don't know why you're bothering me with this," he said to Will as he eased himself down in front of a small rolltop desk burdened with stacks of invoices, job orders, carbon receipts, and a glass ashtray full of cigarette butts.

"I won't take up much of your time," Will said. He lifted a push broom off a second chair, placed it next to a large bin of discarded plywood, and took a seat.

Moise pulled a smoldering cigarette off his ashtray that sat next to an old inkwell and a small can of leftover nuts and bolts. "Time I have. But the painting was stolen from the gallery, not from me. I don't understand why I should be involved."

"I have to consider every scenario, Mr. Schneller."

"You're a cop?"

"No. Not exactly."

Schneller peered at him.

"Elaine's my client," Will said, his voice calm, trying to soften Schneller's mood. "I insure her gallery and anything in it. If there is damage or theft, I'm responsible. I have to find the original painting because the cops won't bother."

Schneller lowered his eyes. "Terrible for Elaine. I couldn't believe it myself when she told me. And a Pollock."

"Do you remember the painting?"

"Not that one specifically, but I'm familiar with Pollock's work. Looks like ugly wallpaper, in my opinion." Schneller shook his head. "I would have expected one of the impressionists, like Monet down at the Carter Gallery, to be stolen—not any painting from Elaine's."

"They took the canvas out of a crate. Can you think of a reason someone would do that?"

"There's no sense. I can't image how much time it took to pry open the crate, and you'd have no idea of the contents inside."

"They drilled out the lock of the storage entry door and went straight to the one specific crate."

The frown on Schneller's face deepened. "So what do you need from me?" he asked.

"A list of your employees. Anyone who might have known which paintings were in which crates."

"There's no need for a list," Schneller said, pointing to his temple. "I have three employees. Six if you include the loaders. But you're wasting your time. I would never let something like this happen. It would put me out of business."

"Do you know who worked the exhibit that day?"

"Of course. All of them. We did the exhibit over several days because of its size. Thirty-four paintings. But let me try to find who did what on which day." Schneller turned to his desk, narrowed his eyes, and began lifting several manila folders. Then, moving them aside, he sifted through the papers underneath.

"Don't be fooled, Mr. Oxley. I know where everything is. I've been in this office for forty years. Not always in art, mind you, but storage of one kind or another. There's always something to warehouse. There are two of us in the city that provide art services. Hanging, crating, transporting, that sort of work. Feels like people are buying art every day now. I would never have considered a business like this ten years ago. There wasn't any interest. But now …" Schneller let out a soft whistle. He reached into his stack of job orders.

"Where's your son, the other Schneller?" Will asked.

"Off somewhere in California. Motion pictures. Warehousing still, but it's better money out there, and he likes to be around the movie stars. Said he saw Grace Kelly the other day," Schneller continued while thumbing through the job orders. "She walked right past his warehouse on her way to her studio, filming one of those Alfred Hitchcock films. Have you seen any of those?"

Will nodded. "*Strangers on a Train.*"

"That's right. Crisscross. You do my murder and I do yours," Schneller said, quoting the movie. "Terrible what's happened out in Hollywood. My son knew a B-grade actor out there. I forgot his name, Johnny or something. My son wasn't friendly with him, mind you, but this Johnny has a bit part in a movie ten years ago. He's standing on a submarine waving to somebody as it submerges. He shouts out *tovarich,* which means 'comrade.' It's right there in the script. It's the line they gave him. Anyway, they review the film last year and he gets named as a Communist." Schneller looked at Will. "He had to write a letter to the House Un-American Activities Committee explaining the charges against him. Of course he denied it all. He explained that the accusations were false. But it didn't do him any good. He lost his contract and hasn't worked since." Schneller shook his head. "So many careers ruined." He stopped flipping through his papers and pulled out a stapled set. "Here it is. Right where I put it."

Will stepped forward. Schneller's finger danced on top of the paperwork, marking the days and the jobs. "The two brothers, Samuel and Isaac, packed up the crate."

"What do you mean?"

"Paintings can be rolled or crated, depending on how careful you want to be. You run the risk of cracking the paint if you roll them, especially if they are rolled for a long time, and they must be stretched back onto the frame afterward. I like to crate paintings, but it's more expensive. So if they aren't taken off the frames and rolled, I build the wood crates here in the shop based on the painting's measurements. It's easy work for me." He lifted his hands toward Will. "I'm still good with my hands." Then he let a small smile escape. "Samuel and Isaac help a little bit, of course."

Will had no experience transporting pictures. He typically insured small but expensive living room paintings that owners rarely moved. Schneller explained that paintings for exhibits had to be crated, transported, and protected. They had to be logged in and given lot numbers. If a picture was on loan, it had to be picked up from the owner's house or museum and transported to the exhibit location.

"I send Samuel and Isaac to the owner's apartment to pack the paintings into crates. A loader goes with them to help load the paintings in the truck." Schneller read through the job order, his finger repeating the earlier choreography.

"Most of the paintings were brought to the gallery by the artists. With an exhibit like Elaine's, with newer, younger artists, the painters usually bring the canvases themselves, and we're just responsible for hanging them. That was the case for all the paintings here but six. Those six were on loan from private collections.

"Owners usually don't want the responsibility for moving their art," Schneller said. "So we do it for them. The one you're missing we brought from the Bower apartment, of course. We built the crate, packed the painting, and delivered it. Nothing else.

We hadn't had a chance to hang it yet." Schneller pointed to his papers. "They're all listed here." He showed Will the paperwork.

Clearly outlined were each painting's lot number, the artist's name, the owner's name if the owner wasn't the artist, the size of the painting, and the title. Any additional information that was meaningful to Schneller was scribbled in the margins. Will reflected on the six wooden crates in the storage room of the Stable Gallery. They had all been identical.

"What information is labeled on the outside of the crate?" Will asked.

"Usually the lot number and the owner's name. We match that back to the paperwork to know what's what." Schneller brought his hands together, closing the loop.

"Other than Samuel and Isaac, do any other employees have access to the paperwork?"

"Other than me? No. But those two I trust the most. They do all the framing and hanging. That's the skilled work. Samuel also drives the truck. He's in charge of the job, making sure the pieces get picked up and moved, unpacked properly. Everything. They've been with me the longest, almost seven years, and they're from the neighborhood. They would never be involved in anything like this."

The two boys may have appeared trustworthy, but Will never trusted anyone. Ferreting out the truth amid the lies was his job. And it was typically how he found his leads. "That's two. Who else?"

"Antonio is the third. He stays here in the warehouse and manages the inventory and the loading dock. We warehouse other items besides art. Sometimes if Isaac can't come in, Antonio will help with the packing. He's good, but not as good as Isaac."

"Okay. That's three."

"Then there are the loaders. They tend to come and go, especially with all the construction these days. There are so many new jobs now that the war is over. But I always have two or three on hand. I don't mind losing a loader. I can hire a new one in a day or two. It's the framers and handlers I try to keep. They're skilled and hard to come by. I don't know what I'd do without Samuel and Isaac."

There had to be something else, something for Will to narrow down. Anyone else who had access to the records? Someone who knew which paintings were in which crates. Schneller would know, but Will couldn't picture the old man drilling through the gallery door on his knees. He couldn't even imagine him leaving his warehouse, escaping from beneath his papers.

"Anyone not show up for work the next day?" Will asked.

Schneller looked down and tapped his finger on the desk. "I've been thinking about it since you came in. One of the loaders had been here a few months. He checked out okay and was working out too—a little flashy for my taste, but he did his work. He didn't show up after the Stable Gallery job, but that's not unusual. Like I said, the loaders come and go. I might have one for several weeks, and then they take off, usually for a better job somewhere else. He was a colored boy. Barnett, if I remember right."

"You have an address?"

"Sure. I make everyone fill out one of these cards." He reached back into the depths of his desk and pulled out a shoebox full of index cards. He pulled out a small, yellow card and handed it to Will.

Clyde Barnett. 2D, 63 W 132nd Street. Harlem.

Will stepped out of the dark warehouse and back out onto Riverside Drive, his spirits lifted with a lead. The white sun blinded him for the first few moments like an interrogating spotlight as he raised his hand to flag down a cab and head back to 80 Broadway.

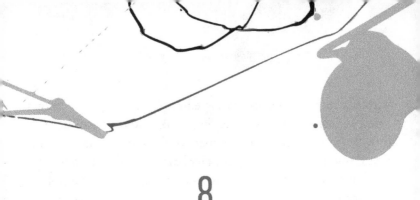

8

WILL HAD BEEN TO FUNDRAISERS and worn tuxedos before, but the crowd that filled Liz Bower's Park Avenue apartment exuded a different air of entitlement. Men in tuxedos talked among themselves in clusters of three and four throughout the apartment, picking stuffed mushroom appetizers from silver trays and drinking martinis. They were the titans of industry, venture capitalists, heirs to publishing companies, owners of broadcasting networks, and members of the Knickerbocker Club. The women stood apart in their separate conversations, laughing quietly together, cocktails in hand. The air smelled of sautéed butter, strong cheese, and expensive liquor.

The apartment itself was a piece of art. The few interior walls were a cool white that complemented the black-and-white spotted terrazzo floor. Low-rise tables and black cantilevered chairs seemed to thrust the apartment into the future. The mirrors were spotless. Heavy silver cigarette lighters and knickknacks were placed on tables exactly so. Everything seemed frozen in perfection, as if Liz had meticulously planned every detail and left it out for display like a stage set.

She stood at the far end of the foyer, directing her house help and wearing a black sheath dress. He had been right, Will thought. The plain black dress was her uniform, eliminating the decision making from her choice of attire. He found himself enamored

with her intricate details. As she entertained her guests, she gestured with small sweeps of her fingers like she was brushing away
dust floating in the air. Her upper cheeks had a subtle coral hue
that flushed when she laughed. Her hair was tucked into its usual
knot; the long tresses flowed in and among themselves, folding
underneath, enticing Will to follow her long neckline down to the
collar of her dress. She stood firm with her feet well planted, not
slouching or leaning to one side. But once or twice Will caught
her rolling her foot on its side then back again. And he found that
he cherished the intimate detail.

Will drifted into the small study to the right of the foyer.
Like the rest of the apartment, the room was decorated to perfection. A collection of books was organized on the shelves—not
enough to crowd, but enough to give more than a decorative
impression. Most titles were centered on art—Picasso, the impressionists. Novels accompanied other academic books, all appearing
relatively at home with their political undertones—Hemingway,
Faulkner, Huxley. The rest were poetry—Ezra Pound, E. E.
Cummings, Yeats.

Framed photographs covered one wall displaying select fragments of Liz's life: one of her as a young girl in a swimsuit jumping off a low bridge into a glassy lake, another of her smiling
arm in arm with two other girls at a Wellesley graduation. One
at a party at Coney Island, and another on the steps of a vaguely
familiar building, maybe in Washington or Boston.

He stopped in front of one photograph. In it, Liz leaned
against a low rock wall, gazing across the Seine, which glistened
with late afternoon sun, toward the Eiffel Tower. In the foreground,
rows of chestnut trees lined a pathway with their autumn leaves
of burgundy and cadmium orange and yellow ocher. Shoulders
back and chin up, she was poised with pride and confidence. Her
whole demeanor gave the impression that she belonged among
the beauty and energy of Paris.

He gazed at the photograph as though he were a boy with a crush, wondering what her life had been like along the cobbled streets. Paris seemed to suit her. He could imagine her sitting in a white wicker chair at a café, holding a small porcelain cup of cappuccino.

Will saw Liz out of the corner of his eye when she stepped into the study and turned, feeling caught in his intimate curiosity. His face felt flushed, although she did not indicate that she noticed.

"You seem to keep turning up," she said, stepping next to him, closer than she maybe would have with other guests. He could almost feel her arm against his.

"I guess I'm like a bad penny," he said and laughed. She tightened the corners of her mouth again, trying to hold back a smile.

"I wouldn't say that. More like a stray dog, full of curiosity." She nodded at the photograph of her at the Seine. "That was taken right before I left. I felt alive there, a part of the world, right in the middle of the excitement."

"Why Paris?" he asked. But he couldn't help but think about her next to him, and he had to be careful not to stumble on his words.

"I was in the Wellesley literary club, and some of my friends were going to Paris after the war, so I joined them. Everyone wanted to be in Paris then. I lived in a small apartment in the Quarter, on the Left Bank." She pointed to a location on the photo far in the distance, past the Eiffel Tower. And when she did, she gently held on to his arm. "On Saturdays, a little market would set up down the street, and I would buy cheese from a portly man who sold it out of a refrigerated cart that he pulled behind a bicycle. You could buy anything: flounder, sausage, tongue, fresh bread, or lobster. I would walk through the market in the morning, talking with vendors and shoppers, and end up at a café on the corner of Rue des Carmes by lunch. I could spend hours tucked away there, watching people rush by, creating the world."

Will studied her for a moment, considering her confession. "You don't seem like someone who sits and watches anything rush by."

Liz smiled. "Well, it's a beautiful idea, isn't it? Paris is beautiful."

"I haven't been back since the war."

He did not mention not wanting to return, not wanting to relive the war. Nonetheless, when Liz looked at him, her gaze pushed past his words and into his eyes, as if she understood the depth of his simple confession. "I'm glad you came."

"I'm a bit out of place," he said, lightening the moment, and gestured toward the crowd in the living room.

She laughed and smoothed the lapel of his tuxedo by running the edge between her index finger and thumb, then gave it a quick pat. "That's why I invited you." She gave him a wink. "Just pretend you love art, money, and politics, and no one will know the difference."

Alone with her in the study, Will became more aware of her than before, the touches on his arm, her playful smile. He could detect interest in her eyes, the way she focused on him when he spoke. She had invited him as more than a distraction, more than someone to talk to when she got bored of the tuxedos and empty conversations, someone to spend time with when she had had enough of the money and politics, of which Will was neither. Suddenly he wanted to be amusing, to make her laugh and place his hand on her side or the small of her back. He wanted to show that he found her interesting.

"When you went to Paris, was it for work?" he said, now wondering where to put his hands. By his side? In his pockets? His appendages suddenly became conspicuous, almost separate from his body. He decided to leave them by his side, thinking the position appeared most natural, although he still felt awkward.

"A Parisian magazine. Art and politics."

Will raised his eyebrows.

"Surprised?" Liz said.

He considered what he knew of her and surveyed the photos on the wall. "I don't think so," he said. "It's just that the women I grew up with always gossiped about what they read in the latest *Lady's Home Journal* or, at best, *Look,* and they all married young before their boyfriends left for war." Will had not gotten married before departing. When his transport ship pulled out, the other soldiers hung over the railing, proud to be heading to the fight, and waved goodbye to their new wives. With the same exuberance, Will waved to his dad, who stood in front of his Buick in the car park.

"Where did you grow up?" Liz asked.

"New Jersey. Morristown." He looked back at the photographs, at the one of her as a young girl jumping off a low bridge. "Is that Rings End Bridge?"

Liz nodded. "I had a childhood friend there. We were ten or eleven. I was a bit of a tomboy then," she added as if admitting a little-known secret. Will had already guessed as much. "He and I would wear swimsuits underneath our school clothes," she continued. "When the bus dropped us off at school in the mornings, we would slip through the crowd, duck into the bushes, and walk the two miles to Gorham's Pond. Sometimes our fathers wouldn't round us up until lunchtime. But most of the time they came after an hour or two. I loved that freedom, and the hiding and sneaking made it even more exhilarating."

Will imagined Liz young and wide-eyed, pulling off her school uniform with a striped bathing suit underneath, then racing toward the bridge to jump off into the glassy lake. They weren't having party conversations, small talk that two guests would have,

Will thought. They were getting to know each other, exploring backgrounds and commonalities. Liz lifted a cigarette out from a tabletop dispenser and lit the tip with a silver lighter. Her lips tightened and cheeks indented softly as she pulled. She blew out a puff of smoke, which floated above them as she returned his gaze. Then she said, "Any news on the Pollock?"

Will nodded. "I visited Schneller & Schneller yesterday. Did you know an employee named Clyde Barnett?"

She shook her head. "No. I dealt with Samuel. Why?"

"He was a loader over there and didn't show up for work the day after the Pollock was stolen. It might be nothing, but he's one of a few on my list."

"Sounds promising. Who else? Me?" She laughed softly, giving him a playful smile.

"Not yet." He returned her smile.

Feigning offense, Liz let her jaw drop. Will offered his arm in mock apology, and they abandoned the study.

They stepped into the sunken living room. On the right, a wall of windows overlooked Park Avenue, and a large marble fireplace wrapped by a low cantilevered bench framed the far end. A large Kline painting hung dramatically on the white wall opposite the windows. Will guessed sixty or seventy guests crowded the apartment, although several had spilled into the hall toward the kitchen. A buzz of quiet conversations filled the air.

"Is everyone here to fund the MoMA exhibit?" Will asked, lifting a martini from a butler's tray as he passed. "The paintings from the Stable Gallery?"

"They're involved in one way or another. Some are on MoMA's board, others are donors. A show like this takes money. You would never believe how much foreign governments tax us to ship the pictures into their countries. We're lucky Nelson can be persuasive with his friends." With wine glass in hand, she gestured discreetly to a man near the front window. "I'm sure you can spot him."

In tuxedos most men looked the same—uncomfortable. But Will recognized the large head and pocket square and the magnificent presence of the man. Though small, Nelson Rockefeller seemed to tower over the three men with whom he spoke. The men appeared drawn to him as he laughed and flashed a wide smile. His gestures matched a voice that was fast and quick. Will could imagine Nelson standing at a conference table in a Windsor knot and pinstripe suit, loud and ambitious, talking animatedly with his hands.

Liz leaned toward Will. "Nelson's been president of MoMA for several years. When he's not working in Washington, of course. He calls it his mother's museum, and he's right. She practically built the institution from scratch herself. Nelson loves modern art, and he's a major donor. He's been a tremendous help with the international exhibitions because of his appointment as Coordinator of Inter-American Affairs under President Roosevelt. He's sponsored nineteen art exhibitions sent to Latin America as part of his cultural diplomacy program." She pointed with a nod toward a few other guests. "That's the CEO of Life. Occasionally, we use the magazine to publish important articles. And there's the head of Chase Bank," she said, gesturing across the room. "Both of them are strong supporters of what we're doing." She scanned the room a second time. "Ah, and there is Dad." She pulled Will toward the back of the living room near the fireplace to join two men.

Her father, Frank Bower, was a barrel-chested man who stood almost a head taller than Will. He stuck out a large hand and greeted Will with a warm smile and a firm handshake. The shorter man to the right of Frank was Porter McCray.

"Porter is director of MoMA's international program," Liz said. "He runs all of the international exhibits."

Porter laughed. "Yes, it's an immense task that everyone seems content leaving to me. I deal with the catalogs, flying over the Atlantic, setting up the shows, and negotiating with the governments. Except that, at the moment, I can't figure out how we're going to transport these enormous pieces around Europe."

Liz squeezed his elbow. "I'm sure you'll work something out."

"Well, they're going to have to be crated because we can't roll them for such an extended period, and they are gigantic. The planes aren't big enough, so we'll go over by ship. I'll accompany them myself. But that's not the hard part. Once we get on land, moving them through Europe will be the challenge."

"What about passenger trains?" Will asked, trying to imagine transporting an entire exhibit—thirty or forty paintings, most of them sixteen feet in length—across the Atlantic and through Europe.

"I considered that, but they're too short. No room inside, and the loading doors are in the center. I can't get the larger paintings in, not even diagonally. But I've been on the phone all day with the Swiss shipping company we use, trying to find a solution."

"Porter knows most of the foreign governments and logistic companies," Frank said. "He worked for the American Field Services during the war. It's like the Red Cross."

Will nodded. The AFS made runs to the various field hospitals during his fighting at Saint-Lô. The medics carried as many bodies out as best they could.

"After that," Frank continued, "he was in the recovery efforts. They shipped him around to areas like Calcutta, Britain, and Berlin, working with governments to procure reconstruction supplies. If anyone can get this exhibit across Europe, Porter can. Something will turn up." He patted Porter's shoulder.

"Did you serve, Will?" Porter asked.

"Thirty-Fifth Infantry."

"Where did you fight?"

"I came in twenty-nine days after Normandy, pushed through Northern France. Battle of the Hedgerows at Saint-Lô, and the others along the line. Gremecey Forest," he said, hoping the conversation would shift.

Frank raised his eyebrows in respect. "One of our heroes."

"Just a survivor," Will said. "I was proud to fight. But luck brought me home, that's all. It could have gone the other way." Will shifted and glanced in a different direction, trying to break the flow of conversation. A new man with a stocky build and a strong, wide jaw joined the group, giving Will relief. He wore his black hair plastered to his head with pomade. And if he had been wearing aviator goggles, Will would not have been surprised.

"A lively party your daughter throws, Frank," he said, lightening the mood.

"This is John Whitney," Frank said to Will. "Jock to most. He's chairman of the museum's board."

Will knew of Jock from the papers and gossip; most New Yorkers did. He had inherited his family's wealth, making him a multimillionaire overnight. That fortune increased through his private investment firm, J. H. Whitney & Co., and through business deals with the Rockefellers. He had escaped from a German POW camp during the war, which continually impressed the women who were already taken by the fact that he raced horses, produced Hollywood films, and flew airplanes.

Jock shot back a gulp of whiskey from his tumbler. "I'll tell you what. It's going to be a goddamn uphill battle with this exhibit. Congress would never support a show like this. Ike may be a war hero, but he's got a Congress filled with right-wing extremists running amok. Hoover's feeding Congress all this bullshit, with his spies building lists. The American Legion is leading the charge. I tell you he's turning the whole goddamn country on itself."

"Spies?" a fourth man said as he joined the group, laughing. "The FBI doesn't have spies. Not real ones anyway." His sandy-blond hair swayed as he spoke, appearing disheveled yet somehow still barbered. His face and build were of movie-star quality.

He turned to Will. "Richard Lang, but call me Dickie, ol' boy. Everyone does."

Dickie shot an inquisitive glance at Liz, and a change washed over her face. Frustration, Will thought. Maybe panic or annoyance. Intrigued by the awkward yet familiar combination, Will thought Dickie might be an old flame. But something else made him uncomfortable. Dickie seemed insincere, as if he wore a false veneer. His words and glances appeared calculated.

"Gentlemen," Liz said stepping back, "I've heard it all before, and I must be a good hostess. I trust you'll keep Will abreast of your plans to save the world." She winked at Will with an amused smile and strolled away, leaving him feeling empty as she abandoned him. As she sauntered away, Will followed the line of her legs, the tautness of her calf and curve at the thigh. He yearned for her to return, to stay next to him. And without intending it, his thoughts jumped to images of her slender frame stretched out on his bed, her arms tossed above her head, bathed in moonlight through his apartment window.

"Are you with the museum?" Dickie asked.

Will turned, flushing, as if his thoughts could be read on his face.

"We've had one of our paintings stolen," Frank interjected matter-of-factly. "Will is investigating the theft for us."

Dickie's eyes narrowed and focused on Will longer than Will would have liked. Then his demeanor changed in a snap, as if someone had flipped a switch. "And here I am spouting nonsense when you couldn't care less. Sorry. Occupational hazard. Don't pay any attention to a thing I say."

"What is it you do?" Will asked.

Dickie did not answer at first but studied Will with intent, as if working through a problem in his head. Then he finally said, "Journalism abroad. You know, American papers in foreign lands. I'm always digging up dirt by stirring it around myself. But tell me, anything interesting with your painting? Have you got a line on the ol' bandit?"

"Not yet."

Dickie lifted a finger as though he was thinking through another question but then dropped it. "Well, good luck, ol' boy." He pushed the air with his hand, dismissing the entire topic. "Can't be an easy thing to do, finding a stolen painting."

He slapped Will on the back. The air turned thick with elitism. The four men seemed too close—a boy's club of which Will was not a part, connected in a way he could not put his finger on, through unspoken words and old references, familiar with the same storied, Ivy League cloisters. A web of connections that appeared at first like the haphazard lines of a Pollock painting, yet when studied closer, became somehow deceivingly cohesive, as if entirely planned.

Feigning the need for the restroom, Will excused himself and walked back across the foyer, past a waiter emptying an ashtray and a small group of men smoking pipes.

When he returned to the gathering, the groups and conversations had changed, shifting into different rooms and different topics. He spotted Liz again, this time separated from the crowd in a small pantry, talking with Dickie. Her gestures were agitated, almost angry, nothing like the slight wisps from earlier in the evening. She seemed to be questioning Dickie. In turn, his responses appeared short and defensive. Curious, Will drew nearer, unable to refrain from eavesdropping, and their voices became clear.

"I was out of town," Dickie said. "There was no other way."

"You should have told me. I could have taken care of it. You've put me in a bad position."

"It wasn't for you to know."

"But you're telling me now? And why shouldn't I have known?"

"Let's just say it's above your pay grade."

Then from behind, a waiter asked if Will needed a drink. Afraid Liz might glance in his direction, Will walked away with the waiter, requesting a vodka gimlet, and then stepped out onto the balcony.

Will gazed out over the city at the mosaic of white lights that flickered and danced among the buildings that housed corporations whose owners were currently drinking scotch and sidecars inside Liz's apartment. The *Hearst Daily* sign gleamed high in the black sky, crowning a building that towered above the other: the Empire State Building, Rockefeller Plaza.

Pay grade. What bothered Will was not what Dickie had said but how he'd said it, like he and Liz worked together. Will took out a cigarette and pressed a match against the side of the box, forcing it along the striker until the small flame sparked bright on the balcony. He pulled on the cigarette and let the smoke roll out slowly.

Below in the deep gorges of the cavernous city of skyscrapers, red and yellow and white cab lights streamed down the avenues against the black pavement, leaving long trails behind them in his mind. The longer he stared, the more abstract they became, flattening in space and reminding Will of the whips of paint in the Pollock paintings—long and viscous and without end, some thick, others thin, releasing an energy that if not contained could explode. The earlier work by Pollock would rise in value, Will thought, and Clyde may have known the painting was worth stealing. And maybe he had a network to bring it to the right buyer. But Will had his doubts.

As he leaned against the railing, the click of the balcony door latch broke his train of thought. He turned to find Liz stepping out onto the balcony, wrapped in a black shawl, her arms folded, keeping the shawl closed tight. The bright city lights danced across her face, shimmering against her fair skin, a color that reminded Will of a soft pink pearl. But her color varied with subtle shades of white and apricot. A loose strand of hair fell in front of her eyes. Her hair was brown as dark mahogany that deepened into a midnight black as the tresses flowed underneath into a knot.

"It's not so bad in there, is it?" she said.

"Not my crowd, that's all."

"I didn't think so. But I will say, Mr. Will Oxley, you can hold your own."

He offered her a fresh cigarette, lit it, then leaned against the iron railing, looking back toward the skyline. The noise from below whirled up and around them as they stood in silence, smoking, comfortable together.

After some time, she turned to him. "So, what's your story?" she said simply. "I don't know a thing about you. Are you in the city?"

"I'm on Eighty-Third between Second and Third."

"By the Lexington Diner?"

Will nodded. "I'm on the second floor of a five-story walk-up."

"That's perfect. You're not on the first floor with all the noise—"

"But I don't have to walk up more than one flight of stairs." When he said it, he felt like they had said the same sentence, and he gave her a questioning look.

"I lived on the second floor in Paris, when I lived in the Quarter," she said.

Will turned and glanced inside her apartment. "Well, don't kick yourself. This place isn't too shabby. The waiters are useful."

"Oh, yes, but they aren't always here," she said with a dry wit.

"Well in that case ..." he said, teasing.

"And you grew up in Morristown. A football star?" she said.

Will chuckled. "Yes, I was quarterback, but they didn't choose me because I was good. In fact, I wasn't. We lost every game we played. But I was the only one who could remember three plays: run right, run left, and up the middle."

She laughed.

"The problem was, there were six plays."

She laughed harder. "I wish I were there," she said and covered his hand on the railing with hers.

"From there I went to Rutgers, drank a few beers. Then, about a year after I graduated, I went to war. Now I work at the same insurance company as my dad."

"And you like it?"

"I like the paintings, not the paperwork. And it becomes a game, tracking these guys down. You have to find the pieces and put them together."

"Pieces?"

"Pieces of a puzzle," he explained. "It's how I think of the investigation, as pieces that need to be put together. It's a puzzle to solve."

"Put the pieces together until the picture comes into view? Until the answer comes to light?" she said. Will caught a hint of sarcasm in her voice.

"Simplified, yes, but I have to find the right pieces. I have to know which color goes with which number. That's the tough part, knowing what's what. Each painting is one of a kind, and each deserves to be found. That's a challenge."

"And that's it? That's why you do it?"

Will hesitated, the candid answer too difficult to give. "I find comfort in paintings," he said, letting the explanation stand on its own. "And I get a sense of purpose protecting them."

She looked at him deeply. "They are more than paintings to you, aren't they, Will." Then she added, "There is something more to art than just what we see, isn't there?"

He turned to the skyline, not wanting to discuss the war, not ready to explain his need to find the quiet moment in a painting, a respite from the nightmares and pain. Instead, he savored standing next to her and feeling the closeness of her body, their arms brushing against each other once and then again. The subtle intimacy made him shiver inside. He gazed out over the skyline, but in his mind's eye he pictured the radiance and elegant angles of her face. The touches, the playful words between them, now took on a different meaning. She was investigating, as women do, exploring the possibilities. Will felt a sense of comfort standing next to her and began to hope there would be more nights like these, together.

He angled his head toward the inside. "Who's the movie star?" he said.

"Richard? I always hated the name Dickie. He's in media—newspapers, magazines, that sort of thing. He'll cover the exhibit when it tours Europe."

"Are you two close?" Will asked, the conversation he had overheard fresh in his mind.

Liz flashed him a curious smile. "Am I to become one of your puzzles?"

"Maybe. The mysterious Liz Bower." A warm current raced through him as they teased.

"See what picture appears as you put my pieces together, is that it?"

She studied his face, and Will noted a mischievous glint in her eye. Her words hung in the air, connecting the space between them, and they stood locked together in an intimate standoff. She took a long, slow pull from her cigarette as she stared at him, their eyes playfully challenging the unspoken words. He ached to kiss her, to feel her supple lips press against his. He imagined his hand around her waist pulling her in close, the touch of her dress's thin, smooth fabric. He could almost sense the slight curves of her back. Would she reach for him if he leaned forward or took a slight step toward her? Was she waiting for him to make that bold move? Then she broke the gaze.

"Easy, tiger," she said, her voice teasing, almost suggestive. She stubbed out her cigarette on the railing and flicked it over the edge. "I've got a lot of pieces."

She grinned and walked away, leaving Will wanting and alone with the city's skyline. He turned back to the balcony railing. The white windows beautifully decorated the glass-and-steel skyline, creating a consistently irregular pattern. Will breathed in slowly, catching the perfume that still lingered in front of him. He closed his eyes and could feel Liz leaning into him.

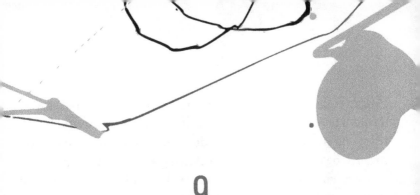

9

IRA OPENED HIS COAT and slipped the small notepad back into his shirt pocket. He stood across from the Bower residence on Park Avenue and scanned the street from one corner to the other. He'd seen a few passersby, including several women walking their dogs, but nothing out of the ordinary. The street stood empty aside from a few parked cars whose license numbers he had already jotted down. Through the glass doors, he could see inside her building. A doorman stood behind a front desk, greeting residents as they entered. He had left the desk twice to fetch packages, leaving Ira little chance to sneak past.

The cool air had wormed under his collar while he watched tuxedoed men and their wives enter and leave the building. A half hour was enough, he thought. He pulled up his coat collar, stepped off the curb, and crossed the street to wait against the building near the entrance. Soon after, when an elderly couple approached and pulled open the door to walk inside, Ira dropped his cigarette to the ground, leaving a thin trail of smoke floating behind, and followed them inside. As the doorman tended to the couple, Ira scooted past unnoticed.

The mailboxes were in an antechamber leading to the elevators. Walnut and copper plated, each was the size of a shoebox, with beveled glass doors and a small keyed lock. Open-slot boxes would have allowed Ira to pull out the mail, but this was a

Park Avenue building, and he was not surprised these boxes were secure. He could pick the lock, he thought, but that would be too risky, and he hadn't intended to do more than scout out the place. Instead, he peered through the beveled glass door of box 30F. Two or three envelopes lay inside. From the markings he could tell they were bills and of no interest to him.

To the left of the mailroom antechamber, an open door led to an adjacent room where there were two large empty trash bins on rollers, a few dollies, and a second door marked Exit. No central trash chute led from the wall, which meant trash was picked up on each floor. That would make their job easier when they conducted a trash cover on Bower because her trash would be directly outside her door. Ira considered riding the elevator up to her floor but decided against the decision given the number of people going in and out of the party. He didn't want to risk being seen.

When he walked back through the lobby, he stopped at the counter. The visitor book lay open, so he took the opportunity to scan the names. Finding ties to the Communist Party was a matter of making connections, one name leading to another. Ira figured she wouldn't work alone. She likely had a partner, someone to help make connections and record information. He pulled his notepad from his suit pocket and started jotting down the first name on the page, but the doorman interrupted before he could finish a second.

"May I help you?" he said.

Ira looked up from the book and met the doorman's eyes. "Wrong building, I guess. Sorry," he said matter-of-factly and moved past the counter and out onto the street.

He buttoned his coat and began trudging up Sixty-Eighth Street toward the Third Avenue el, hunching inward, closing the neck of his coat to protect himself from the gray wind blowing off the East River. He had researched the Bower daughter over the past week. She was a liberal, an intellectual, precisely the type of person the Russians would convert. Typical of what he expected of a Communist woman, she acted strong and independent. From what he understood of Communist marriages, the woman was the more dominant partner. The Rosenbergs were a perfect example. People said Ethel had planned and orchestrated the entire plot. Although Liz wasn't married, Ira figured the same held for father and daughter. She ran the foundation. And, with tonight's party as proof, she appeared to be using her father's business connections for clandestine fundraising. Every dollar she swindled out of these rich people, she probably sent to the Kremlin or used to fund her subversive plans. When she lived in Paris, she'd rented an apartment in the Left Bank, which Ira knew was home to leftist intellectuals and artists. It's probably where she was turned to Communism, brainwashed. When she returned four years ago, she started the foundation, which had quickly funded plenty of international art exhibits—several in Europe and South America. All the exhibits were in countries the Russians were trying to take over. There had been seventeen shows in the last three years, and Ira could not help but wonder if the Bower daughter was sending out military or government secrets. Why else would her foundation focus on the same countries as the Russian Commies?

The close relationship between Bower Manufacturing and the US government concerned Ira as much as the international exhibits, given the opportunity for infiltration and subversion. What if the Bowers gained access where they should not and extracted military information? Bower Manufacturing supplies the government with uniforms and gas masks. What if the Bowers send faulty equipment to the military? Ira could imagine any number of possibilities. When he crossed Park Avenue, he turned down the boulevard to pass the Waldorf Astoria. Commies snared weak-minded sympathizers, manipulating them to carry out their dirty work, and to Ira, the Bower daughter fit the profile.

By placing fellow travelers and spies in strategic positions, the Communist rats could take over the country. Spies existed. He never questioned that fact. And Bower Manufacturing would be a perfect vehicle to steal military secrets and industrial information.

He climbed the stairs to the el train platform, proud he had made a clear connection. Other cases had proved more challenging. The associations to Communism were more subtle and hidden, requiring creativity to uncover the proof and flush out the pinkos. The el train screeched into the platform, steam jetting out from below its boiler as the brakes brought it to a stop, and Ira stepped into the front car.

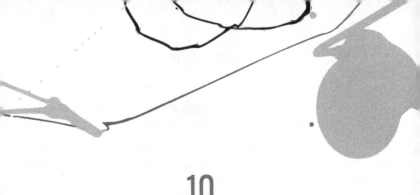

10

THE MEMORY OF LIZ hung in Will's mind the whole next week. He had not expected to be so enamored by her, for her to linger in his mind for so long. He sat back against the plastic seat of the cab on his way up to Harlem and replayed their conversations in his head. He pictured her standing next to him on the balcony with the city lights illuminating her face. Their shared moment on the balcony had given him an odd sense of familiarity and comfort. The soft touches were not what captured his interest but the silences between them. The feeling of standing next to someone and forgetting where you are, other than with that person. And in the moment, feeling that nothing else mattered.

When his cab pulled to a stop at 132nd and Lenox Avenue, Will forced himself to break his thought of her in the black sheath dress. Apartment buildings stretched along the avenue, and passersby filled the sidewalk. Storefront windows displayed chocolate layered cakes and rolls of fabric; their green awnings reached out over their windows with accordion-like metal arms. Clothes hung on lines, and kids leaned over fire escapes, shouting down to overalled friends on the street. Will pulled a piece of paper from his pocket, rereading Clyde Barnett's address. Following the numbers above each building's stoop, he made his way along the avenue.

The brown brick building at 63 West 132nd was guarded by trash cans and a black iron railing weathered by street dirt and age. On the stoop, four young Black boys—twelve, maybe thirteen years old—studied Will with keen eyes as he approached, one of them tapping a splintered stick against the step's edge. The boy was thin and tall. Another, maybe the youngest of the four, wore an oversized coat and whispered to another.

"Is this 132nd Street?" Will asked.

"That's right." The young one was quick to respond.

Will glanced up the stoop to see inside the building. "You know Clyde Barnett?"

The boys stared at their shoes, fidgeting, and the tallest kept tapping his stick like he had not heard the question. Will pulled a cigarette pack from his coat pocket and lit one, letting the moment settle. Then he bent down and offered the open pack to the younger boy. These boys had smoked before, he thought. There was no novelty here, and they would welcome the handout.

Will jingled the pack. "I'm not a cop, if that's what you're wondering."

The smaller boy looked up. "Don't usually have folks like you comin' through here asking questions is all."

Will shook out a single cigarette as a gesture that he did not mean any trouble. The boy did not move. He scrutinized Will for a moment as if considering his options, then reached toward the cigarette.

"Otis, don't," the other boys said in unison.

Otis's hand froze. He glanced at his friends and back at Will for a second, then took the cigarette. He was a lanky, pigeon-toed kid who seemed the most adventurous of the four, if not the smartest. He studied Will from head to toe as if judging whether he could hold his own against Clyde, then pointed up the stoop.

"Second floor. Apartment D."

Will started up the steps but stopped, turned, and stuck out his hand. Otis had probably never shaken a white man's hand before. "Thanks, Otis."

The boy considered Will's hand a moment, then he slowly reached out and shook it with caution, his eyes widening when their skin touched.

As Will entered the building and climbed the stairs, the smell of hard living surrounded him. Decades of dirt and snow from work boots. Cigarette smoke and sweat from years of manual labor and nights out at the Savoy. He ran his hand up the railing as he climbed, smooth like a river rock under his palm, worn from years of use. Will worked his way down the narrow hall, the ceiling pocked with empty light bulb sockets, to Clyde's apartment, 2D. Finding the door ajar, he edged it open.

"Hello?" he said, announcing himself.

He gave two hard knocks on the door, and when there was no answer, he stepped into the one-room apartment. A stillness hung in the air, quiet and empty. A small table with two folding chairs was in the middle of the room. In the corner, a twin mattress stripped of sheets lay askew atop its box spring. Next to the bed, the drawers of a tattered blue bureau had been pulled out and emptied. Clyde had left in a hurry.

Will stepped further in and eyed the room, hoping for a piece of the puzzle to present itself, but he did not expect to find anything. Contact names, drop-off locations, buyers— those types of clues were never found. He worked his way around the apartment, checking the empty drawers. Inside the closet, hangers hung empty. He checked the bathroom, and when he turned back, he found Otis standing square in the front threshold.

"You ain't gonna find Clyde here, mister."

"I can see that. What happened?" Will asked, sitting down in one of the folding chairs to encourage the kid to relax. Otis studied the room and shrugged. Will figured curiosity had brought the boy up to the apartment and that he had lost interest upon seeing the room empty.

"You live nearby?" Will asked and, noticing Otis no longer had his cigarette, offered the open cigarette pack again.

"Next door." Otis stepped closer, pulled out a cigarette, and stuffed his other hand into his jean pocket.

"Have you seen Clyde or talked to him lately?"

Otis shifted his feet. "Kept to himself mostly. Heard he did some time up in Buffalo. What are you searching for anyways?"

Will lit Otis's cigarette and ignored the question. "Anyone else lived with him?"

"I see other people come and go, but he's probably sharing rent. Most people on the floor have to take in a lodger every once in a while." Otis took a pull on his cigarette and leaned back against the door frame. "The lady up on three, Mrs. Jackie, she collects rent. I've heard her complain that Clyde paid late every month. I guess he finally took off."

Will tapped his ashes onto a discarded plate resting on the table, his mind turning the pieces and trying to bring the foggy image into focus. More than likely, Clyde had spent time in Buffalo for petty theft—taking jewelry or boosting a car. He was an amateur who had come into a windfall with the stolen Pollock.

"Where'd Clyde hang out, Otis? Where might he spend some money?"

Otis studied Will for a long time. He glanced at Will's cigarette pack, then stood there silent. Amused, Will slid the pack across the table, and Otis tucked it into his pocket.

"The Palm," Otis said matter-of-factly. "Everybody's down at the Palm at night, mister. If Clyde hangs out anywhere, it's there."

Will walked the seven blocks down Lenox Avenue toward the Palm, past brown brick apartment buildings, a small grocery, and a variety store. Two old men slumped in folding chairs underneath a barber pole stared at him as he walked by. Their shop window advertised the newest straightened, flattened, or greased-down hairstyles. He was an unusual sight, Will knew, a white man walking down Lenox Avenue in a suit. Everyone had to be questioning his purpose, and he couldn't help but do the same. Would the bartender of the Palm even be a lead? Was he wasting his time? He had to admit it was a long shot, but an amateur thief could never keep his mouth shut. They always bragged.

When he reached the neon sign flashing *Palm Café*, he stepped inside and crossed the black-and-white checkered floor to the bar that ran the length of the restaurant. Opposite the bar past the dance floor were the dining tables where the hustlers and lindy-hoppers would be eating later that night, jazz playing and drinks splashing out of their glasses.

Will asked for a beer from the bartender at the far end of the bar, who wore a crisp white shirt with the sleeves rolled high and a black tie. The bartender looked up from talking with two well-dressed men, and all three of them stared. They didn't want him here. He had been careful with his voice, not to sound threatening, but he couldn't read their faces, not from this distance. After a moment, the bartender collected himself and crossed the bar with a dishtowel in hand, easing the tension in the room. He grabbed a beer from a cooler under the bar and dropped the bottle in front of Will. Maybe he thought Will was a bookie or a cop. What other white man would walk into the Palm in the middle of the afternoon? Will was too clean-cut for a bookie, so the bartender probably pegged him for a cop.

"That'll be fifty-five cents," he said, wiping the bar with his dish towel.

Will placed a ten-dollar bill on the worn oak bar, worth a week's rent for the bartender, and as he slid the bill to the back edge of the bar he asked, "Do you know Clyde Barnett?" The bartender gave little outward reaction but studied Will, twisting the rag in his hand. Cops usually did not pay, so Will guessed the bartender was now figuring him for a bookie, which was good because most people talked to bookies.

The bartender shook his head. "Can't say that I do, mister. A lot of folks come through the Palm," he said, picking up a glass and wiping the rim clean.

Will placed another two dollars on top of the ten, but the bartender made no move toward the money. Instead, he turned and strolled to the far end of the bar, where he rejoined the men nursing their bourbons. Will took a slow sip from his beer and, over the edge of the bottle, watched the men whisper among themselves. Will needed the bartender's help. He needed more pieces to his puzzle because all he had was an open crate, an abstract expressionist painting, and a missing truck driver. Now Will found himself sitting at the bar of the Palm Café under the bartender's judging eye, hoping he would talk if he knew anything at all. After a while, the bartender returned and started slow, apparently trying not to commit too much. He must have concluded that the threat of not cooperating with Will was greater than doing so. Will was thankful either way.

"Clyde comes in pretty often. But I haven't seen him for a week or so."

"How can I reach him?"

The bartender shrugged and offered a blank stare. He wasn't offering much and hadn't taken the money. Will had already placed twelve dollars down and didn't want to go any higher. He didn't have enough for a cab ride as it was. He would be taking the subway home.

"Did Clyde ever say anything interesting?" Will asked, hoping to pry out some information.

"Mister, I wish I could help, but I wasn't involved in anything Clyde did. Don't know anything about it." He said it as if trying to close the door on the subject, not wanting to get further involved.

But Will considered his comments incriminating. The bartender knew Clyde had done *something*, and Will guessed that something was the same something he was after. "What did Clyde do?" Will said. He gave the bartender a moment to work out his options. On the one hand, if he thought Will was a bookie and didn't talk, someone would return, and he'd have to pay in a worse way. And if he thought Will was a cop who bribed, then Will was a crooked cop, which meant just as much trouble.

Eventually the bartender sighed, slid the twelve dollars off the bar, and leaned toward Will.

"I don't know much about it, but Clyde came in maybe a week ago. The boys down at the end of the bar said he kept talking about how he had come into a big score, said he kept shouting about stupid white folk and their art. But man, Clyde was always shouting. You can't take any of it for the truth."

"What else?"

"Nothing. Like I said, haven't seen him since."

"Do you know where he went?"

"Detroit, Chicago. Who knows, man? Folks move all over for all kinds of reasons, especially if they've got trouble following them." His eyes fixed on Will as if pointing to the obvious.

Will took the last few swallows of his beer then stood. "If you hear something, give me a call." He pointed to the bartender's pocket. "There'll be more of that if you do." Will wrote his number on a napkin and placed it on the bar. "And if you don't call, I'll know. Then I'm coming back, and there won't be a conversation."

Will caught the Eighth Avenue subway and slumped on the rattan seat, his palms resting on the corncob pattern. The interior lights of the subway car flickered, and advertisements flew by as they rushed past local stops toward downtown. The ceiling fans hung still. Petty theft was different than fencing a stolen painting, Will thought as the subway shot through the tunnels, the metal cars clanking at each turn. And judging by the condition of Clyde's apartment, he did not seem like a guy who knew art or had a network. Clyde was not sophisticated enough to bring a painting back into the market, to work the small galleries and disreputable antique shops. If he had stolen the Pollock, he would have to know how to fake provenance and negotiate pricing and buyers. It was professional work and would take a professional fence. Will figured if Clyde had moved the painting through the market, he had to have done it through Lorenzo Marzano.

As a fence, Lorenzo might pay Clyde two or three percent of the painting's value before collecting ten percent selling to his buyer. Lorenzo acted as the middleman between the art thief and the broader black market. But Will always paid Lorenzo fifteen for information that led to a recovery. Turning on his sources was not something Lorenzo wanted to do, but greed always took over, and fifteen for less work was better than ten.

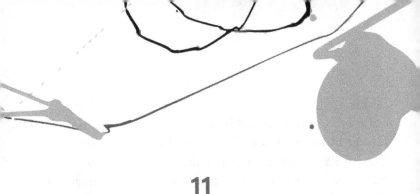

11

BY THE TIME WILL MADE IT BACK to the office, the sun had crossed over and begun to spread along the Hudson River, its golden rays stretching between the tall buildings and creating shadows that darkened the corners of the city. Charlie's folders were straightened and placed on the shelves behind his desk, which meant he had already left to make it home to Poughkeepsie for dinner. Will's first phone call was to Lorenzo, but no one answered. Will figured he would have to call the restaurant several times before reaching him. Alternatively, he knew he could meet him at the Fulton Fish Market at five in the morning. Will had found Lorenzo there several times before, buying that day's menu for restaurants in Little Italy.

Next, he called the police station again, asking for transcripts of the investigation.

"We're busy with real cases," the cop said. Will had heard the same answer every week and was ready to give up on ever obtaining a report. "We had over a hundred and twenty-five murders last year in Manhattan, and the last case we're going to bother with is a lost painting."

"Stolen," Will reminded him, but the phone had already clicked dead.

With Lorenzo not answering and no police report, Will turned to the details of a new client to keep the Pollock dead ends off his mind. The week before, he had met Mrs. Harcourt over tea at her brownstone and learned she was a descendant of a Sir George Harcourt, Earl of Berkshire. She had spent ten days on a Cunard ocean liner crossing the Atlantic to be near her one daughter, whose husband worked in advertising, mostly household items like Tide laundry detergent and Tupperware. Mrs. Harcourt had jewelry of exquisite craftsmanship, silver serving trays, and scalloped warming dishes from the family estate at Windborne, none of which Will would typically insure. But on her blue living room wall hung a simple frame, no more than eight inches square. The frame contained a sixteenth-century engraving of a monk sitting at a writing table, the delicate pages of his bible open and a halo of light emanating from a candle. Moonlight poured in through the windows and across the wooden floorboards.

The engraving would require research because Will had no comparable pieces to help determine the replacement value. So he turned to his folders on the floor, searching for examples of similar engravings sold in galleries. In the middle of reading an article, the harsh ring of the phone startled him; he reached out and grabbed the receiver.

"Want to have a drink?" Liz said on the other end of the line.

Will's breath quickened at the sound of her voice. "How about the Monkey Bar?"

At seven o'clock, Will pulled open the etched glass door and stepped into the Monkey Bar. He crossed the intimate space, slipping through the high tables with miniature candles that flickered yellow, and slid onto a barstool. The sprawling wallpaper throughout the bar portrayed colorful caricatures of monkeys mixing banana daiquiris and serving martinis under palm trees. At the far end of the room, carpeted steps led to a sunken dining room bustling with waiters in white dinner jackets.

"Good to see you, Mr. Oxley," the bartender said as he flipped a coaster down, placing a beer on top. The bottles of his trade glistened behind him.

"Evening, Darcy."

"Paper?" Without waiting for a reply, Darcy pulled a newspaper from underneath the bar and dropped it in front of Will.

Will flipped through the paper, reading nothing in particular until he noticed an article on the group of artists the papers had named "The Two Hundred." The article singled out several artists who'd been accused of Communist affiliations and provided detailed descriptions of their paintings and union memberships. Alongside the article was a photograph of the Roschin mural at the New York Post Office—the same mural Will had seen in the *Hearst Daily*. Will studied the images depicting New York's early history: the Dutch buying Manhattan Island from the Indians, the Flour Riot of 1837, the opening of Ellis Island to immigrants. The article claimed Andrei Roschin had used red paint in subversive ways—red books, red ties, red everything. The article used this notion to label him a Communist and quoted local politicians' demands that the mural be removed.

Will laid the paper down, took a sip of his beer, and stared into the dark mirror behind the bar. The candles' flames reflected in the glass, dancing like stars shimmering off a lake. He saw the image of Liz standing at the entrance of the bar, collecting herself. The candlelight danced against her face, and a sense of warmth spread through Will as if he had known her for years. She struck him as lovelier than when he saw her last, and he expected he might feel that way each time he saw her. She had set her hair differently, no longer a haphazard knot at the nape of her neck but smooth and manicured with the hair falling straight down then curling inward just above her shoulders. Pinned on top of her head was a leopard-print pillbox hat. Her eyes seemed to be of every hue of blue, a deep ocean of ultramarine and cerulean. He imagined her as a muse to a painter and all the details on which the painter might obsess. To create the brightness she radiated around her cheeks and the bridge of her nose, the painter would smoothly blend pink, white, apricot, and light browns, then pink-grays, blue-grays to turn the shape of her jawline and create the shadows on her neck. How many times would he paint and repaint the curl of her hair to reflect the subtle transitions from aged mahogany to dark chocolate, then struggle to keep the warmth of her personality as her hair deepened to a coffee black in the folds? The painter might fuss over her eyes for months to capture the essence of her soul, until they could belong to no other muse but her.

She hung her black wrap on a hook then straightened her pencil skirt. She navigated through the high tables and down the long bar toward him. "Scotch, neat," she said to the bartender as she slid onto the barstool.

The casual, elegant way she ordered her scotch made Will want her more. Will had ordered scotches before, but they were just scotches. When Liz ordered one, the words seemed to take on a different meaning, stirring feelings of exhilaration and excitement, of adventure and exploration. Darcy poured her a lowball glass, and she took a slow sip, savoring the smokiness.

"I'm glad you called," he said.

"I wanted company." She smiled and placed her hand on his forearm.

She stared into his eyes as if wanting to say something different, more meaningful. For the first time, she appeared before him unencumbered, without the partygoers and the foundation wrappings, simple and straightforward. Honest.

Girls had pursued him through the years, but none of the relationships lasted. That element of trust was always missing, knowing someone so completely that you could divulge your secrets without fear. So Will had stayed single while his childhood friends came home from the war and bought Chevrolets and washing machines and moved out to the suburbs to raise perfect families behind white picket fences.

Then she turned away and focused her eyes on the back bar. The moment was brief, but when she turned back, whatever concern seemed to fill her mind had disappeared. She pulled out a cigarette from a silver case, and Will lit the end, watching her lips as they tightened and pulled. She exhaled a thin stream of smoke that floated in front of them.

"Tell me about the Pollock," she said. "We're a team, remember?"

When he described the visit to Clyde Barnett's apartment, she leaned in.

"If you find this Clyde, can he lead you to the painting?" she asked.

"He can lead me to the buyer."

"And if he hasn't sold it, are you certain you can find it?"

Will nodded with confidence. "He'll sell it. There would be no reason to steal it otherwise."

"But how does one buy a stolen painting? How would this Clyde sell it?"

"I don't think he has a buyer. He's an amateur without a network, which means he'll have to go through a fence, a middleman, and the best fence I know is Lorenzo Marzano." Will explained how Lorenzo gave him access to a loose network of thieves and disreputable art dealers.

She asked more questions that would have customarily aroused suspicion in Will, a client's unusual interest in specific details of the case, but she seemed to enjoy playing the part of the partner, a team.

"Not all my cases are dramatic," Will said. "Last year, I recovered a French sculpture in a pawn shop on North Broad in Jersey.

The collector had made his money in tomatoes of all things—he sold them to Campbell's soup. Anyway, he receives a call from a friend who says he spotted the sculpture in a pawn shop. I go over to the shop and the sculpture is sitting on a back table. It was a simple sculpture of a woman floating atop a wave with a flowy dress, the wave and dress seamlessly flowing from one to the other. When I told the pawn shop owner it was stolen, he quickly said he bought it from a man named Ronny. I never found Ronny, but it turns out the collector's housekeeper was paid by someone to make copies of his house keys."

Darcy brought them a shrimp cocktail hors d'oeuvre, and Will spoke of other cases. She listened intently and laughed at times when he described the more ridiculous ones. Will felt he could sit with her forever, enjoying the conversation that seemed to come naturally to them. They easily jumped between topics, finding shared humor in different stories.

"Do you miss Paris?" he asked over the flicker of candlelight.

"Yes. You should return some day. We could go together." She smiled. "But I love it here. This is home. And the Foundation is doing important work. I've provided funds to coordinate several MoMA exhibits in Latin America and now we're going to Europe. It's exciting work."

"Why do you send the exhibits overseas?"

"It's important for other countries to see American art, don't you think? The freedom the artists have, the freedom of expression, of spirit and character. I believe the artists and their paintings embody what our country is about. The paintings are more than pigment on linen canvases, Will. They could change the world."

She spoke freely and with excitement. They ordered another drink, not paying attention to the time, and only when Darcy said the bar was closing did they realize the evening had passed without them noticing.

Liz took a long sip of her scotch and then said, "Let's take a walk."

Will stood and held out his hand. She clasped his fingers, pulling herself off the stool, and he led her back through the Monkey Bar. He lifted her wrap for her to slip into, and they stepped outside.

The air smelled like New York: fifty years of rubber tires rolling over old concrete, wet bedrock and construction and steam, perfume and cigars. It smelled like life repeating itself a thousand times. She said she wanted to walk along the park, so they went up Fifth Avenue past the fashion stores and the Plaza, its flags flowing in the cool breeze. They crossed Central Park South, slipping in and out of the glow from the streetlamps. Along the east wall of the park, with its rough-cut interlocking stones, tree roots had uprooted the cobbled sidewalk, and Will made sure Liz was careful with her step. He reached out for her hand, and her fingers found his, delicately sliding between them. They strolled along the park wall, unhurried, stretching the evening further. A sense of comfort settled in Will when he walked next to her. He placed a hand on the small of her back to turn her toward Park Avenue, and a shiver spread through his hand and up his arm at the feel of her shape, the delicate bend in her back. They passed the cigar stores and shoe repair shops, commenting on knickknacks in the windows, and walked down Park Avenue toward the entrance of her building. "This is me," she said, placing her fingers delicately around his wrist to slow them to a stop. She reached for the door and then turned to him as if in unfinished thought. She remained fixed on him for a moment, and Will sensed she wanted to tell him something. Then she smiled at him as if shaking off the thought.

"Goodnight," she said and gave him a soft kiss on the cheek. Then she pushed open the door and walked in.

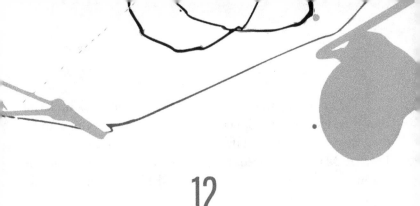

12

AT FOUR IN THE MORNING, buildings flipped past Will's cab window like a motion picture show as he traveled down to the Fulton Fish Market. The driver approached each light as it turned green, cruising down the empty avenue during the one quiet moment when Manhattan took a quick breath, shifting from late-night bohemia to early morning frenzy.

Along the street, diners were opening, their lights still dim as the owners prepared for the early morning regulars, and Will could not help but wonder if Liz was still in bed fast asleep, warm and dreaming under the covers. Walking together along the park wall, talking of Paris, feeling the curve in her back, had been blissful. He gazed out the window, imagining similar moments with new ends and different beginnings.

When the cab pulled into the parking lot of the Fulton warehouse, Will paid the driver then planted himself near several wooden barrels to wait for Lorenzo. Diesel exhaust mixed with the smells of salt and fish that settled in the air around him like a dense fog over the East River. Delivery trucks rumbled over the cobbled pavement under a deep blue haze of early morning.

Liz had asked about the Pollock, but she wanted something more than the stolen painting. He could not help imagining the possibilities ahead of him.

The knocking motor of a white refrigeration truck broke his thoughts. He dropped his cigarette, pressing out the end with his foot, then stepped toward the vehicle. The door swung open, and Lorenzo Marzano stepped out looking like he'd stuffed four too many layers under his dark wool coat, the buttons straining like caps on a soda bottle.

"Will Oxley. Always a surprise when you show up." He smiled at Will, keeping a short cigar clenched between his teeth, and took in the stench of the market with a deep breath. "Do you smell that, Will?" he yelled as a forklift rattled by, yellow light circling as it carried ice-packed boxes of fish. "Fresh fish, my friend. Fresh fish." Lorenzo reached out both hands and gave Will two firm pats on the shoulders, as if they were old friends.

In reality, Will had met Lorenzo six years ago when a small warehouse he insured caught fire in lower Manhattan. When he reviewed the contract, Will noticed that Lorenzo was the beneficiary of the claim but not the building owner, which pointed to insurance fraud. And because cases like Lorenzo's were difficult to prove and carried a significant legal cost, Will knew All American would pay the claim and figured Lorenzo knew the same.

The more interesting fact that had caught Will's attention was Lorenzo's knowledge of the growing art market. Lorenzo knew the most sought-after painters—Picasso, Kandinsky, Matisse—and the value of their work. He considered paintings as if they were a form of cash themselves. The notion occurred to Will that, as prices in the market began to climb, and gallery owners, dealers, and collectors had taken notice, so too had the criminal underworld. Lorenzo spoke fluently about cash value and provenance as if he were an art aficionado. Will hesitated to jump to conclusions, but Lorenzo did not seem like a man who frequented the galleries.

Taking advantage of the situation, Will threatened to report Lorenzo for insurance fraud unless he helped him from time to time. In return, Will would ignore the fraud incident and pay Lorenzo the occasional recovery fee. And thus began their relationship.

"Have you heard anything about a stolen Pollock?" Will asked.

"We're late," Lorenzo said, ignoring the question and pointing to the packed trucks in the lot as he moved toward the loading-dock doors. "Fish get unloaded at midnight, selling starts at four, and they'll be hosing off the floors in five hours. Place'll shut down until tonight." He led Will onto the concrete loading dock and through the first bay, where men in high rubber boots and flannel shirts were shouting and packing ice into Styrofoam boxes. Grappling hooks hung from iron beams, and coffee stains colored the floor. A black water hose wrapped around the stalls, disappearing and reappearing as it ran along the aisles like a snake.

There were as many tattoos on the fishmongers' arms as there were varieties of fish at the market. Cod, bluefish, mackerel, and halibut were sold in the front. Lobster and soft-shell crab were sold on the far side with the other shellfish: oysters, mussels, and snails. Smaller packages were wrapped and taped in brown paper, while larger orders were boxed and rushed across the floor on dollies, loaded into trucks, and shipped away.

As Lorenzo moved through the front of the market, vendors acknowledged him with a nod or tip of the hat in a way that didn't say good morning as much as it signaled respect. He stopped at one stall and shook hands with an Irish man with Celtic script tattoos on his arms and what Will assumed was an inmate number cut into his wrist.

"I need twenty-five snapper and as many cod," Lorenzo said then turned to Will. "Kelly's been here forty years."

The Irishman nodded. "Started when I was a boy. Took over the stall when my father died. Most of us have."

Lorenzo clapped his hands together. "Best fishmonger at Fulton," he said. Kelly began to pack up an icebox without handing Lorenzo a sales ticket, which reminded Will the market was still riddled with corruption, steeped in a subculture that harkened back to when sailors and prostitutes filled the wharf. This was partly how Lorenzo kept informed of criminal activity.

As Lorenzo moved on, pointing to the different stalls, he spoke under his breath. "I haven't heard much about your painting. I heard it happened, but nothing more," he said then stopped at the next stall, picking up a shrimp and smelling it for freshness.

"Who bought it?" Will asked.

"Don't know." Lorenzo signaled to the shrimp vendor, who filled his order of twenty pounds. "We haven't heard that the painting has changed hands. All we know is a colored boy stole it."

Lorenzo moved to another fish cart full of iced-down halibut. He fingered one or two, checking the slick of the skin. "Listen," Lorenzo said after stepping away from the stall. "You can't keep coming to me. If the guys knew I'm working with you, they'd cut me out. My sources would dry up."

"You've got your fingers in more than I care to know about, Lorenzo. I don't get into your business, but I still need your help. That was the arrangement we made."

"You are in my business, though, see? And it can't last forever."

"This one's important, Lorenzo. What do you know?"

Lorenzo was silent for a long time then finally said, "Nobody seems to know anything. The colored boy isn't anyone we know, not a regular. And the painting hasn't surfaced, which means the boy may not have sold it yet."

"He has to come through you," Will said. "He has no network. This guy's an amateur."

Lorenzo began navigating the aisles of stalls through the brick columns and back toward the parking lot. As Will followed behind, he considered the likelihood that Clyde did not sell through Lorenzo. Clyde had pulled the painting from a crate—*this* specific painting. He hadn't bothered with any others. To get the money, he would have to sell the picture into the market. He'd have to have a buyer. And to have a buyer, Clyde would have to have a network or someone who did. Lorenzo has the network to get these paintings back into the market. Anything else didn't make sense.

They reached the white refrigerator truck, and Lorenzo jumped in, shutting the door behind him. He stuck his head out the window. "Listen, eventually the painting will surface, and I'll get information on it. But maybe he had a partner. Maybe the deal didn't go as planned. Maybe he got paid and gave the buyer the slip. Any number of scenarios are possible, Will." Lorenzo pulled his head back into the truck, and the engine rumbled as he turned the key.

"You owe me, Lorenzo."

"And you never let me forget that, do you?"

The smooth whitewall tires rolled backward, and the truck drove out the lot. The morning sun began to peek over the metal roof of the fish market warehouse, and the mongers started mopping their stalls. After a day's sleep, they would start again at midnight. Will headed down Fulton Street toward the office, frustrated, feeling like he had gained nothing from Lorenzo.

Will worked his way back through lower Manhattan, down Water Street and up Pine toward his office. The speed of the cabs had picked up and with it the pace of the city. He stopped for a coffee at Peal Street Deli, the brass bell on top of the door chiming as he entered and left. He rode the elevator to the twenty-third floor of the All American offices, and when he arrived he saw Pritchett had placed another stack of paperwork on his desk with a note that read, *Where are you on the Pollock?* Charlie was out making morning sales calls, asking businessmen and middle-aged women to sign up for a promise in exchange for a monthly payment to All American.

Steam rose from Will's cup of black coffee. He leaned back, propped his feet up on the desk, and glanced at the miniature landscape painting hanging on the wall. He had bought it for almost nothing in a West Village shop four years ago. The image appeared before him like a mystical photograph, a rugged yet sublime creek winding through a beautiful rock formation. The majestic detail conjured up images of Lewis and Clark on their transcontinental expedition across the beautiful, pristine land-scape. The American frontier. A soft and peaceful image that stilled his mind.

Will decided Pollock's paintings were landscapes of sorts—abstract, vast spaces spread across a canvas with no borders, like the open planes of the American West. They exuded the same sense of yearning, the same sense of unbridled passion and free-dom. The open canvases were expansive, powerful works with a dramatic display of wild and majestic self-determination.

He studied the small photo of the Pollock tacked on his wall. Truth be told, Will had started to like the painting. Having reflected on the Pollock paintings since he started the case, he decided the paintings were more complicated than he had appre-ciated at first. While remaining two-dimensional, they achieved both flatness and depth. No brushstrokes could be seen on the canvas, only paint, but the physicality of it, the act of pouring and splattering paint on the massive canvases, could not be ques-tioned. The gestures were sweeping, large, and aggressive. But all the Pollock paintings appeared similar to each other. Impossible for someone without a trained eye to tell the difference or pick out the most valuable, which brought Will back to the same ques-tion: Why did Clyde steal that specific painting?

Will imagined Clyde circling the crates at Elaine's, reading the exterior labels to find the right one. He wouldn't have known which painting to steal without help. The theft was not opportunistic. Clyde had picked a specific painting at Elaine's, but he did not seem like a person who planned. He must have had a partner making the decisions for him. He'd stolen the painting either with a buyer in mind or in hopes a buyer would materialize. However, the possibility of either of those two scenarios occurring narrowed if Clyde did not have a network.

The sun grew bright, and Will stepped out to grab a pastrami sandwich from the Bull & Bear nearby on Wall Street. Sitting at the counter, he gazed out the front window. The runners for the traders raced out of 11 Wall Street and into the deli, ordering sandwiches wrapped in white butcher paper and then darting back to the Stock Exchange.

Will remembered a schoolmate from Rutgers who had become a trader saying they worked in teams. One trader worked the phone on the trading floor, taking trades and signaling to his partner, who stood deep in the pit. The pit partner flashed signs, buying and selling stock, and wrote the information on his notepad, then signaled back to his partner on the phone to close the trade. Unless you paid close attention, you would never know they worked together. The entire scene appeared to be complete pandemonium. At first, the action—arms flying in the air, the shouting—might appear random. But after time, patterns emerged as teams of two and three worked together to create a network from buyer to seller. Choreographed chaos. Sitting at the deli window, watching the traders rush by, Will decided these tactics could be used to steal the Pollock. A team of two that at first seemed random. Partners. Someone with a network, with connections. Someone on the inside.

And why not Charlene, Will thought, recalling Elaine's sole employee at the gallery. What if Clyde and Charlene had worked together? Clyde was a thief, as amateur as he might be, and Charlene had the network, the buyers.

Charlene could have used Clyde to rob the gallery and set up the buyer herself. That would explain how Clyde could sell the painting without Lorenzo in just a few days. Charlene had the network and the buyer prearranged, which explained why that specific Pollock was targeted. Simple. In fact, quite cunning for a young girl who presented herself as such a waif. Will wrapped up the rest of his sandwich, tossed it in the trash, and stepped out onto Wall Street, raising his hand for a cab.

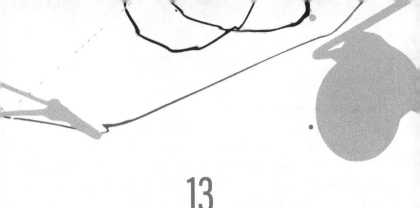

13

AS WILL HAD EXPECTED, the Stable Gallery stood empty at one in the afternoon. Standing alone in the vast space, with paintings looming on the walls around him, he found himself drawn again to the back of the gallery where the large Pollock hung, an expansive landscape spread across the canvas. He stood squarely in front of the picture and studied the composition. The strands of paint appeared as if they'd been whipped and flung together, rising and falling into a dense tangle of arteries, pulsating in front of him with a kind of life energy. They twisted backward as if trying to pull Will's subconscious deep into the painting with them. He followed one loop into the next, shifting across the painting with no place to rest, no edge to keep him contained. If it weren't for the canvas edge, the paint strands would have stretched on forever.

The painting seemed to grab Will and pull him inside, penetrating his whole body. He felt as though he'd become part of an inner world he'd known nothing about, inside Pollock's mind. His pain and struggle, his passion and anger, had all been bottled up then exploded onto the canvas.

He imagined Pollock moving around the gigantic canvas with bucket and brush in hand as he splattered and moved, splattered and moved, his feet dancing like an Indian around a ceremonial fire, sometimes quick and spontaneous, other times slow and deliberate. With a gentle wrist, he swirled the black paint onto the canvas, ending in a small, soft pool of black. Then, grabbing a stick, he violently flung more paint down. White and black. Layer after layer. Lines and puddles. Lines and puddles. Then a series of violent splatters. Methodically shifting around the painting, lost in his own mind, the Pollock of Will's imagination moved in a state of semiconsciousness.

When Will pulled himself back and took in the painting as a whole, he could not question the cohesiveness of the piece. It reminded him of ancient Indian pictographs painted on sandstone walls, of tribal wars and mystical rituals. Pollock had created a crystalline network of paint in which each sinew stood on its own yet joined with the rest to create a field of balance and cohesion. Perfect balance. The effect engulfed Will, leaving him almost in a trance. Only when Elaine glided out from around the back of the gallery did he break away from the painting.

"Oh my God, how fabulous. I thought I heard someone," she said before turning and yelling toward the back of the gallery. "Charlene, Will's here."

Elaine gave Will's arm a hard squeeze. "What are you doing here? Oh, who cares. How absolutely fabulous. We're starting to pack the MoMA exhibit tomorrow. They've picked all the pieces. Schneller is bringing half the crates tomorrow and the other half next week, but it will take us forever to get organized."

"Is this one going?" he asked, motioning toward the large Pollock.

"Yes, of course. It's fabulous, isn't it?" Then she pointed around the gallery. "The de Kooning will go. The Motherwell, the Newell, and the Rothko. They're all absolutely fabulous."

"Why are they all so large?"

"Aren't they fantastic? It is a way to make the experience more direct, more impactful. These are no longer tiny paintings, like the French. They swallow you, don't they? And once Pollock went large, everyone did." Then she laughed. "It also helped that we were knee-deep with canvas after the war. Central Art Supply on Tenth has hundreds of rolls for sale. You can get eleven yards of a ten-foot roll for twenty-five dollars."

Will couldn't argue. These painters had no money. They were eating ketchup and water as tomato soup. Finding large rolls of canvas at those prices would be a steal. They could experiment on a large scale without losing much money.

"But that's not why you're here, is it?" Elaine asked.

"I wanted to take another look around, ask you a few questions," Will said, careful not to reveal his suspicion of Charlene quite yet. "Sometimes you miss something the first time around."

"Clues? You're on a trail. How exciting!" She squeezed his arm again and led him to the couch and chairs in the back corner of the gallery near the office.

"Charlene," she called out as they sat, "bring some white. I am not about to talk to this beautiful man without some wine."

As if on cue, Charlene sauntered through the back office door carrying a bottle of white wine, two glasses, and a beer. She couldn't have been more than twenty-three, with a small face and a perky nose. Thieves can come in all shapes and sizes. Will could not discredit the fact that she knew which paintings were in which crates, and he was sure she knew buyers.

"Beer, right?" she said brightly, handing him his beer and placing the wine bottle down. Thin as a rail, she reached up to fiddle with her black boy-cut hair, elbows sharpening as she did. She appeared playful, carefree.

Will thanked her for the beer, and Elaine immediately asked about the Pollock.

"I think the thief had a partner to sell the painting," Will said, glancing at Charlene. He expected a sign of nervousness but saw none. Then, as Charlene leaned in to pour Elaine a glass of wine, he noticed her hand slide smoothly across the small of Elaine's back, a tender gesture signaling an intimacy he had not expected. The gesture ran counter to his suspicions. Most thieves don't steal from their lovers. The touch seemed genuine, not one with an ulterior motive.

"Obviously," Charlene said with exaggeration as she plopped down on the couch. "I could have told you that." She took a good sip of her wine. "But the question is, who would buy the Pollock? Everybody talks about Pollock, but nobody *buys* Pollock. Inspect our records. I can't sell one, certainly not a smaller, earlier painting. The critics fight over him. They love him and hate him. The artists are jealous. They say he's broken through, done what they've all wanted to do. He's America's Picasso. People come to stare at the famous painter. But the gallery makes no money off any of that." She took another sip of her wine. "Now his paintings simply hang on walls, and he's isolated himself up in Springs, near the Hamptons. We might be the one gallery left showing him. I don't know. The Janis maybe, but even they're dropping him. He sold one painting at the last show, that's it."

Will frowned. He suspected Pollock paintings would be hard to sell, but he assumed there would be a small market. There had to be a market; otherwise, what was the point of stealing the Pollock.

"Yes, yes, you're thinking of the murals," Charlene said, apparently noticing Will's confusion. "*Autumn Rhythm, No. 1.* Peggy Guggenheim bought one. MoMA bought another. But that was three years ago. What has anyone bought since then? Tell me, what has he done since that one great summer? He's completely imploded."

"So you don't have any buyers of Pollock paintings?" Will asked, dumbfounded.

"No." She slammed the word down as if closing the lid on the subject.

Charlene's words took a minute to register, but when they did, the puzzle Will had been constructing broke. Pieces he had recently connected decoupled like derailed train cars. Without buyers and a partner to access them, Clyde would have been challenged to sell the painting for quick cash. There had to be a market and a buyer for Clyde to make money. If there was no money, why steal the Pollock?

"Pollock has become a tough client," Elaine added. "And as you can see, Charlene's a bit tired of it."

"A bit? He asks for advances all the time, when he knows his paintings aren't selling. But who does he blame? Me. Cursing at me. Telling me I don't know what I'm doing, I don't know how to sell. Threatening to take his paintings to another gallery. But he can't, and he knows it. Then he starts apologizing like a little boy. It's strange. *He's* strange, and I don't like him. People have moved on. De Kooning and Kline, that's who's selling. Galleries with those artists are making money."

"It's a fight to the top," Elaine said, "between Pollock and de Kooning, to be the best, and everyone's watching. Everyone wants to see who's going to be the greatest American painter. The pressure gets to them, but it gets to Pollock the most. De Kooning's quiet about it. He's much more controlled."

Charlene laughed then swallowed most of her wine. "Oh, it's vicious, and their wives fuel it—sometimes it seems like they're competing more than the artists! The critics fuel it, too, Greenberg and Rosenberg, and this MoMA exhibit isn't helping, sending these paintings throughout Europe as symbols of America. There are others, of course, the whole group down in the village. Ten or twelve of them, all abstract, all pushing the limit. Paris is dead, I tell you. Everyone wants to be *the* great American artist."

"Oh, yes. And you know Pollock was on the cover of *Life*. Oh, the article was fabulous. His photo came with a daring title—'The Greatest Living Painter in the United States' I believe it was." Elaine tapped her lips, considering what she had said. "Is that right, Charlene? No, no, I don't think so. They posed it as a question, not a statement. 'Is He the Greatest Living Painter in the United States?'" She laughed. "As Charlene said, there's always a bit of a fight over him. Or else *he's* the one fighting. All those guys live to fight and drink."

After finishing his beer, Will left Elaine and Charlene to finish their bottle of wine and stepped outside the gallery. Charlene had no buyers. Clyde had stolen a specific Pollock, but without easy access to a market, quick cash couldn't have been his motive. A piece of the puzzle in Will's head had now turned on its side.

As Will stood on the curb thinking through different possible motives, he noticed a man across the street staring at the gallery, staring at him. The man stood against the building wall, his long afternoon shadow stretching out beside him. Will tried to make out his face, but the brim of his black fedora shadowed his features. Will stepped to the curb and squared himself to the man like they were nose-to-nose. Now he could see more of the man's face. His beady eyes were like those of a dog who hadn't eaten for a day or two, anxious and quick to bite. Was this man watching him? Was he watching the gallery? The man tucked a small notepad into his pocket, turned up his collar, and started down the street.

Certain the moment was not a coincidence, Will scrutinized the man until he turned the corner out of sight, and then Will headed in the opposite direction. Will tried to piece together why the man was watching the gallery, turning the question over in his mind all the way to the el platform. The buildings cast large swaths of gray shadows as the afternoon sun set behind them, the corners of the city disappearing into the darkness. Being associated with the gallery could raise suspicion, Will knew that, however unwarranted. The Stable Gallery was modern, and so were the painters. They were too far off the edge for some, neurotic and unruly, a wild pack of radicals wallowing down in the village. Will raised his arm for a cab. Could Clyde have stolen the Pollock for a reason other than quick cash? What could be Clyde's motive? Any other scenario did not make sense.

Will's boots sank in the mud, then the mud squished between his fingers as he fell forward into the trench on the other side. He pulled himself out on his hands and knees, out of the mud and crimson blood, until he was on the other side of the hedgerow. The only audible sounds were calls for help, but he couldn't tell from where they came. But somehow he could see his fellow soldiers' eyes, the glassy, liquid eyes pleading for help. He climbed out of the trench toward them but slipped on a lifeless body, then again on another. A sea of dead soldiers covered the land. Bodies lay everywhere, their calls ringing in his ears.

Will shot up out of bed, his heart hammering, his sweaty shirt stuck to his chest. The clock read 2:30 a.m. He reached back and wiped the sweat off the back of his neck. The glassy eyes of the dying soldier surfaced in his mind. The soldier stared at Will, pleading without words, though both knew there was no help to give.

Will dropped his legs to the floor and reached for a cigarette. He took a long pull, then exhaled and stared out the window. Leaves on the treetops fluttered in the soft night air. He closed his eyes to see Monet's warm orange-red sun spreading its arms over the bay and kissing the boat sails and undulating water as it rose over the horizon. He breathed in slowly and waited for his mind to calm. With ease, his thoughts drifted to Liz, and he could picture her in his mind, her mahogany hair that was smooth and full, the subtle pinkish hue of her skin like a pearl, her cheeks with the coral hue just below the eyes, the roundness of her face and chin. Her ears were small and slightly pointed at the top. He could still feel her delicate fingers around his wrist from the night before and wondered when he could walk the avenues with her again. A part of him was glad the Pollock had been stolen. Liz brought a freshness to his life. He knew there were facets to her life he wanted to explore and felt a desire to experience the next day together, and then another.

Will curled his toes against the soft carpet and waited for the morning sun to filter through the buildings and into his apartment, that familiar anchor that tore the night away and lifted the darkness to reveal a new morning.

14

STROUT SHOT FORWARD IN HIS CHAIR when Ira threw open the door and walked into the ALERT office. Sam Rainey, the junior at ALERT, followed behind. They crossed the floor with pinched faces, each carrying a large black garbage bag.

"Shit, Ira," Strout said, "not here. Down the hall in the other room."

But Ira had already dropped his bag, splitting open the plastic and spilling out a dirty coffee filter and grounds, groaning at the sight of it. They typically used the trash room near the chute, which always made sifting through the trash easier, but today was the one day this month the cleaning lady decided to show, and they couldn't afford to have her asking questions.

"Jesus, I hate this part," Rainey said, kicking one of the bags away from his foot.

They had surveyed Liz Bower's apartment building for a week, paying attention to the comings and goings. Pickup was on Thursday afternoon, so they had pulled the trash that morning. Ira stood with Rainey, both staring down at the bags, reluctant to dig into the trash.

"They're not going to open themselves," Ira said, leaning over to tear open the split in the first bag. When he reached in, his fingers wrapped around something wet, and he yanked back his hand, wincing. He would never get used to digging in someone else's trash. And nothing ever came of the disgusting effort, not like the wiretaps. Those were easier to glean information from, even though they were harder to place. All the tactics were illegal, though, so Ira figured there wasn't much difference. Rainey had already started to separate his bags into piles on Strout's floor—food scraps in one, containers in another, and paper waste in a third. Tentatively, he picked up crumpled wads of paper, unfolded them, and stacked them in a pile.

If no wiretaps were set, Ira preferred to go through the target's mail rather than the trash. With the mail he got straight to the paper—the letters and the union memberships—without having to sift through nasty remnants of decaying food. But since the mailboxes in Liz's building were locked, pulling the mail had proved too difficult. Besides, simply going through the envelopes did not give them access to the little notes jotted down during a phone call and then tossed, or the pamphlets collected at Communist meetings and thrown away at home. Inevitably, every target required a trash cover.

Liz Bower was no different from Ira's other targets, and neither was her garbage. The pile on the floor contained carrot peels, aluminum trays from frozen dinners, and a lot of paper. They spent a good thirty minutes trying to decipher paper scraps with coffee stains that had bled the ink into purply-brown abstractions. Ira hoped for a letter or note from any of the already identified Communists, something to tie Bower directly to the party through concrete, subversive actions, but nothing substantial jumped out at him. No incriminating letters or union rags.

"There's nothing in here," Rainey said, giving up on his bag and moving to sit in one of the folding chairs in front of Strout's tanker desk.

But Ira kept at it, determined to find a connection. He pulled one piece of paper out at a time, shaking off the occasional food scrap. He was lucky because his bag seemed to be from days when Liz had eaten outside of the apartment. As trash goes, hers was clean, with little evidence of cooking. Communist women were typically promiscuous, so he wasn't surprised by the notion that she would dine out with all manner of sordid company. He found a *My Home* magazine with Audrey Hepburn on the cover, but he'd expected more than torn up newspapers and magazines, an apple core, and a few breakfast remnants. Ira stared at the trash, shaking his head. To Ira, the collection spread out on the floor appeared staged, as though it had been arranged for a theater set. Had it already been culled? Did she know people were watching her? Probably. If you were a Communist in America, you covered your tracks. Ira decided he had to pay close attention to each piece of paper because Liz would have attempted to conceal any incriminating evidence, which may account for the torn newspapers. He continued sifting through the trash, picking out anything he found suspicious. Near the bottom of the bag, a small fragment caught his attention. The torn paper appeared to be the top corner of a larger document. Ira could read the words *Chase Bank*. The line below, cut off at the beginning, read *Foundation Account*, which he assumed meant the Bower Foundation.

Ira figured he had found part of a bank statement for a Bower Foundation account. He needed the rest. Using the toe of his shoe, he spread the trash out to see everything simultaneously, hoping to connect different sections of images or text to make a whole.

Rainey came over. "What'd you find?"

Ira handed him the scrap. "We need to find the rest of this bank statement. Start digging."

They spent another ten minutes examining each piece of paper, but they couldn't find the rest of the statement. Ira stood above the trash, perplexed. The discovery—or lack thereof—did not seem right. He found it odd that just one piece of a statement would be in the trash, as if it had been accidentally dropped in the bag.

"Curious," Ira said to himself, working the rationales in his head. He turned back to Rainey. "Let's go through your trash again. Maybe she separated the pieces."

"Why would someone do that?"

To Ira, the only possible answer was that Liz Bower knew she was under surveillance. Either that, or she had an odd practice of keeping her trash clean of personal information.

They began sifting again with greater attention, finding more food scraps and containers of one sort or another. After a while, they finally found three other pieces of the statement, one of them quite large. Ira placed them on Strout's metal desk and tried to arrange the pieces, putting the torn sides together in a patchwork configuration so they could see several transactions. "It's a lot of money, more than I expected," he said. "But I can't tell where it's coming from or going."

Strout leaned across his desk. "Let me see."

Ira pointed at the pieces. "See here? There are several transactions over a couple of days, and it's a significant amount. I can't tell anything without the whole statement, but it's definitely an active account."

"Of course it's active," Strout said. "Banks don't send statements for closed accounts."

Ira ignored the slight and studied the little evidence, trying to make sense of the information. He had no doubt the complete statement would lead him to more prominent Communists or their funding source, and likely both. "The account doesn't seem to be performing like a typical foundation account. There's too much money flowing in and out of the account and on too regular a basis," he said.

Tapping his glasses against his palm, Strout stepped away from the desk and gazed at the document. Pride warmed Ira inside. He had not found a clear connection of any sort, but what they had found might lead to one.

A knock on the door startled them all. But the shock on the cleaning lady's face when she opened the door led Ira to believe their mess on the office floor startled her more.

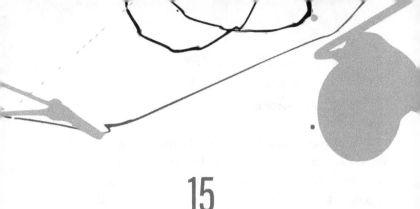

15

LIZ SUGGESTED THEY MEET at the Cedar Bar when Will had begun asking questions about the artists in the village, about Pollock and de Kooning. She stood at the curb waiting when his cab dropped him on Eighth and University, looking surprisingly different dressed in jeans with her hair tucked under a red bandana. It was the first time he had seen her downtown. He admired how she seemed to adapt to every situation without constraints or concern, confident in her ability to belong.

The nondescript bar disappeared into a nondescript street where most of the metal storefront gates had been rolled shut by this time of night. A blue neon sign flickered *Bar* above the entrance, and six or seven tattered young men hovered near the door, smoking cigarettes.

"This is where they all live," Liz said, motioning to the four- and five-story apartment buildings lining the street. "Franz Kline's on Fourteenth Street. De Kooning's a few blocks down on Tenth. Jackson Pollock and his wife, Lee Krasner, used to be here on Eighth. The artists move around a lot—Ninth Street, Tenth Street, Avenue B—trying to find the perfect lighting, higher ceilings. Of course, half of them get evicted for not paying rent, so they relocate to the next cold-water flat."

Across the street, raucous yelling came hurling out an open window of a loft apartment, then the building door slammed open, and three men stumbled out.

"No, you're wrong. That's not what a painting is," one of the men yelled.

Will recognized Willem de Kooning from Elaine's gallery show. Even at forty, he had the features of a youthful sailor, and his faintly freckled face and prematurely white hair gave him an angelic appearance. Liz said the shorter man—small but athletic, with dark hair and a mustache—was Franz Kline. The two men picked up the third, who had fallen to the curb drunk, and arm in arm they all stumbled into the Cedar Bar. They seemed close, like brothers, tied by time and experiences. They'd probably spent the depression years painting murals for the WPA Federal Art Project and barely making enough money to eat.

Liz pointed to the apartment building from where they'd come. "They're finishing up at the Club. They like to drink, give speeches, and get worked up about art theory, Freud, and existentialism. They get together to talk about what they're doing in their studios. I think it's a way for them not to feel lonely and isolated after painting by themselves all day. They've usually gotten out of control by the end of the night, and that's when they move to the Cedar Bar." She grabbed Will's hand and followed the artists inside.

The bar was long and narrow, with smoke-tinged air and bare pea-green walls. The place smelled of stale beer. They squeezed through the loud crowd of college kids dressed in jeans and work boots, past several small booths upholstered in cracked maroon leather, coats hanging on meager racks at the ends, and headed toward the bar. As Will passed, one kid jumped over the back of a booth and dropped into the booth on the other side. A brazen woman reached after him.

"Jesus Christ. Your face is as red as my fucking tampon," the woman said and proceeded to pop herself on the top of the booth's back, laughing, her foot pressed against the table's edge.

Liz didn't give them a glance but continued toward the back, keeping hold of Will's hand as she pushed through the crowd. The bar carried emotional energy that seemed to hover at its breaking point, as if at any moment a fight would erupt or laughter or crying would engulf them all. When they reached the back of the bar, Liz ordered two beers and dropped thirty cents down.

"They only serve beer," she said, handing him a bottle and clinking the bottoms in a toast.

Behind them, a booth of kids talked in hushed voices among themselves. "Is he going to show up?" one of them said.

"God, do you want him to?"

"Yeah, kind of."

Will took a quick swig of beer. "Who is everyone waiting for?"

"Pollock," Liz said as they squeezed back through the crowd, past a game of quarters. "It's a bit like a car crash. You don't want to look; you don't want to see what's going to happen, but for some reason you're drawn to it. His therapist lives in the city, so on Wednesdays Pollock comes running to the bar afterward. The kids hang around hoping to catch a glimpse of him."

They reached the front of the bar and slid into a booth in the corner. Two men sat across from them with six empty beers before them. Will pointed to the broken pay phone hanging from the wall. "What happened?"

"Pollock trashed that a year ago," the one with brick-red hair said. "He was pissed off at Kline or de Kooning. Who can remember? He was screaming, calling everyone worms, yelling that he was the greatest painter. Then he kicked the phone until it separated from the wall."

"Jesus," Will said.

"That's normal."

"Will, this is Raymond Ellis," Liz said. "His paintings were at the MoMA preview at the Stable Gallery."

Will shook the artist's hand. Ellis had paint under his finger-nails and around his cuticles, which looked as though they had been stained that way for ages. Splatters and spills of paint covered his jeans. His boots were a flat black, and in different spots where the original polish had worn off Ellis must have painted over the leather. He gave off the undefinable manner of *painterliness*, a sense of detachment from the world gained from hours alone with himself and oil paint and canvas and theory. Ellis's voice was loose and slow from alcohol, and Will guessed he had started drinking in the late afternoon like the rest of them, then spent hours at the Club and was now settling in at the Cedar for the long evening.

At that moment, a head flashed at the window. Someone peered into the bar, and then, as quickly, it disappeared.

"Was that Pollock?" Will asked.

"I hope not, but maybe," Ellis said. "He checks to see if the crowd is large enough before he comes in. If it's not, he waits."

Moments later the door slammed open, and Pollock swaggered in with a bottle of bourbon in his hand, wearing a jean jacket and T-shirt, a two-day-old beard covering his square jaw. Whispers and chatter rippled through the bar like firecrackers.

"Apparently the crowd is large enough," Ellis said, rolling his eyes.

Pollock bumped through a group of kids as he waded in. A scowl hung on his brooding, weathered face.

"Worms!" Pollock yelled. "Frauds, all of you." His roar bounced through the bar, causing some kids to cheer under their breath with their friends while others cowered lower in their booths, hiding from the wrath. Pollock stumbled toward de Kooning, who was leaning on the bar with Kline, their arms over each other's shoulders.

"De Kooning!" Pollock continued, stomping through the crowd. "You've betrayed it all. You're still doing the same fucking thing!" The crowd stared, and Pollock turned to them. "You're all cheap and lousy fakes. You're whores and worms! De Kooning and I are the only ones painting, the only ones doing anything real." He stumbled around like he was on a ship, unsure of his footing and thrown off balance. Then he yelled out again. "I'm the greatest! I'm the greatest painter."

Ellis downed the last of his beer and pulled another from the floor. "Don't think they don't like each other; they do. But there's history. Pollock always eclipsed de Kooning until recently." He spoke as though he were announcing a sporting event as it unfolded in front of them.

"What do you mean?"

"Pollock's struggling. He can't sell; nothing's happening for him. He hides out in his barn up in Springs. De Kooning has stepped out from behind the shadow of the great Jackson Pollock."

"No one likes Pollock's paintings anymore?" Will asked, wanting to confirm what he'd learned from Charlene.

"Fuck, I didn't say that. He's a genius, don't get me wrong. But the last few years …" His voice trailed off, then came back. "The critics can't get enough of his good shit, like *Autumn Rhythm* or *No. 1*."

"Why the numbers?"

"It makes them more abstract. If I name a painting *Man with a Hand Plow*, you're going to expect to see a man with a fucking plow. But if I name it *No. 30*, what the hell can you expect? Nothing. You don't expect, you *see*. Total abstraction. Anyway, it got too goddamn confusing, all the numbers. So, for a few, he added names, like *Autumn Rhythm*."

Then, without warning, a burst of commotion came from the back, and Pollock beelined toward Kline, parting the crowd as he moved. When he reached him, he grabbed Kline around the neck, and Kline shoved back, knocking Pollock against a table. Beer glasses crashed onto the floor, shards flying in every direction. Pollock charged Kline again and grabbed him around the waist, then lost his balance, pulling them both to the floor. Eventually, Kline pinned Pollock with a knee on his chest. They exchanged quiet words, and a wide grin returned to Pollock's face. He worked himself to his feet and slapped Kline on the back as they leaned on the bar. Once they poured themselves a bourbon from Pollock's bottle, the crowd lost interest.

The artists ridiculed each other like brothers, Will thought, but there was tension. They competed. There needed to be a greatest painter and they knew there could only be one.

"Why would someone steal his painting?" Will asked himself aloud but wondered if stealing the Pollock could help an artist reach greatness.

"Beats me," Ellis said with a laugh. "Seriously, I don't know. I mean, you can feel something's happening. It's not like before when no one cared. First, *Life* publishes an article on Pollock, then MoMA buys one of his paintings and then one of de Kooning's. People are starting to notice.

"Liz and the foundation have put a lot behind us. They gave the money to MoMA and pushed our art. We're starting to get some real attention. And now the *Twelve Modern American Painters* exhibit. Shit, it used to be the same twenty people at all our shows. But now we're getting a bit of attention and a little money in our pockets. Not much, but more than before. De Kooning and I used to paint with gloves on because we had no heat."

Will felt Liz watching him, a glance too long to be casual, and when he turned he caught her eye. She smiled at him. She had a subtle dimple on her right cheek that he hadn't noticed, a feature one could miss, noticeable to only the discerning eye. To know the intimate details made him feel closer to her. How her round chin protruded out slightly so that delicate shadows formed when she smiled, the roundness of her shoulders and slight concave shape of her collarbone. Her gaze lingered a moment, then she glanced down as if embarrassed by her thoughts.

The second man in their booth, small and thin, almost boyish, leaned forward, breaking their moment. "No one is stealing my fucking paintings; I'll tell you that much."

"Nobody *wants* their paintings stolen, Andrei," Liz said. Then, turning to Will, "We're helping Andrei fight the removal of his mural at the New York Post Office."

A quick panic shot through Will. He recognized the name from the newspaper article, the Russian painter he'd read about in the news, part of the Two Hundred. Without the distinctive proboscis, Will would not have been able to pick Roschin out of a crowd. His accent was the one Russian characteristic about him. But the fact that Liz associated with Roschin, helping him fight the protesting of his art, twisted the pit of Will's stomach. Pritchett's words echoed in Will's mind: *None of this better come back to the firm.*

"They picket my work," Roschin said. "The goddamn committee said my images were monstrous, like Frankenstein. They commissioned the mural five years ago, for Christ's sake, through the WPA, and now Congressman Dondero's Committee on Public Works is demanding it be removed? What the fuck?" He took a generous swig of his beer. "I was happy to get the commission from the New Deal plan. They were all about helping us unemployed artists during the depression, but apparently taste has changed in Congress," Roschin said with contempt. "Goddamned Dondero. He's on a witch hunt, trying to label modern art and all the artists Communist. He's just trying to make a name for himself, grandstanding, fucking self-promotion. It's bullshit." His accent came out more pronounced when he cursed.

"I read about it in the paper," Will said.

"Fucking article. The committee said my paintings incite subversion. They actually used the word 'slanderous.' Said I failed to show the beauty and glory of the State." Roschin swigged down the last of his beer. "It's not helping that I'm Russian, either.

'Soviet psychological warfare' is what they're calling it. Can you fucking believe it?" He paused. "Do you know what I have to do now, Will?"

Will shook his head.

"Go on trial. I have to stand before the fucking House Un-American Activities Committee. Prove I'm not a Communist. Prove I'm not a spy trying to overthrow the goddamn government."

Will turned to Ellis. "What about your work?"

"That's it," Liz said. "They might hate his work because it's modern, but he has no political references. None of them do. Take Pollock, Kline, de Kooning. There are no images, no figures, and without any of that, it's politically neutral—or it appears as much."

Will admired how passionately she spoke; to her they were more than paintings. He remembered one of Kline's paintings at Elaine's exhibit. Using a wide housepainter's brush, Kline had dragged the raw house paint across a huge stark white canvas, evidencing the action of his painting, the physicality of it. But no religious symbols, no images. Nothing political. Pollock too—absolutely no images or symbols that one could construe as political. He remembered others, too, like Rothko's canvas covered with single fields of color. Two softly painted red and yellow rectangles with blurred edges covered the stark ocher orange canvas, light emanating from the very core of the painting.

"Pollock's got no problems," Roschin said. "He's been stamped by fucking *Life* magazine." He pointed across the bar. "Look at the guy. He's the fucking Marlon Brando of painting. He rivals Hemingway in drinking. He taught himself how to paint. He drinks. He fights. He grew up on a ranch in Wyoming, for Christ's sake. How much more American can you get? No wonder *Life* chose him. I'm the one who has to go up in front of HUAC."

"McCarthy and Dondero are okay with Pollock?" Will asked.

"Jesus, no, of course not. They hate him. But they can't point to anything. There are no underlying images to declare he is subversive. Maybe they believe there's some hidden map or secret message, but how can they prove it? They aren't like my paintings. I painted good early history of New York, you know. But now they say the Indians look like the government starved them. They say the labor organizers are rallying workers holding hammers. So what happens? I'm suddenly a Communist, that's what." He shook his head in disbelief. "You have to be really fucking careful. You never know what the fuck's going to happen anymore." He slammed his beer down. "These guys are real dickheads," he said, almost to himself.

Liz slid out from the booth and scooped up everyone's empty bottles, offering to grab everyone another. When she returned, she slid next to Will, her thigh brushing against his. She placed a hand on his knee so naturally that Will thought she did so absentmindedly. He placed his hand on hers, and she gave it a soft squeeze.

Then another roar ripped through the bar. Pollock charged after a young artist, picking up a glass and throwing it at him. He chased the man right out of the bar but gave up a few steps out the door. Then, through the window, Will saw him leaning against the building. He pulled his jeans down to his thighs and pissed all over the front wall and onto the sidewalk.

"Is that normal?" Will asked, shocked.

"Jesus," Ellis said, shaking his head. "He pisses everywhere. Pissed in a fireplace at Peggy Guggenheim's one time. It's like he's claiming his territory or something. He's a fucking wild man. A freak, I tell you."

"So it might be true that he drinks paint and pisses onto the canvases," Will said with a laugh.

"Stop it." Liz laughed, then gave him a soft slap on the inside of his knee as if in a playful spat. Will's heartbeat quickened. He elbowed her delicately.

"I'm just saying. People do wonder." Everyone laughed.

She left her hand there for a moment. Her touch, her lingering, could only be from a wanting, Will thought, a sign that she would accept an advance. Inexplicably, the desire to kiss her overwhelmed him, and he wanted to press his lips against hers, against her smooth skin.

The hours slowed as the night wore on, and the conversation shifted back to who was the greatest painter. The less-spirited drinkers retired early, unable to give what the night asked of them. In the early morning hours, Kline sauntered over to their booth with a bottle of bourbon.

"How about some shots?" he said.

Kline appeared good-natured and youthful, but nervous. He dropped his arm around Ellis, who beamed the brightest he had all night, and Will got the sense that when it came to wives and girlfriends and boyfriends, painting came first, and they did whatever they wanted afterward. Will listened to the stories of their time together at Black Mountain College, drinking coffee and learning how to paint, how the bridge of the nose molds into the eye socket, and how the flesh of a leg expands when you sit.

As the beer warmed his body and he listened to Roschin and Ellis and Kline, questions swam in his head. Suspicions wormed their way in. The Two Hundred were being accused of subversion. Roschin was being targeted and he was scared. No one knew how far the accusations might go. Who else might be targeted, and for what? Incriminating evidence would be information someone might want to hide.

At some point in the dawn hours, Liz crushed out her cigarette and stood. "I'm tired, boys. You'll have to continue without me." She turned to Will. "Walk me out."

They stepped out of the Cedar Bar and into the cool air. Will hoped she would give him a moment to kiss her, to pull her in tight. She had wanted him to see the painters up close, he thought, to hear their struggles and understand their motivations. And in showing him their world, she had shared a part of herself.

Liz sauntered toward the curb and turned. She stood there waiting. Will stepped to her, their waists almost touching, which sent a shudder of energy through his body. This was his moment. But before he could lean forward, Liz placed her hands around his face and kissed him, long and slow, pulling her body in close. Her soft lips were wet and passionate and fit neatly with his. She continued almost selfishly, as if satisfying an urge that had built through the night. Will kissed back almost as selfishly. She lowered her hands and interlocked each one with his. Will wrapped them around her back and held her tight. Leaning forward, she shut her eyes and pressed her body against his, savoring the kiss. It was as though he had never kissed before. Every touch and movement felt new and exciting. Will wanted to stay in the moment forever. But then, without notice, she pulled back.

"I can't," she said, almost a whisper, then kissed him again, her lips exploring his, before stepping away. "I'm sorry, Will. This was a bad idea."

"Why?"

"I'm sorry. I want to, but I can't." She gave him a soft, slow punch on the chest. "I didn't expect this." She smiled in apology, then turned. Will reached for her but let her fingers slip through his hand as she slowly pulled away as if forcing herself to leave. Why had she changed her mind? Will struggled to understand what stopped her. What was preventing her from getting involved? She raised her hand and signaled for a cab that came too quickly.

Will walked down the avenue under the glow of the streetlamps, confused, repeating her words. *I want to, but I can't.* A light rain began to fall, glistening in the lamplight, and the early spring wind blew the droplets sideways, carrying them farther than they could have gone on their own. The wet pavement

shimmered with lamplight, appearing before Will like a long mirror, and the air smelled of new rain when it first begins to fall,
mixing with the dirt and oil of the street.

When he returned to his flat, Will lifted heavy footstep after heavy
footstep up the wood stairs toward his second-floor apartment,
the kiss with Liz still fresh in his mind. He had hoped for another
drink or a longer kiss. He already wanted to see her again. She had
kissed him with her whole body. But she pulled away, and Will
couldn't understand why.

The boards creaked under his weight as he ascended, and he
tried to pick the quietest spot on each step. Too tired, he abandoned the effort and continued to climb, holding onto the railing
and the memory of their kiss. The el clattered outside as it rushed
along its track.

When he reached the landing, Will stood for a moment to
catch his breath, warm and tired from the liquor. As if from out
of nowhere, a force spun his body around, knocking him off balance, and a pain shot through his shoulder. A man tore down the
stairs past him, his shoes sliding off the edge of each step as he
grabbed the rail for support.

"Watch it!" Will shouted.

He rubbed his shoulder and turned toward his apartment.
At the sight of the door thrown wide open, his stomach lurched.
He ran inside. Papers were strewn across his small desk, the
drawers overturned, and the contents scattered on the floor.
Couch cushions lay askew. He ran into his bedroom. The mattress leaned off the box frame and clothes were thrown across the
floor. He stood in shock for a fleeting minute, then adrenaline
kicked in and he raced back out into the hallway. Leaning over
the stair rail, he peered down the two flights to catch sight of the

front door closing. Will leapt down the stairs, taking them two and three at a time.

Outside, Will scanned the street on both sides through a thin sheet of rain. Rounding the corner onto Second Avenue was a man in a black fedora and dark coat. The memory of the man outside the Stable Gallery flashed before him. This break-in was not a burglary, he thought. The man had been searching for something.

Will raced across the street and turned down Second Avenue, struggling to gain traction on the wet pavement. Two blocks down, the man tried to jump the curb but landed short and stepped into the slush. With his feet soaked and slowing him down, Will thought he might have an edge, but not much.

Will bolted after him, adrenaline clearing the booze out of muscles that tightened and fired Will's body down the street and through the rain. What would he do if he caught him? Ask him who he was? Ask him where the painting was? Or was the man following him for some other reason?

When the man ran past Seventy-Ninth Street, Will knew he was headed to the Seventy-Sixth Street stop of the Third Avenue el. One block up, three streets down. Will needed to catch him by then, or he was lost. The Third Avenue el could take him anywhere.

Will turned on instinct at the first block, hoping to avoid the scaffolding on Seventy-Eighth and maybe gain a yard or two. He forced his legs to push his body up the sloped street. His chest and throat burned as air rushed in and out.

He reached the top and glanced down Third Avenue, but no one appeared at the corner. A cab rushed under the el, water splattering off the wheels as they rolled down the street. Then the black fedora appeared one street over. When the man reached the corner, he stepped off the curb, but a cab sped through the green light, and he jumped back, stumbling another few steps. His heels hit the curb, and he fell backward, his hands catching his body in a sitting position.

Will took the chance and bolted toward him. At the sound of Will's feet, the man looked up. Will locked onto his beady eyes, the eyes of a man with no dignity left, fighting to take it back from whoever had stolen it. This was undoubtedly the man he'd seen outside the gallery. Will sprinted to catch him, mustering all the energy he had left, the air burning his chest.

But the man had jumped to his feet and darted across the street and underneath the el. The stairwell entrance loomed two blocks away, the lights flickering on the platform. Farther down the track, the train's headlight glowed through the rain as it approached.

Under the elevated track, gray sheets of rain fell through the slat openings of the green iron girders and onto the cobbled street, darkening as they dropped away from the dim floodlights over-head. Under better circumstances, Will could catch the guy, but at three in the morning, hampered by the rain and bourbon, he wasn't sure. The horn of the el blared as it approached, yards in front of the man.

Will darted toward the other side but stumbled on the cob-bled street. A sharp pain shot into his kneecap as he landed on the corner of a dislodged brick, his hands landing in a puddle of water. He shot up, pushed away the pain, and headed for the plat-form stairs. But when he reached the steps, he found them empty. Will stopped, turning slowly, searching in all directions. There was no movement on the street. The man had disappeared. Will checked behind the stairs. Nothing. He peered into the dark shad-ows of the iron girders, scanning the street. The pain in his knee throbbed. He had been down for no more than a few seconds.

The rhythmic knocking of the train clattered above as it entered the platform, brakes hissing as they locked into place. A familiar announcement slipped through the air. *Seventy-Sixth and Third. Next stop, Sixty-Seventh Street.* Will raced up the wood stairs, pulling himself up by the wet pipe railing. A few men lingered at the back of the platform, hiding from the rain. A man and a woman ran off the train, squeezing together as they opened their umbrella and ducked under the platform cover.

Will ran alongside the train, peering through the windows for a dark coat and black fedora. Finding neither, he spun around. The same people huddled under the same umbrellas. He went back to the top of the stairs and surveyed the street below, searching. He peered into the shadows, near the girders, along the building edges. Nothing.

Limping to the first bench, he dropped down, unable to move farther. The last fifteen minutes caught up to him. His heart raced, and his chest burned as if it had been ripped open, raw and wind torn. A metallic taste hung in the back of his throat, and he leaned over, coughing. He tried to move his legs but could not. Leaving them stretched out in front of him, motionless and heavy, he dropped his head back, trying to catch his breath, but the weight of the break-in, the implication, pressed down on him. He waited, breathless, for the next train to arrive.

Soaking wet but sweating, Ira lay four inches underneath the chassis of a Ford sedan. His breath had finally slowed. The soles of his feet throbbed from running on the cobbled brick street in black dress shoes. His ankles, soft and weak, ached as though they would snap if he made one more quick turn.

He had counted on Will Oxley spending the night with the Bower slut, never imagining he would chase him down the street in a seven-block sprint.

How long had it been? Twenty minutes? Thirty? Ira turned his head as much as possible to peer out from underneath the sedan. No shoes walked past. Nobody was nearby. He rolled out from under the parked car and picked himself up off the pavement. He headed up the platform stairs to wait for the next train. Oxley was nowhere to be seen, and that was how Ira wanted it.

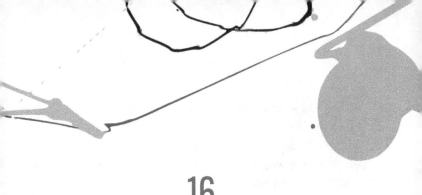

16

WILL SAT ON A GREEN VINYL STOOL at the Lexington Diner next to James Palmer, waiting for his answer. Behind a counter crowded with a coffee maker, salt and pepper shakers, and a lime-green milkshake blender, the cook scraped a fork rapidly against the sides of a metal bowl, yolks and whites wrapping around the tines as he drubbed the eggs. He spooned a block of butter on the small grill that sizzled and popped when it landed.

"You don't think it could have been a robbery?" Will asked again, fearful he already knew the answer.

Palmer shook his head. "Doubtful. Guy looked like me, right?"

Palmer resembled a quartet singer in high school—baby-face skin, shiny black shoes, and a necktie with a perfect knot.

"Older. Less clean cut. But same black fedora." Will pulled out his pack of cigarettes and tapped two out. Palmer reached for one out of habit, the rhythmic routine ingrained after a year in the trenches together with the Thirty-Fifth Infantry. Palmer had been there during Saint-Lô and when they seized the Gremecey Forest sector eight weeks later, through all the rain and the mud, the freezing air and misery. The tree bursts killed hundreds. They learned to hug the tree trunks rather than lay flat on the ground, which gave them a better chance of avoiding the exploding shrapnel as it rained down.

When they returned to New York after the war, Palmer applied to the Federal Bureau of Investigation. The process took a year with the background checks and phone calls to neighbors, so he spent the time with the New York police department until the FBI accepted his application.

"Hoover's gone nuts," Palmer continued, placing down his coffee. "He has every agent collecting information from all kinds of informants and private investigative groups. He's digging for information on party members' activities—anything to prove Communism is illegal. I'm buried under press clippings, stacks of union newspapers, and union meeting notes. You should see the file room—union newspapers everywhere."

Palmer worked in records administration at the FBI and cataloged files based on type or individual. A file beginning with 091 was bank robbery, 047 was impersonations, and 065 was espionage, which was where Palmer spent most of his time these days.

"And Hoover has thousands of informants," he continued. "You wouldn't believe it. Bank tellers, school administration officials, company employees. You step into a taxicab and the driver could be an informant. Who knows who's watching and for what reason?"

The cook dropped two plates in front of them, each crowded with scrambled eggs, link sausage, and toast. Palmer began stabbing at his eggs. "Then there's the new agency. Nobody knows what the hell they're doing."

"Which one's that?"

"The CIA. Central Intelligence Agency. It started five years ago, came out of the old OSS."

Confused, Will shook his head.

"The Office of Strategic Services," Palmer explained. "God knows what they did. Gathered gossip, that sort of thing. They considered themselves spies, but they weren't real spies. People called it the *oh-so social* because most members were social elite, people who could travel to different countries without appearing suspicious. You know, real clubby, all rich and Ivy League." Palmer waved his fork dismissively. "I'm not sure how much of the rumors are real. Anyway, they disbanded the OSS right after the war. And now there's the CIA. No coincidence, in my opinion, just official spy business rather than a social club."

Palmer did not wait for Will to comment. "Hoover hates it," he said. "He hates not knowing everything and everyone. We don't know who these Communists are or what they look like. They could be anyone. And the CIA appears to be composed of the same guys the FBI is against: liberals and foreigners launching covert operations through back channels. Jesus. Hoover suspects everyone." As he cut his eggs and scooped a bite onto his toast, Palmer explained how the CIA believed the country was in a cultural war as much as anything, using words like *psychological warfare*. Hoover couldn't keep tabs on anyone at the CIA, he said, but suspected them all of being spies. "Who the hell knows, Oxley. I just keep the records. I'm not cut out for that spy shit."

The implication of what Palmer had said shuddered through Will. Taxicabs and bankers. Doormen. The guy in the office next to him. Thousands of informants watching, learning, and reporting. A network of informal snitches operating under their own assumptions, sending information up the chain to fill rooms full of dossiers cataloged and tagged by agents like Palmer. The investigations were something everyone knew existed, but most people didn't talk about. Maybe husbands and wives whispered together at the dinner table after the kids went to bed about a neighbor who lost his job, a teacher at the local school who was blacklisted, or a union worker down at the plant. But the scale of the effort and the infrastructure must've been more extensive than anyone knew. Will hadn't considered its scope until now.

Palmer pushed back his plate and picked up his cigarette. "But why would someone be investigating you?"

If Will was honest with himself, he knew the answer—the gallery show, the Two Hundred, and the association with Roschin would all catch an informant's attention. Will explained the Pollock case, and Palmer fingered the last corner of toast on his plate, popping the piece into his mouth. He didn't speak for a while but sat watching the cook and sipping his coffee. Then he turned to Will. "Maybe it's not you they're investigating."

The possibility had been in the back of Will's mind since the Cedar Bar with the talk of political subversion and secret maps. He'd been trying to ignore the suspicion but no longer could. Maybe someone believed Pollock should be on the list of Two Hundred. Maybe the painting hid a secret. But Will wasn't going to stop doing his job. He wasn't going to stop searching for the painting or back down because he felt threatened.

Palmer dropped his napkin on the counter, a white flag of surrender. "I don't know. It's your choice, your job. And mine's waiting for me back in the file room." Palmer shook his head. "Jesus. If the public knew what I was spending my time on." He jumped off his stool, took another sip of coffee, then said goodbye.

Will left the diner soon after Palmer and walked past Gristedes Grocery, where ScotTissue rolls were stacked in a pyramid in the display window and an advertisement for Surf detergent hung on the glass. He moved through a light crowd of men in gray flannel suits and stopped at the corner to grab his morning newspaper. The paperboy pulled a folded newspaper out from a white canvas bag stamped with the Hearst logo and handed it to Will.

"We've got a hot extra this morning, sir," he said, wiping his ink-smudged fingers on his pants. His bright tangerine hair stuck out from under his cap.

Will scanned the headline's bold lettering. *Atom Spies Rosenbergs Refused Clemency. Execution Set for June.* The grainy picture had placed Ethel and Julius's mug shots side by side. With a round face and small mouth, Ethel Rosenberg resembled a librarian more than a Communist spy.

"Mom says these Commies are brainwashed in Russia," the kid said. "She says these two are the tip of the iceberg, and if the Communists take hold of the unions, they could disrupt rail service and control the newspapers. That's their whole plan. I ain't gonna work for no Commies. I'd drop my bag right now if I knew a bunch of Commies controlled the newspapers."

"Easy kid," Will said and flipped him five cents. He thanked him for the newspaper and continued down Lexington toward the el stop. The Rosenbergs had sent government secrets out of their apartment to the Russians. Maybe Palmer had a point. Maybe the painters could be doing the same, maybe there were messages or secrets hidden within the paintings, but Will could not connect the pieces in his head. The Two Hundred artists had painted images and emotions, but all in all they were simply pictures. Will could not envision a Communist connection. He climbed the stairs to the platform and dropped down onto a bench. The el train came rattling along the rail and into the stop. Palmer was right though. Will needed to be careful.

17

WILL WANTED TO IGNORE the fact that Palmer might be right, that he might be under investigation. But when he suggested to Charlie that the man had turned his apartment over because he didn't have anything worth stealing, Charlie choked down his bite of sandwich and leaned forward as far as he could over the double desk.

"That doesn't sound like a robbery. They were searching for something, Will. Someone is watching you," he said in a low whisper. "You know what I mean?"

Will had accepted that possibility. The guy who stood across from him at the Stable Gallery had been in his apartment. He had ransacked his desk and searched through his papers, but nothing had been stolen. Will stood up, eyed the main room outside his office, then shut the door. Other than Charlie, Will could not trust anyone. Anybody could draw false conclusions and turn him in. Like Palmer had said, informants were everywhere: a doorman, the neighbor, the colleague at the office.

If someone comes asking," Will said, "just be honest. We don't know why there was a break-in, if it was a break-in. That's all. That's the truth."

Charlie couldn't afford to get involved. He was the kind of guy who made sure he was home for dinner, tucked his kids in bed, and kissed them goodnight. He couldn't get blacklisted. Charlie needed his life to be predictable, safe. Will was about to say as much when the phone rang, and Charlie grabbed the receiver. After a few seconds, he handed the phone to Will. "It's the bartender from the Palm. Says he knows where Clyde Barnett is."

An hour later, Will stood outside the door of another dilapidated apartment in Harlem. He laid three hard knocks on the thick door and waited. He listened for voices inside, but the yelling from the apartment next door overpowered anything he could have heard. Then a shadow broke the sliver of light underneath the threshold, and from inside came the sound of sliding metal as the door unlatched. When the handle turned, Will's adrenaline spiked, and with it his boot camp training from the war. His foot landed squarely on the door and kicked it open. The door bounced back after a dull thud, and Will kicked it again, hard. He pushed his way in to find a man lying on the floor holding a bloody nose.

"What the hell's going on?" the man said as he scrambled back on his hands and knees, blood dripping onto the worn wooden floor as he moved. He crawled up onto a small cloth-upholstered couch.

"Clyde Barnett?" Will asked.

"Who the hell is asking?" Clyde struggled with the blood dripping out of his nose. Will pulled a handkerchief out of his back pocket and tossed it to Clyde, who squeezed his nostrils tight, trying to stop the bleeding. He was about Will's age but skinnier, with thick curly black hair cut short on the sides and piled long on the top like a Q-tip. Clyde was making little progress, the blood now dripping onto his white undershirt, pooling and expanding into cranberry-red splotches.

"You have to stuff it up there," Will said as he dropped onto a folding chair next to the couch. After lighting a cigarette, he set the pack down on the table and let the moment simmer, staring at Clyde, who had pushed the handkerchief into his left nostril. He and Clyde stayed like that for several minutes, staring at each other with Clyde breathing out of one nostril. "I need your help," Will said finally.

Clyde snorted, a spot of blood splattering onto his upper lip. "Fine way of asking."

"You never know what's on the other side of the door. And I couldn't let you run."

"We're on the fourth floor, man. Where am I gonna go?" Clyde twisted the handkerchief and began to tend to his nose, wiping the crusted blood off the edges of his nostrils. After a moment, he grabbed a pack of his cigarettes off a small side table and nimbly plucked one out with long and thin fingers like a pianist's. He pulled on the cigarette several times, bouncing his knee up and down, and Will waited for the situation to settle in Clyde's mind. "You ain't a cop," Clyde said finally.

"Why do you say that?"

"If you were, you wouldn't have quit beating me. You'd have kicked me until I couldn't talk anymore, then wrote down whatever answers you wanted."

"Is that what happened to get you into Buffalo?"

Clyde grunted. "Yeah, that's what happened." He rolled his eyes. "Something like that." Clyde's eyes darted around the room like he was trying to avoid the fact that Will sat across from him. Will had seen this before. Clyde was trying to sort through the angles, trying to find a way out. He had something to hide. Will decided to let his anxiety build for a moment, so he stood and surveyed the one-room apartment for any place Clyde may have hidden the Pollock. If Clyde did not have a buyer, he may still have the painting tucked away in hopes that he could determine a way to get rid of it. Will inspected behind the refrigerator, then moved to the closet, then under the bed, but there were no spaces to hide a six-foot-long painting, even if Clyde had rolled it up. The apartment was too small. Will turned back to Clyde, who had resigned himself to staring at the floor.

"We both know you took the painting," Will said. "And you're right. I'm not a cop, and I'm not here to catch a thief. But I am going to recover that painting, and you're going to help."

Clyde raised his head. "Listen, mister. I ain't got what you want, and if you ain't a cop, why don't you get out."

Will dropped back into the folding chair and stretched out his legs. With calculated effort, he took his time to respond, pulling another drag on his cigarette and staring at Clyde. He moved the cigarette pack to the edge of the round table and dropped his lighter on top. Then, he started again, but slowly, trying to get Clyde on his side. "I'm your way out of this, Clyde," he said matter-of-factly. "You help me, and most of this problem disappears for you. Or at least I do. And unless you want me to get the cops, get them searching all through your apartment, get them asking you questions that land you back in Buffalo or worse..." He paused to let his threat take effect. "Then you'd better answer my questions."

Clyde slumped on the couch, shaking his head slowly. "You ain't a cop?"

Will leaned back and waited.

Clyde twisted the handkerchief into a point and poked around in his nostril, cleaning out the blood. He stared at Will, then back at the floor. "Ask me what you need to, then get out," Clyde said, dropping his shoulders and giving in.

"Okay. Let's start with the painting. You've got no network, so where is the picture, or who'd you sell it to?"

Clyde started shaking his head back and forth, fidgeting with the cigarette between his fingers. "I never saw them. Honest, mister. That's the truth." He spoke to Will directly, as if trying to convey his willingness to cooperate.

"Who gave you the money then?"

"I put the painting in the trunk of a car out in Brooklyn and took the cash like they told me."

The last few words connected in Will's head, but complete thoughts took another minute to process. Clyde never met his buyers but was instructed on how to get paid, which means he hadn't been in control of the situation. Clyde did not know his buyers, which would make finding the canvas more difficult. "Clyde, how'd you find your buyer?" Will's words were deliberate.

Clyde dropped his head back against the couch and began rocking it back and forth. "They found me, man."

"What do you mean? How'd they know you had the painting?" Will's words came out slow as he tried to process the information.

"They called me. *They* set it all up. *They* told me which gallery, what painting, where to drop it off, when, everything."

Will went numb. A made-to-order job. Clyde had no partner, no plan. He had been following instructions. He was a puppet, used to create distance between the theft and the people who needed the painting. The blood rushed back into his vessels, and his face flushed as he considered all the time he'd lost following the wrong lead. Had they planned the diversion intentionally, known he would follow the obvious lead? And why? Will stubbed out his cigarette and walked to the window; the afternoon sun cast long shadows down the avenue.

Clyde was a pawn, nothing more, Will thought as he gazed down the street. He got paid, yes, but he was instructed what to do, and now the painting had changed hands to an unknown buyer. And why did they need the painting? He turned back to Clyde, hoping to ask the right questions but not knowing what they were. He needed to find a point of intersection.

"How'd they contact you?"

"I told you. They phoned me." Clyde started tending more to his nose than to Will, apparently letting go of the fight, automatically answering questions as they came.

Will glanced around the apartment again. "You don't have a phone here. Did you have one before?"

"No, I ain't got no phone. They called over at Schneller's. Asked to speak with me."

"Just the once?"

"Two times. The first time they called to feel me out. I told them no. I had got out of Buffalo State two months before and didn't want to get involved in any of that shit no more. But they kept me on the phone. They kept prying and talking and asking questions, making me real nervous. They kept asking about my sister up in Chicago." He shook his head. "How'd they know I had a sister? I didn't like any of that." He pulled fast on his cigarette a couple of times. "I don't know, mister. I figured they didn't call asking; they called telling. So I said yes. And that's about it. They called back a few nights later."

"For what?"

"To set it all up."

"They gave you everything?"

"The man gave me the address, told me to steal a painting, gave me the crate number and everything. I ain't never stole a painting before, didn't know what I was supposed to do with it. They told me to bust open the crate and roll it up. Painting was damn big, too. Tall as me. I pulled it off its frame and rolled it up. Don't understand white folk, why they'd want to steal a painting. But that's what I did. I took a train out to Brooklyn that night, dropped it off, and made my money."

"They told you to drop it in a trunk? And you did?" Suspicion wormed its way into Will's head. Clyde seemed like the sort to figure he could make more money by doing something stupid, like take the money and keep the painting, try to make money twice. Clyde sat on the edge of the couch fidgeting with his cigarette, unable to stay still. "Why are you nervous, Clyde? Did you take the money and keep the painting? Are you hoping they'll give you more? I can tell you that's not how it will go down. They're going to find you. I did. And it won't end well when they do."

Clyde stilled and almost stopped breathing. His eyes held a mix of fear and pleading. He slumped on the couch as if realizing his predicament, the trouble he had brought on himself. Then, he lit another cigarette off the end of his first and mumbled under his breath.

"Is that why you moved? You're trying to hide?" Will asked.

Clyde let out a long breath, his eyes weary.

Will waited a minute, then began slowly, his voice honest and soothing. "I'm your way out, Clyde. If you have the painting, give it to me; otherwise, help me figure out who you sold it to and how to contact them. You give me that, and you don't have to hide anymore. You can go out and visit your sister in Chicago."

"Why would I give it to you, mister? That would make it all worse." Clyde seemed to catch himself and double back on his words. "Anyway, I don't have it."

Will stood up. Whatever trouble Clyde was in, he needed help. Maybe he had the painting, maybe he didn't. Maybe he took the money. Maybe he stayed in town when he shouldn't have. Will picked up his cigarette pack off the table, walked to the door, and then turned back. Clyde had not moved. His face hung long. Will wanted to make Clyde's choices real for him to be sure he understood. "They're going to find you. I'm your way out. I'll give you a few days to think it over." Then he walked out.

Will met Liz for dinner several nights that week, tucked away in corners of little neighborhood restaurants. Whatever had held her back before had faded into the background, although Will still heard a hesitancy in her voice. She accepted his invitations, and each night after dinner they returned to the Monkey Bar, where they talked over drinks and warm candlelight until Darcy closed, time always slipping away from them. She asked about the case and what leads he had, and he worked through the details with her.

"What if Clyde still has it?" she had asked one night.

So the next day they visited a few of the less reputable Pawn & Loan shops in Chelsea to search for the Pollock on the off-chance Clyde had tried to resell the canvas. The stores typically had questionable paintings without provenance or original purchase receipts. If Clyde wanted to try and sell the canvas on his own, doing so through a pawn shop would be his best bet. He wouldn't be paid much money for the painting, though, and therefore Will was not optimistic they would find it.

They strolled through the small rooms, squeezing past hickory cabinets and between dining tables with their chairs stacked on top. Shelves were stacked with silver trays and clocks and porcelain figurines, but they found no paintings resembling the Pollock.

"Why art?" she asked when they stepped back out onto the street. "What do the paintings mean to you?"

He did not want to discuss the war or the memories that stayed with him at night, but he knew if anyone could understand how the paintings helped, Liz could. He wanted to share that part of him with her, but doing so would expose a torn part of his soul, a weakness and pain that he had tried to hide. He did not know if he was ready for that openness, that raw truth. Still, he turned toward her. An orange-red haze from the setting sun silhouetted her face as they stood outside the pawn shop. The rays from the sun shadowed her form on the right side so that the pink pearl color of her face turned a warm purple-gray. He could not help but be drawn in by her radiance.

"I don't know why people are drawn to different works of art, but they are," he said, continuing down the avenue. "Some aspect of the painting triggers an emotion. It grabs hold and doesn't let go. It could be an image or the colors or the message. Either way, a painting can have a meaningful effect." Will stopped walking and stood silent for a moment. Then his eyes met hers, and he tightened his jaw to stop himself from breaking down before her. He swallowed hard and took a deep breath, afraid that if he spoke too soon he would be unable to control the pain he had carried by himself since the war. He worried it would pour out of him, a deluge of emotion. But he wanted to share this part of him with her. He took a breath to remain steady. He struggled to form the words, to bring them out from the dark corners where he had buried his feelings for so long.

"The war stayed with me when I returned," he said finally. "We all came back different, broken. I find solace in paintings. I need them." His voice was soft, almost apologetic. "Paintings help quiet the memories. I can spend time in front of one and be taken away from the images of bodies and trenches." He described the dreams he had at night and how he woke with sweat on his face, how he could still hear the bullets ripping past his head and tearing into the dirt next to him, and how if he envisioned the sunrise painting—the orange-red glow of the sun, the soft rolling water, and the rocking boat—he could push the visions away. "Maybe a different painting does the same for someone else. Recovering stolen works of art, paintings that had been torn away from somebody, became important to me. I protect them, in a way."

Liz had not moved as he spoke, but when he stopped talking, she placed a hand on his cheek. She looked directly into his eyes and held his gaze, giving him a sense of security. "I like you, Will. I like that you're straight and honest and true. It's a quality I don't see often." Her soft fingers brushed against his skin. She was close enough that the subtle hint of perfume lingered between them, sweet and sharp. Will brushed back the single strand of her soft hair that seemed always to have a mind of its own, tucking it behind her ear.

"So where do we go from here?" he asked.

"Let's just keep walking together."

She held his hand as they walked together down Eighth Avenue toward Rothman's Pawn Shop. A part of Will felt like himself before the war, without the pain and anguish he had carried for years. He felt he could take deeper breaths again with a light chest. The air felt fresh and new with bright sunlight filtering down. The tree leaves suddenly appeared a hopeful, bright-yellow green.

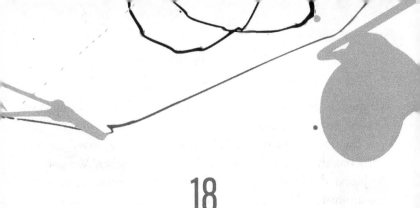

18

IRA STOOD next to the white marble podium clock in the lobby of Chase National Bank on Park Avenue. The air echoed the quiet tapping of Comptometer keys and footsteps on marble floors. Six girls in matching blue scarves stood behind the teller counter, separated by short partitions, waiting with smiles, ready for someone to approach. Ira watched one of the girls as she counted off a series of crisp bills, handing them to a man who thanked her and walked away, his heels clicking against the floor as he crossed the lobby. Past the podium clock, near the bank vault door, several men with tired eyes sat behind mahogany wood desks topped with deposit slips, ledger books, and gold pen chains. Ira had the contact's name from Strout but no additional information.

He scanned the faces of the account managers, hoping to receive a signal. Their features appeared the same, young and eager, but one of the men had a receding hairline that made him look out of place. He caught Ira's glance and stood up from his second-row desk. When he approached, he spoke in a low whisper. "Ira Fenton?"

"Keller?"

Keller nodded and moved back to his desk with Ira close behind. "I signed up for this because you guys threatened my brother," he said, crouching into his chair. "He's the party member, not me. I'm not the bad guy here, and I don't like breaking laws, certainly not breaching people's bank accounts."

Ira pinched the bridge of his nose. "Don't be naive," he said. "This was the deal you made to help your brother. We got you the job at the bank so you would give us information on other Communists. What did you think we were talking about?" Ira handed him the portion of the bank statement made up of three or four pieces taped together.

Keller studied the paper and, after writing down the account number, handed the taped pieces back to Ira. Then he turned to the drawer on his left but, shaking his head, reversed his direction and leaned over to the one on his right. He mouthed words under his breath as if coaching himself through the situation, which signaled weakness to Ira—clearly the same weakness the Communists had targeted in his brother. Keller pulled open the larger bottom drawer and thumbed through the first few files. After a moment, he pulled out a document folder and scanned the paperwork with his finger, then flipped the pages, checking to see that everything was in order. He turned the paperwork around for Ira to see.

"I have account documents, articles of incorporation, bylaws, and bank statements. I can tell from these that the account was set up four years ago—March 1949. There's been significant activity since, including fund transfers and payments. Several transactions, debits and credits." Keller continued to study the documents. "The account appears to be funded each month, depleted by fund transfers, then replenished again, which is somewhat unusual."

"Do foundations usually fund on such a regular basis?"

"No, they usually fund in big chunks annually or quarterly, or after a major charity event. Here we have a few major funding events but also large regular payments. That doesn't make sense."

"Let me see." Ira grabbed the paperwork out of Keller's hand, certain the imbecile did not have a trained eye to spot what was important. He flipped through the pages and noticed several regular incoming payments and several outgoing payments. The MoMA exhibit could require significant funding, and maybe on a regular schedule, but nothing long-term, and these payments had occurred since the account was opened four years ago. "How do your other accounts perform?"

"Other foundations have several deposits as well as several outgoing payments. But they are typically from different donors and usually during specific periods, like after fundraising events or before the end of the year for tax purposes, and they're usually always made by check. These are by wire transfer." Keller pointed to the bottom of the page. "And consider the outgoing payments. Several are to other foundations, but others look like they're going to magazines and newspapers, many of them overseas. This account performs like a conduit of some sort, possibly a shell account, receiving and dispersing funds regularly."

Ira shook his head, not understanding. He continued to read through the pages, hoping to find an explanation. In fact, he hoped he might find the right question to ask because he wasn't sure what Keller was showing him. "What does this mean?" he asked, pointing to Elizabeth Bower's name, which hovered over a line next to the word *incorporator*.

"That means she created the corporate entity of the foundation." He pointed to a separate article in the document. "This shows she is also the director. She can sign documents, make payments, those sorts of activities. Usually the director is also on the board."

"Who else is on the board?"

Keller flipped to the foundation bylaws. "The bylaws won't include names, but they will provide the structure." He reviewed the papers twice, then studied them a third time.

"Odd. In my other foundations, the board is large, typically made up of the president, vice president, treasurer, and several other members. But this foundation doesn't appear to be set up in the same way. They don't list the board positions."

"What does that mean?"

"It means it's different, that's all. It operates without a board. I would think it has to have one, but I guess not if it isn't defined in the bylaws."

"Is that unusual?"

"Quite."

Ira reviewed the documents one last time. Why couldn't it have been easy? An account, a name, some proof of what the Bowers were doing, and if he were lucky, a trail straight to the Kremlin, or at least a local leader. Instead, he found confusion, the obvious answers hiding from him. He scanned back through the paperwork, studying the names and dates. As he considered each piece of information as evidence, he made a connection. "When did you say the account was set up?"

Keller flipped the pages. "I think …Yes, 1949. March 1949."

A wave of suspicion rattled through Ira's nerves. He dropped the papers on Keller's desk, grabbed his hat, and thanked the man. There had to be a connection. The date was too coincidental and one he'd never forget.

The cab dropped Ira on Park Avenue across from the Waldorf Astoria and continued down the wide boulevard, through the rectangular canyon of red brick and cream-colored molding. The metallic sculpture of the glamorous winged woman was poised on top of the hotel entrance, standing in front of the gold grill facade with her back arched and toes pointed as if seconds from flight. Ira marveled at the hotel's provenance, a real estate achievement of dueling industrial families, a representation of America's elite and powerful.

How a hotel of this stature could host an event like the one in March of 1949 still baffled him. They had called it the Cultural and Scientific Conference for World Peace, with the purpose of holding intellectual discussions in the search for paths to lasting peace. His lip curled when he said the name aloud under his breath. What a ruse. But nobody could stop the event. He had tried. He had stood in this spot four years ago. He could still hear the picketers' chants in his ears as he replayed the day in his head. *Stop the Reds! Stop the Reds! Stop the Reds!*

On that dreary March day, as Manhattan struggled to shake off the cold gray blanket covering the city, Ira had stepped into the picket line circling in front of the entrance. Several protesters were handing out leaflets titled "How and What to Tell a Communist." His cold, bare hands held tight to the wooden stick attached to a sign that read *Agents of Moscow, Get Out of America*, and he continued the drumbeat of the chant, feet stamping as he circled with the men. One of the other New York Steam Union members sidled up to him and joined the march.

"Can you believe this? How the hell did this happen? All these Commies right here in our city. Who the hell dropped the ball on this?"

"Beats the hell out of me. I'm just glad we found out before the conference ended."

"Jesus. This is the third day. I was here Friday, and there weren't many of us—twenty, tops. We should get more protesters today since we put the word out."

They shook their heads and continued shuffling along the picket line, chanting. Ira had received the call from the American Legion that morning. The Legion needed more men to protest the conference, which was sponsored by the National Council of Arts, Sciences, and Professions. By the afternoon, the number of protesters had grown to almost four hundred. All anyone could talk about was the fact that the conference was an initiative of the Communist Information Bureau and that the Soviet Party was planted inside the Waldorf. The conference was supposedly held in the name of peace, which was bullshit. They said they wanted to figure a way for the two cultures to live together. They wanted to avoid a third world war. But the whole event was a ruse to spread Soviet propaganda, connect spies with weak-minded artists and writers and intellectuals, and infiltrate the country to find Americans willing to spy against their people. The Commies were breeding spies right here in the Waldorf. A week before, the State Department caught on and began denying visas to the Russian delegates, but the conference had too much momentum. Picketing and disruption was the only way to stop it. Ira stepped out of the picket line and joined a small faction of men gathered at the street corner.

"We should storm in, riot or something," one of the men said.

Ira nodded. "I agree. It's been speech after speech, and no one's done anything to stop them. Time's running out. The conference will be over in a few hours." Ira motioned the men closer. "Listen, we'll go in like we're attendees, with our umbrellas and such, and no one will think anything about it. We'll filter in and spread out. Any other way and they'll stop us before we get started."

The others signaled their approval.

"Then," Ira continued, "during the next speech, we make hell. Pound your umbrella tips on the ground, open them if you must, disrupt it all. That's enough to make havoc. If we do it right, we'll be able to end the conference early."

"The weather's dreadful. Nobody would think another thing about it."

"Do we have enough umbrellas?"

"We each have one, and we can grab twenty more protesters who have more. It can't be that hard."

After ten minutes, they had collected twenty-five in all. There had to be hundreds of participants inside, but twenty-five would do, Ira thought. He edged himself in front of the group to see for himself, to see the Russian Communists. Even though he had never seen one, Ira was certain he could pick one out of a crowd. They'd have beady eyes behind heavy-rimmed glasses. Their cheeks would be red, and they'd smell of sauerkraut.

They were to go in a few at a time to avoid suspicion, and Ira decided to go through the hotel's side entrance, expecting less of a crowd there. However, when he got there, access was blocked by a police barricade. A group of four nuns knelt in front of the door, making the sign of the cross and chanting about the savior and demon souls of the Communists. He stepped past them, around the barricade, and through the bronze-plated revolving door.

Inside across the far wall hung a banner that read *Cultural and Scientific Conference for World Peace*. Men in dark, felt-wool coats, fedoras, and ushankas ran from one side of the lobby to the next, in and out of the conference rooms. Each exuded energy, an excitement that Ira knew came from making their Communist connections. These intellectuals from Russia, connecting with the liberals in America. The Soviet spy handlers made connections here with potential moles.

How could anyone have let this happen? How could anyone let these weak-minded groups gather under such a subversive and clandestine hoax?

Now, Ira stood outside the Waldorf Astoria once again, his heart racing furiously from the memory. This was where it had all begun, where the connections were made. This was where the Soviets had found their spies. They had started their plot to take over the minds of Americans right in the heart of Manhattan. They had connected with the artists, the writers, the newspaper men—the liberals and the intellectuals—right on that exact spot on that cold March day.

Ira stepped past the doorman, pushed through the bronze-plated revolving door, and climbed the entry stairs. He stood in the expansive lobby directly underneath the crystal chandelier, its electric candles and glass beads dripping down from its center crown. Elizabeth Bower's name had to be on the registry from that weekend four years ago.

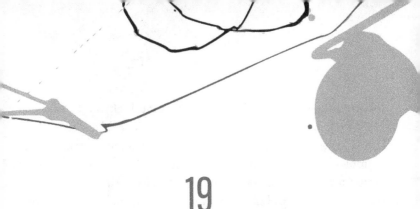

19

WHEN WILL RETURNED to Clyde's apartment in Harlem, he found an eviction notice taped to his door for unpaid rent. He walked back down the four flights of stairs, around the front, and down to the basement apartment where he found the building super. The super told Will that Clyde had mentioned going out to Chicago to visit a sister, and since she had a stable waitress job at a small diner on Maxwell Street, Will was able to track her down.

"Arrested?" Will said when he reached her on the phone.

"That's right. He came to visit a week ago and up and stole a car while he was here. I don't know where they took him, but he's gone, baby. Sorry."

Will slammed the receiver down. He could research the prison records to find where Clyde was jailed, but what would be the point. If Clyde did have the Pollock as Will suspected, he would have hidden the painting somewhere, and it wasn't going anywhere now. And rather than tell Will where the picture was, Clyde would wait out his time in prison and then try to resell the painting once released.

The facts that Clyde had disappeared and the Pollock case had stalled could wait until Monday. So Will stepped onto the bus for the four-hour ride down the two-lane highway to the East Hamptons looking forward to a weekend with Liz. The weather had warmed overnight as it did in Manhattan, and rentals in the Hamptons had opened along the five-mile strip providing an escape for those who wanted out of the city. When Will reached the Hampton stop, Liz stood in sandals and high-waisted shorts at the station curb, shielding her eyes from the sun.

"De Kooning's place isn't far from here," she said, grabbing his hand as he approached with his small travel case. They naturally fell into a kiss, one that was simple and uncomplicated. The sandy air smelled humid and salty as it blew off the beach three miles away. At the curb, Ellis sat behind the wheel of an old Ford pickup, and it was a tight squeeze to get the three of them in the cab.

"We started yesterday and haven't stopped since. You've got catching up to do," Ellis said as he pulled a six-pack of Pabst Blue Ribbon from the floorboard and tossed a can to Will.

Will grabbed a church key off the dashboard and poked two holes in his flattop can. The Ford bounced along Main Street, which was lined with giant elm trees that arched over the road, past the traffic light in the center of town, and along the pond. East Hampton had a mix of wealthy New York residents whose large houses wrapped around Hook Pond and artists who rented dilapidated farmhouses on the outskirts of town that offered ample studio space and a quick escape from the city.

"You'll like East Hampton," Ellis said as he guided the truck with his knees, trying to light a cigarette. "There's a bunch of us out here, and there's always something going on. The older houses rent cheap, and we bunk three or four together. You can crash wherever you find a spot. Suits me fine. You can find a party anytime you want, so you don't sleep much anyway. And nobody minds that we're here. Everyone's real friendly. Nothing like Springs."

"What's in Springs?"

"That's where Pollock lives. Out there everybody is a cousin of someone else, if you know what I mean. The whole town was built off potato farming. It's a few miles up the way but worlds different. I've been out to his studio. Living out of the city helped him for the first few years—getting away from the art scene, the ridicules. But what helped the most was getting away from the bars. He stayed sober for the most part. He did magnificent work. But now ..." Ellis let his voice trail off and pulled on his Pabst. "I don't know. Nobody goes out there anymore. He's still painting sometimes, but he can't repeat what he did a few years ago. I think it's killing him."

"Will he show up tonight?"

"I doubt it. Nobody invites him." Ellis laughed and whirled the truck down the road. They drove up Jericho Lane, which held a loose collection of simple houses with weathered barns, and approached the wood-planked house de Kooning had rented. The house was shaped like a bowtie, with two gray wings rising from the center. The ceilings at each end were at least twelve feet high, with long windows breaking up the space.

They parked along the street behind a row of Chevrolets and Buicks and headed to the house, where jazz drifted out of an open window. When they stepped to the front porch, de Kooning threw open the screen door.

"Supper's almost on," he said over the noise with a warm voice that held a strong Dutch accent. When he stepped back to let them in, the chaotic energy from inside enveloped Will. The sound of Miles Davis's horn bounced against the walls as the turntable filled the room with music. Beer cans littered side tables, and empty bourbon bottles covered the kitchen counter. A young woman was placing mismatched platters full of tuna noodle casserole, hamburger stroganoff, green-bean bake, seven-layer salad, and meatloaf onto an oversized table already crammed with wine and beer bottles and ashtrays full of cigarette butts. Paper plates were stacked on one end next to the paper cups. Laughter rolled out of every room.

Elaine sat on the edge of a couch, dressed in a blue gingham bathing suit with her arm wrapped around the neck of a shirtless young man. She laughed and whispered in his ear. Kline moved into the room and dropped his small frame into a chair. Ellis joined him quickly, and they seemed to continue a conversation they had started long ago.

As de Kooning approached the supper table the others began to descend, taking their places wherever they could, and Will joined Liz at the far end. The conversation popped around the table like a spontaneous improvisation as they all reached for the hodgepodge of dishes.

Ellis raised his glass of bourbon. "Here's to Liz helping with the MoMA exhibit. It's about time everyone knew American art," he said, spilling his drink. "Across the pond, all they focus on is the figure. It's bullshit. We need a new subject matter. It needs to be about painting, the action of painting, our creativity."

"That's what Pollock's done," another artist said, agreeing with Ellis. "He put the act of painting right on the canvas. That's why he's the greatest. That's why he's in the show."

"The greatest?" said a young girl with black ringlets. "Maybe he *was* the greatest. But Bill's the real painter." She put her arm around him and pulled him close. "Pollock's a genius, yes, but he's a one-time freak."

Another at the table broke in. "Here we go again. It's all we can ever talk about. Bill or Jackson, Bill or Jackson. Don't we get enough of it from the critics?"

"Pollock's a great artist," de Kooning said with respect. "He's broken the ice."

"Well, I think he's absolutely boorish," said the girl with black ringlets, as if protecting de Kooning. Then, in what must've been her best Pollock imitation, she frowned into her beer, lifted her head, and mumbled in an almost inaudible voice, "Wanna fuck?" The table erupted in laughter.

They continued to eat and debate their art, illusion, and truth, and Will listened as the dinner livened. The liquor bottles emptied, and the screen door slapped regularly as people came and went. Fueled by liquor, Ellis argued with Kline about foreground and cubism. De Kooning popped up with questions about the line and something about the figure, then receded again into the background. Will let the conversation whirl around him as he cast his eyes on Liz from across the table.

He would catch her glancing at him, or she would catch him doing the same. They would smile and quietly laugh between themselves. He loved the intricate details of her face, the dimple on her right cheek, the hue of her cheeks. When he closed his eyes, he could remember each one. Her image provided him a sense of respite and calmed his nerves like the sound of trickling water in a garden. The shape of her eyebrows, the indention above her collarbone, the slenderness of her arms.

After dinner, when Will broke away to one of the smaller rooms for a smoke, the girl with black ringlets joined him.

"They live separately," she said, answering a question that hadn't been asked.

"Who does?"

"Bill and his wife. He doesn't live with me, but he doesn't live with her either." She followed his gaze out the window, lighting her cigarette. "Everyone here knows, but I guess it seems strange as an outsider. It's a bit of a triangle, I suppose. Painting comes first to them. Bill sits in his dilapidated apartment and paints all day. They all do. They spend what money they have on paint, eat nothing for dinner, and spend their nights drinking at the Cedar. That's their life. We girls simply try to fit in." She gave a half-hearted smile.

"And his wife doesn't mind? She doesn't come out to the Hamptons?" Will asked, not really caring but wanting to be polite.

"She will. She can't stay away from the parties. It's half the reason she's with him."

"And where does that leave you?"

"In a different room." She paused, then added, "Usually." She let out a brassy laugh, waiting a minute for the comment to register, then finished. "He usually sleeps in the studio anyway. It's not an arrangement any of us likes, but no one's willing to let go. I wish the situation weren't this way, but it is. Bill is everything to me."

"Seems like painting is everything to Bill."

"He wants to paint, nothing more. He wants to get it right."

"He's doing well. He's sold paintings."

She let out another brassy laugh. "Yes, but there's no money. Not that money is why he paints, but it helps. His wife takes whatever money there is, anyway."

"MoMA bought one."

"That was two years ago. And he's been working on the series of paintings ever since. People expect a lot this time. There's one spot at the top, and everybody's waiting to see who will take it. The critics have chosen sides and pitted them against each other." The girl relaxed her arms. "But Bill's the best. He is."

Then, from outside a blaring horn startled them both, and Will turned to the window. A dark blue Cadillac convertible swerved up the drive, the round headlights bouncing over every rock in the road. The car weaved from side to side like a carnival ride trying to stay on the rails. The speed didn't let up as it approached, and Will considered running, envisioning the car crashing straight into the house.

"Oh, fuck," the girl said under her breath. She turned and shouted back through the house. "It's Pollock!"

The room stopped in midmotion; the jazz left to bounce against the stillness. Almost immediately, a low hum of whispers and groans began to circulate, and comments started from all directions.

"Shit. I hope he doesn't come inside," someone said.

"Bill, you should go upstairs."

"If he comes inside, we'll deal with it," de Kooning said. "He's still a friend."

"He could tear the place apart," the girl with ringlets said.

De Kooning frowned at her. "Or he could sit here and do nothing."

"Right, sit there and say nothing, do nothing, making everyone uncomfortable. And we'll wait, wondering when he's going to explode, which he will. He always does."

Will turned back to the window. The car had reached the house. The Cadillac, with its massive grille and huge front fenders, spun around the circular drive, horn blaring. The car popped up over the edge of the driveway and into the yard, then jolted back as if the steering wheel were spinning on its own. As it passed the front of the house, the scene before Will seemed to advance in slow motion. Pollock leaned over, his square head ducking low to peer out the far side window, eyes squinting to see inside. Deep creases contoured the man's forehead, and the weathered skin of his face extended into his balding head.

Will expected to see a nightmarish scowl on Pollock's face, unbridled anger ready to explode, but instead, as the car slowed past the front window, a man who appeared lost and confused, almost childlike, peered out the window. An outsider. A loner. Behind the fights and drinks and explosive rage, behind the talk of easy lays and the fuck-yous, behind the stories of nights police picked him up passed out in the gutter and nights he called his wife a cunt and a slut, Will realized the man peering out the window was filled with uncontrollable emotions, uncomfortable in his own self and awkward with people. A man in pain. And beyond that, deep inside the stoic brown eyes, beyond the threats and rage and sadness and chaos on canvas, Will observed a Pollock who wanted to be accepted, a little boy still yearning for the close touch of his mother.

Then the tires spun in the gravel, and the Cadillac exploded back down the driveway, time returning to normal speed. The back end of the car fishtailed, and its horn blared.

Will turned back to the girl, who stood in a room that had returned to its regular cadence, jazz once again muffled by the cacophony of the party. "Does that happen often?" Will asked.

She shook her head. "On the bad nights." And then she walked away.

Out the window, the red taillights faded away in the dark, leaving a blur of madness and beach dust in the air. After a moment, Will moved back through the house, which buzzed again with jazz and laughter, to find Liz. In the back room, two painters stood with Kline, each with a brush in hand. They were trying to paint on a single canvas together, spilling their drinks and paint on the floor as they did. Liz was standing with Ellis, who had begun to slur his speech and use a wall to hold himself steady. She smiled when she saw Will and left Ellis with the painters. They filled their drinks in the den and then squeezed together at the end of the couch. Liz pulled her legs up underneath her and leaned toward Will.

"The Foundation is supporting many of the artists here with grants or through the MoMA funding," she said. She spoke with passion and energy about the art, about the foundation, and Will felt like he could listen to her forever.

She placed a hand on his forearm, and a quiver ran through his body as every sentence, every movement took on more importance than it normally would. The artists who mingled and smoked and shouted around them faded into a blurry background in Will's mind, but Liz stood out clear, curled next to him. The jazz softened to a lull behind their conversation.

After taking a sip of scotch, she pressed her lips together, and he could not help himself from picturing her slender frame naked on his bed, her round breasts lifting as she arched back, flattening her stomach. He ached to kiss her.

She placed her glass on the coffee table and took out a cigarette. Will leaned in close to light the end. A Duke Ellington riff floated between them.

"Do you know why I like art, Will?" Her voice was light and free. He shook his head and leaned into her. "It challenges you to question your own beliefs, challenges the social fabric you live in. You may be attracted or repulsed by a piece, but art forces you to evaluate your world. Art can be powerful. It can send messages and reflect our personal histories."

"Like the missing Pollock? Can it send messages? Change our paradigm?"

She reflected a moment. "Yes, like the Pollock." Then she turned her gaze to the artists in the front room, who were laughing and drinking. "All of them," she said. "Kline, de Kooning, Motherwell, Rothko."

"The Bower Foundation is serious about promoting these artists, isn't it?"

She nodded. "Art needs patrons, Will, people in high places, or it can't exist. Consider the patronage during the Renaissance— the Medici family and the pope. They chose the artists. They commissioned the art. They gave the people the art they believed the people should have. And the people didn't know any different."

"So you're giving the people abstract expressionism."

"Something like that," she said, smiling drowsily as if the answer were more complicated than she had the energy to explain.

He could hear her voice speaking the words in his head: culture and power. They would come to the front and then roll down again. The Medici family. Papal power.

By two in the morning, people began disappearing into bed-rooms—men and women and both together. "Let's go outside," she said. They left the couch and stepped out onto the porch, which warped from years in the humid beach air. She held his hand as they crossed the high spartina grass toward a small studio building at the back of the lot.

Walking next to Liz, a feeling stirred inside Will that he had not felt before. Something he could not identify. Maybe he was falling in love with her. No fireworks or sparks had burst inside him. Nothing hit him over the head. It wasn't an overwhelming desire but a sense of comfort and familiarity. He felt trust. When he was with her, the hectic world went quiet and still, peaceful, and a sense of perfection wrapped around him. The edges of his world blurred, but she remained clear and in front of him. He realized that his world had shrunk down to one person. She was his center. The possibility of a new life stood before him. It was a life different from his own, one built with her, and that new world began to make sense.

They continued to walk across the grass, the chaos of the house fading behind them as Will listened to Liz describe her life in Paris. He pictured himself with her in the city, walking the streets, holding hands under soft yellow streetlights, and eating at cafés.

When they reached de Kooning's small studio, Will opened the frail screen door for Liz, and they stepped inside. The single large room had a bathtub against the wall, functioning as a brush-cleaning sink, and an unmade cot with yellowing sheets rested in the far corner. Brushes were lined side by side on a small rectangular table, every one of them clean. They were arranged by size, large ones on the left down to the smallest pin-sized brush on the right. Will recognized the various kinds of brushes from his few years in the business: camel hair and hog hair brushes, round and flat brushes, mop brushes and fan brushes. There was a Rubens brush and a sign painter's liner brush set off to the side. Art books and photographs sat on a small shelf that hung on the wall. The studio evidenced a sense of discipline and dedication that was almost religious.

Scattered on the concrete floor like confetti lay several pounds of paint flakes, every hue on the color wheel. Variations of canary yellow, violet, peach, and coral brilliantly colored the floor. Then Will took in the six large swaths of unstretched canvases tacked on the walls: paintings of wild-eyed women in vibrant colors, jarring hues of ocher, rose, flesh pinks, grays, yellow, cream, and orange. The fragmented and abstract images surrounded Will as he stood in shock, turning in the middle of the studio. He recognized de Kooning's aggressive brushwork, the muscular movement of his paint.

The images blended into the background, and the background disappeared again into the foreground. They were angular, aggressive, violent, and rough. A thick black calligraphic line circled and caressed a woman's breasts, then hash marks scraped across them. Grotesque teeth leered out of skull-like faces that had gaping eyes and holes for nostrils. Body parts were connected in awkward ways. The hands were like claws. The canvases erupted with manic energy, almost mayhem. The goddess-like women were viscerally sexual.

The paintings had been scraped down and repainted over and over again, as if they were continued works in progress—unfinished, reworked, and reworked again. And the discarded flakes had fallen, covering the floor like rainbow snow.

Liz and Will stood together, staring.

"My God," Will said. No other words could match the images in front of him.

"These are his newest, a series of six women. I'm buying one. MoMA will too."

Will took a minute to recover. "Jesus. What is he trying to do with these paintings?"

"Be the next in line, the greatest," she said with a serious tone. "Cezanne, Van Gogh, Picasso. Now it's time for a great American painter."

"And you'll help them get there. That's what the MoMA exhibit's about."

"Exactly. Great nations need great art." She focused on his eyes as if trying to read his mind, determine what he stood for, what he believed in. "It's kind of like we're still at war, Will, but a cultural war. You served in the war," Liz said. "You know what it's like, why we fight to protect our way of life. It's America's turn. You fought for it. Every generation has. Your dad did before you. I know you can understand."

Will stood quiet, staring at nothing in particular, and a war memory began to play before him. But this one was different, more painful. Blue ink on the card, the simple words: *We regret to inform you.* He'd received the notice during the infantry's stint of rest and rehabilitation in Metz, France, nine months before he returned home. He had lain on his cot, devastated that he hadn't been there, hadn't been at his dad's side at the hospital. He had held the heads of dying soldiers he didn't even know as the blood suffocated their lungs, but he hadn't been able to hold his dad's hand as he slipped away.

The sense of loss had remained with Will through the years, but with no one to tell, he'd pushed the emotions down and numbed himself to the pain. But now, with Liz, he could lay bare his pain, and the weight of his nightmares lifted from his shoulders.

"Are you all right?" Liz asked.

Will shrugged. "When I returned from the war, the doctors said some sort of cancer had taken my dad. They never knew what kind, but it happened fast. Five days from the diagnosis.

I wasn't there when he died. My aunt took care of the funeral arrangements, the phone calls, the thank-you notes." His dad's death had been too painful to mention before, but he trusted Liz with his feelings and wanted to open up. "I wasn't there. I wasn't able to help."

"I'm sorry," Liz said. She laid a hand on his arm, letting the moment take its time. But not too long. Not long enough to make the moment painful.

Her tenderness touched Will, and the moment when desire and trust come together stood there in front of him. He could feel his life coming together with hers, joining like a tightly woven fabric, all the colors intertwined. He ached to be closer, to feel her lips against his. He pulled her close with his hands around her waist, and she leaned forward with her eyes shut and pressed her lips against his, lingering for a moment. She kissed him slow and long as if letting it fill her body. She lifted her head and met his eyes.

She kissed him again and held him tight. Then she wrapped her arms around him with such force that he almost fell over. They both laughed while also trying to kiss and regain their footing. They moved in unison to the paint-covered floor with its brilliant reds and yellows and blues and whites and soft creams. When they rolled to the floor, the flakes stuck to their arms, which were damp from the humid sea air. She wrapped her legs around his waist and he kissed her hard, then below her ear, then along her neckline. He could smell the long day on her, which heightened his excitement. He felt her hot breath at his ear. He had wanted this since the day he met her at the Stable Gallery in her black sheath dress, the day he felt her confidence, her sense of adventure. Her body quivered in his arms as he teased her skin softly with his tongue. Her breath quickened.

Then she pushed him away and propped up on her elbows. "Not like this."

He rolled to the side. "Like what?"

"On the floor of the studio."

His body tingled hearing her admit the act, and he said, "It sounds perfect."

She leaned forward and gave him a long kiss, "Yes, it does. It really does. But you don't know what you're getting involved in. You don't understand."

"I don't need to. Not now. Let's not tell our secrets now. Not tonight."

She placed her hand on his face with a soft touch. "Don't hate me."

"I never could."

"Promise me. Remember this, whatever happens."

Will took in what she said and smiled. A promise. "Trust me." Whatever secrets she had he could let her keep.

She pulled him in and pressed her open lips against his, covering his mouth; in doing so, she showed that she trusted him to be there, to forgive whatever secret she hid inside, whatever she needed to keep from him and maybe from herself. And in turn, he needed to trust her.

Excitement raced through his body. His heart beat rapidly, like he was winded from running a thousand yards. She pulled him back down to the floor, and he pressed his body against her. He kissed her again, excited by the feel of her tongue. He could smell the lust in her breath, the thickness of it.

As he fumbled at the button on her blouse, she pulled at his pants, both working too hard and too fast at the simple tasks. They wriggled out of their clothes and lay naked on the bed of paint flakes, taking each other in for the first time. She was everything he had imagined, perfect in his mind, beautiful and vibrant. He ran his hand along her slender frame. Her chest below her neck was smooth with small freckles along the collarbone, and he noticed how the color of her skin lightened to an ivory white around her small breasts then deepened with a subtle apricot hue toward her stomach. Her belly button was simple, almost flat. Will began kissing the round part of her shoulder, then along her collarbone. He could barely catch his breath, but his movements were slow and tender. He wrapped his mouth around her breast, and she arched with a quick breath, her nipple hard against the softness of his tongue. The shortness of her breath made his heart race faster. The newness of her body alone could bring him to the edge. His hand rubbed across her waist, tracing her curves.

He felt his way down with a light brush of his lips against her skin, moving lower, to her stomach, below her belly button, and, delicately, the inside of her thigh. She clutched his hair. This moment, the spark, the wanting, was different from any other. Yes, he wanted to be inside her, but he wanted more. He wanted the faith that comes with giving yourself to someone. He wanted the moment to bond them, allowing them to know everything about each other. Every detail—the faults, the desires, the fears. And he knew she wanted it too, complete trust. When the secrets didn't matter. He wouldn't hate her, whatever her secrets were.

When he came back up, her heavy kisses, her mouth sucking on his tongue, almost pulled the air out of his breath. Will lost himself in her eyes and enjoyed her lustful gaze, which mirrored his own.

Then she whispered with a heavy breath, "I need you."

She pushed him over and rolled on top, her soft mahogany hair falling over him like a curtain. The heat in her breath caressed his ear. When she pushed up and arched back, paint flakes had stuck to her body, covering her with cerulean and crimson, coral and golden yellow, emerald green and sapphire blue. She appeared before him as a dazzling mosaic of color, a painting herself.

The wild eyes of the de Kooning women glared down at them with their exaggerated almond shapes, like Egyptian goddesses of sex and fertility. Their bodies shamelessly urged them on with their enlarged breasts, their nipples sharp and angular. They were alluring and grotesque and seductive all at once. Vulgar and monstrous. The fragmented images were distorted. Hourglass figures with stick legs, dark strokes of open crotches and arms and breasts and teeth and mouths. The paint had been scraped across the canvas with muscular force. The painter's whole body pushing and pulling and pushing again, back and forth and back until at some point it reached a powerfully cathartic release.

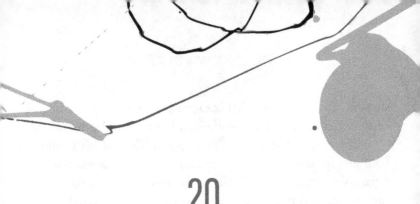

20

THEY SPENT ALL THE NEXT WEEK TOGETHER. The heat of the day kept them off the streets and in the restaurants and museums, lost in the moment when everything was perfect. In the middle of the day, they ducked into a movie house on Forty-Seventh Street and watched Gregory Peck in *Roman Holiday*.

In the evenings, they had cocktails and dinner at the Monkey Bar. When their table was ready, the maître d' would guide them down the carpeted steps to the sunken dining room. A second waiter in a white dinner jacket followed close behind, carrying their vodka gimlets on a round black tray. Fresh-cut roses in silver mint julep cups adorned white cloth tabletops, like tables in a steamship stateroom. They preferred the corner booth with the small round table and maroon leather cushion. A thin gold railing outlined the top of the dark-stained wood. They did not always talk about the Pollock case, although Liz asked questions and kept herself informed. Will had tried to track down Clyde, but the prison transfer records were poorly maintained, and he could not pin down his new location. There were duplicate records of his transfers to both Mid-Orange and Auburn State Prisons, but neither facility had Clyde on the intake list. Clyde's sister had no better information and had grown tired of worrying about his whereabouts. Will admitted to himself that the case had slowed. And even though Liz expressed that she was not concerned, her tone of voice evidenced her disappointment.

One night after dinner, they visited Kline at his studio on Fourteenth Street. Gigantic canvases on massive easels filled the expansive loft. In the middle of the studio, gallon paint cans, turpentine, and roller trays crowded two rectangular tables, and more cans and trays had been placed on the worn wooden floor. Tin cans and glass jars stuffed with large house brushes lined the windowsill. On the bookshelf and in the corner of the studio were stacks and stacks of yellow pages torn from phone books, each with small black sketches, images of furniture, chairs and tables.

Always affable, Kline shared his half empty bottle of bourbon and rambled on with them while he worked. He took his time, first pasting one of the yellow phonebook pages with the black sketches onto a piece of cardboard, then tacking the cardboard next to a canvas. He pulled a large housepainter's brush from the windowsill, grabbed a bucket of black house paint, then copied the lines from the sketch onto the ten-foot canvas with precision, enlarging the image to complete abstraction, angular black strokes covering the picture plane. His arm flowed naturally. He worked confidently as he brushed the paint onto the canvas. From there, he filled the negative space with white paint, then black again on the angular strokes, then white, then black, then white again, over and over until he had created a level of depth and complexity Will had never appreciated. There must have been six different whites—cool whites and warm whites, titanium white and zinc white—and as many different wet-on-wet layers. He worked on more than one painting at a time, which allowed him to revisit the dryer canvases and add another layer, wet-on-dry, always maintaining the image and structure: white and black, again and again.

"How did he come up with the idea?" Will asked Liz as they watched Kline work.

"Like all of them, his style took time, a year or two of changes and evolution. First, he experimented with the black and white palette, then his paintings grew in size. But it was de Kooning who pushed him further and helped solidify the style he paints with today."

They had become close enough that Will knew she detected his surprise. She smiled and explained without his questioning. "De Kooning brought over a Bell-Opticon one night. They projected Kline's phonebook drawings onto the studio wall. They even projected the numbers and letters on the page. Enlarging the sketches on the wall so that only sections and fragments remained on the visual plane pushed the images into abstraction. After that, Kline never turned back."

Will had assumed Kline painted in a rapid, spontaneous manner, but watching him work, he realized each brushstroke had purpose. All the paintings started with the small sketches, images transferred to and enlarged on the canvas with specific intent, coming to life through the broad brushstrokes and physical act of painting. The large canvases forced Kline to use his entire body to make the gestural strokes, reaching from one end of the canvas to the other. These strokes were not made by fine brushwork and delicate fingers. The paintings did not hide the brushstroke as if it did not exist but exaggerated the painter's presence. At times during the night, Kline would climb onto a ladder to reach the uppermost part of the canvas then sweep the brush across the top with one gigantic movement.

At one point in the night, Liz turned to Will. "You should be part of what the foundation is doing. I want you to insure our MoMA exhibit."

By one in the morning, the bottle of bourbon was empty, and they left Kline to paint into the early hours.

Friday night, when the Rosenbergs were executed, they stayed in Will's apartment and ate TV dinners. On the news, a crowd of thousands gathered in Union Square, hoping for one more stay of execution. But at eight o'clock the picket signs dropped to the ground, the protestors' efforts now pointless. Although it wasn't in the newspapers, Palmer told Will over coffee at the Lexington Diner that one electric shock had killed Julius, but Ethel had put up a longer fight. When the doctors pulled down the top of her dark-green prison dress and placed the stethoscope to her chest, they stared at each other dumbfounded because her heart still beat. The guards dragged her body back into the wooden chair and replaced the black belts and straps to her body and electrodes to her head. And the witnesses looked on, eyes wide in fright.

Will worked on Mrs. Harcourt's insurance contract all morning while he waited for Pritchett to decide whether to insure the MoMA exhibit. Although he never found a comparable engraving in his research papers, he had insured a sixteenth century drawing that would be similar in value. The drawing belonged to a young pencil-thin man named Joel Feinmann, who owned Feinmann Gallery on Sixth Avenue, specializing in drawings and prints. He acquired pieces by borrowing his parents' money and preferred throwing parties to managing his business. As a result, he had quickly delegated the day-to-day responsibilities to a family friend. Only months after opening, a customer asked to view the drawing, but it could not be found. Turned out the family friend had sold the drawing out of the store and pocketed the cash without registering the sale. Easy enough to do if the owner isn't paying close attention, which Joel Feinmann was not.

By lunch, Pritchett agreed to let Will insure the exhibit, so Will finalized Mrs. Harcourt's contract and caught a taxicab to MoMA. He pushed through the revolving door and entered the lobby. Through the expansive windows along the back wall, afternoon sunlight shimmered off the outdoor sculpture garden's reflecting pool, which was surrounded by small willow and Japanese styrax trees. A myriad of paintings hung on the walls. Liz stood in the center of the expansive stark-white lobby, waving him over.

"The offices are upstairs," she said.

When they entered, they found Porter McCray, director of MoMA's international program, in his office talking to John Whitney, chairman of the museum board.

"McCarthy's making it too goddamn hard," Whitney said. He sat in a black cantilevered chair at McCray's large, sleek black desk with stacks of paper and a full ashtray. "We're all lined up. We've already contacted the *Musée National d'Art Moderne* in Paris. But this was in the papers this morning." He pointed to an open newspaper on the desk.

On the first page of the local news section, an article named a list of museums that Congressman Dondero had accused of being Communist sympathizers. MoMA was first on the list. Will read the headline and dropped his head at the timing of the bad press. Pritchett would be pissed. Then Whitney turned to Will and frowned as if only now noticing him, the crease in his forehead deepening.

"Why is he here?" he asked.

"If I'm the money," Liz said, "I want the exhibit insured."

"Fine by me. We've got problems as it is with the exhibit, that's for sure," Whitney said, pulling out a cigarette and lighting it. "Congress will eat this shit up," he said, pointing to the article. "That goddamn Dondero is stirring up the public, which means they're in a frenzy, and I've got anti-Communist organizations breathing down my neck. And it doesn't help that they're putting Roschin on trial in two weeks. Congress would never provide funding."

Liz dropped into a chair. "But the foundation is funding the exhibit, so it launches. We all understand the benefits of a private foundation funding the MoMA exhibit. Congress can't do anything about it."

"These artists have a long history, Liz. You know that. Most of them explored Communism during the depression—members of the John Reed Club, the Artists Union. Not all of them are on the list of Two Hundred, but they might as well be. Congress will be outraged."

"But they're the face of the exhibit," Liz said. "They're American art, the new modern art. Pollock, Kline, all of them. And the fact that they can do whatever they want with their art in a free country is half the point. You know that as well as I do, Jock."

Will sat back against the windowsill. Was it possible that Pollock's painting could threaten the exhibit? But before he could dig any further to determine how the stolen Pollock might be related, the phone rang and broke the conversation. McCray grabbed the receiver and placed the mouthpiece against his chest. "Sorry, but I've been waiting for this call all day," he said and then spoke into the receiver. "You found some. Four? That's great." McCray paused, listening to the person on the other end of the line, then began again. "And the doors, they're in the back? That's perfect!" He dropped the receiver on its cradle.

"You'll never guess what we've secured," McCray said, then paused as if expecting the room to answer, a great smile on his face. "I found confiscated German train cars. I've been searching for them for weeks."

"German train cars?" Will asked.

McCray slapped the desk in excitement. "Yes! German cars that were used during the war. The exteriors resemble first-class passenger cars, but they were used for transporting troops and tanks. Camouflage, you see. The cars themselves are extra long and extra wide, and the insides are stripped bare. And the best part is they have huge loading doors with ramps in the back. They're perfect. We'll be able to load the crated paintings right through the back, no problem. We can transport the paintings all through Europe, the whole exhibit. Can you imagine it? We'll be traveling through Europe in confiscated German war trains, but instead of tanks, we're carrying Pollocks and de Koonings. It's quite ironic, isn't it?"

Will hardly knew what to think. He could not imagine the scene. McCray seemed to be suiting up for his own war, his own secret invasion of Normandy, storming the beach by boat and then transporting his oil and acrylic troops into enemy territory. Will imagined the train cars shooting through the mountainous landscape and through the tunnels from Paris to Berlin, Belgium, and Belgrade. Trojan horses packed in their wooden crates. And at each stop, the museums would have to clear out their own current exhibits—European masters, Picassos, and impressionists—to be replaced with American artists, abstract expressionism hung on the walls of Europe. American art taking over.

"That must be an enormous expense," Will said.

"And this is only the beginning," McCray said. "We'll do several exhibits. But the money isn't the problem. That's where Liz comes in. The Bower Foundation. The Rockefeller brothers' fund. There's a consortium of foundations out there funding the exhibit."

The funding made sense. Most museums and art exhibits were privately funded. The Bower Foundation probably received significant funds from various donors. They could fund any exhibit they wished with total control and no oversight, especially if they controlled their board. While he listened, the three of them final-ized the plans for the exhibit. To Will a painting was personal, like his Monet. To Pritchett, it was a dollar amount to recover. But to these three, the paintings seemed charged, a symbol of America, carted through war-torn Europe by train and exhibited in public as a bold reminder of America's triumph while the Parisians were still picking up the rubble. And the foundations were funneling an enormous amount of money to the endeavor, as if paying to spread America itself across Europe.

If Pollock was part of the Two Hundred, or should be, then his painting would be detrimental to the exhibit. But then why steal it? Why not just remove the canvas? And there was another Pollock included in the exhibit anyway. Why steal that specific painting? Will couldn't imagine how any of these questions were related, if at all. Clyde was a dead end, a nickel-and-dime thief for hire. Clyde had made his money, but where did the money come from? Who called Clyde to give instructions, the crate number, the drop-off location—everything neatly packaged in a phone call?

These thoughts were bouncing in Will's head when Whitney picked up the phone receiver. "Yes, I'd like to place a call. No, it's local. Yes. Okay. Ready? It's 26-45-1882." He listened. "No, 1882. Are you writing this down? Say again. Okay, I'll hold."

And as Will listened to Whitney give out the phone number, an idea sparked in his mind like a match dragged across its phosphorus strip into a burning flame. Phone records. How could he not have thought of it before? Each time a phone call was placed, the switchboard operator logged the call into a logbook. Protocol. A record of the call must be made if for no other reason than to ensure the number was captured correctly. If Clyde received a call at Schneller's, the source of the call must be written down somewhere.

But when he posed the question to Charlie back at the office, Charlie laughed.

"Are you kidding? They get hundreds of calls a day."

"But there must be some form of tracking, some way to audit the calls. If a phone call went to Schneller's, it had to come from somewhere. Someone placed the call, and an operator must have logged it in."

Charlie shook his head. "I can't imagine it works that way. There's no need."

"Just ask."

"So, you want me to ask the local switchboard operator to let us go through all the logbooks, which they may or may not have, in hopes of finding some number, which may or may not have been the one Clyde received a call from, to maybe find some connection with a stolen painting?"

"Right."

Charlie laughed again.

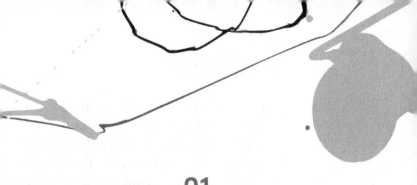

21

"I STILL DON'T BELIEVE IT, but you were right," Charlie said, handing him a black leather logbook with *American Bell Telephone* embossed in gold lettering. "Sure enough, the switchboard operator writes down the incoming number before connecting to the receiving end." He pointed to the logbook in Will's hand. "It took convincing, but they loaned the books to us for the investigation. The rest are on the table."

Will gazed past Charlie at eleven logbooks, each more than three inches thick, and realized at once that the task might be more daunting than he'd expected.

"Eleven more?"

"Sure. One for each of the switchboard operators. You didn't think they would be organized by telephone number, did you?"

Will had hoped so, but he admitted that such an arrangement would be impossible. After settling in at the desk, he flipped through the first logbook, scanning the initial few pages. Rows of numbers, extensions, notes on who dialed in, and the connecting line. Hundreds of pages filled the book, each with rows and notes. Then he considered the stack again. A logbook for each girl, each girl connecting hundreds of phone calls a month.

He lifted his head and looked at Charlie. "This could take weeks."

"And that's if I help you," Charlie said then smirked. "And I don't plan to." He passed the logbooks over one by one.

Will dug into the first book, relieved that most of the notes and numbers were written in clear handwriting. The first page went slowly. He absorbed himself in the notations, wondering about the lives spread before him. He pictured the girls with their hair pinned up, sitting straight in their roller chairs, answering the calls with a cheerful "Number, please" and then staying on the line, silent participants in intimate conversations. They must be familiar with certain voices, keeping up with faceless lives on the other end of the lines—a young man announcing the arrival of his baby, gossip on a fifth-floor walk-up somewhere in Manhattan.

Then Palmer's words echoed in his head. *Thousands of informants watching, learning, and reporting. A network of informal snitches.* Were any of the girls listening for someone else, he wondered? Eavesdropping for someone else would be easy. A contact with a friend who was part of an investigative group, or a member of Congress, a small favor asked over dinner or in whispers on a pillow. Or maybe it went the other way— a union member, a party member with ties to Russia, a Communist spy. His imagination leapt to the Rosenbergs, a seemingly innocent husband-and-wife team.

Will gathered himself and focused again on the logbook. As he continued to scan the pages, he realized that each had separate columns for incoming and outgoing extensions. The incoming column had a variety of extensions but seemed to keep to a specific few.

"Do you recognize any of these extensions?" Will asked. He leaned the book in Charlie's direction.

Charlie shook his head, then stopped and narrowed his eyes. "Wait. I do. Imagine that." He smiled, excited by the game. "There." He pointed at the page. "That one's in Brooklyn where my sister lives. "Those are all variations of the same extension. They must be different parts of Brooklyn."

"You've got the knack." Will grinned and tossed him a logbook. "That book must be for incoming calls from Brooklyn," Will said. "They're calls into the central office needing to be connected elsewhere. Each girl must be responsible for answering and placing calls by incoming location. That means the books must be organized by borough."

He studied the column with notes. There seemed to be two types of calls. The first were local calls, calls within the central office where the operator connected her plug into the receiving jack for the local number. Those calls were marked with *interco,* and the receiving extension was noted in the appropriate column. The second type were connecting calls. These were calls where the operator had to connect to another central office of a different city so that operator could make the connection to the desired long-distance party. Those were marked *transfer* and included the extension of the connecting central office.

The notes and system did not help Will much because an incoming call to Schneller's warehouse could be in any of the logbooks. But at least Will knew on which column to focus. And he knew the series of calls to Schneller's warehouse had occurred two weeks before the night Clyde stole the Pollock, which meant he had a time frame. Finding the right incoming call would be a matter of going through each logbook and focusing on the right column on the pages in the right time frame. He expected they would be done by the afternoon.

But by lunch, they had been through no more than two logbooks. Because the time frame fell over the holidays, the number of calls was more than he anticipated, everyone calling family to wish them happy holidays. A few calls to Schneller had peppered the pages, but nothing helpful.

After a while, Will and Charlie grabbed sandwiches from the Bull & Bear deli, brought them back to the office, and moved to the next book. Again, unrecognizable numbers and handwritten notes. They followed the same methodology for the rest of the day, scanning the incoming column for the right number within the right time frame. But not until the following afternoon, with the seventh book, did Will come across Schneller's number once and then again two weeks later, both calls at 4:15 p.m. He studied the entries again, flipping the pages back and forth to make sure he hadn't seen the pattern in error.

"Found something?" Charlie said, glancing up.

"Maybe. Two calls."

"Ours? From the same incoming extension?"

Will checked again. "The same. This must be the number."

"Where'd they come from?"

Will leaned over to show Charlie the logbook. "Do you recognize it?"

Charlie shrugged, then pored over the page again. "The note says *transfer*. But it says *transfer* on all the calls." Charlie stopped and looked back at the stack of logbooks. "This must be the logbook for all connecting calls."

"I'm not following you."

"All these calls came in from another central office. One switchboard girl must record all incoming calls from other central offices. This is her logbook."

Will considered the extensions and the notes next to the incoming column. Charlie was right. Transfers. The calls did not come from Manhattan or one of the boroughs, but from cities farther away.

Charlie fell back down in his chair and dropped his head. "But to find the incoming extension, you'd need the other central office's logbook."

"Why?"

"Haven't you ever called long distance?"

Will groaned, remembering the last time he had waited almost fifteen minutes to be connected to Chicago. "You're right. To dial Chicago from Manhattan, you might have to go through two different central offices, maybe Philadelphia and Detroit, then after that to Chicago. I'm sure it works the same the other way."

"And that's Chicago. What if it's New Orleans or, worse, San Francisco? That could require five connecting offices. And most of the time the operator rings you back when she's made the connection."

"But maybe the call didn't come that far. Maybe there's one connecting office."

"And maybe there are several." Charlie stood up and rubbed his eyes. "Listen, let's take a break. I can't see straight anymore."

Will and Charlie took the elevator down to the lobby and stepped out onto Broadway. The street was crowded with people, and the cabs rushed past in a flurry, creating yellow streaks as they rushed down the avenue. By now the sun stretched long over the street, and the lights inside the buildings were gaining strength against the fading day. Will reached into his suit pocket and pulled out his pack of cigarettes, offering one to Charlie. "What's going on, Charlie?"

"I don't know." Charlie leaned against a pole. "I mean, what if Clyde lied to you? What if he never did get any calls?"

"Why would he do that?"

"To get you off his back, maybe protect his buyer? I would. And if that's the case, we're wasting our time scrolling through a bunch of numbers, calling different central offices. You need to solve this, but I don't know if I can go through another set of log books."

"You're giving Clyde too much credit."

"Maybe." Charlie gazed out across the street, then turned back. "But if I had a buyer and wanted to sell another painting to him, I'd throw you off his trail too."

"But stealing paintings isn't Clyde's business. He's an amateur. He steals cars and bicycles. He has no other paintings to sell. And why make up a series of phone calls, the made-to-order job? Why not feed me some description of a buyer and say he moved to San Francisco?"

Charlie shook his head. "I don't know. Maybe he couldn't make up a description."

"But he could devise an elaborate cover story?"

"Okay, maybe not. That puts us back to the phone records and a secret buyer, if there is one."

"There's always a buyer."

"Maybe not in this case. Liz thinks Clyde still has the painting, right? And Lorenzo hasn't heard a word about the Pollock. He says it's going through different channels." Charlie shifted off the pole and dropped his cigarette, smothering the ember with his shoe. "I don't know. Something doesn't seem right."

Will couldn't argue. As he stood out on the sidewalk, different conversations began shifting and connecting in his head. *Communist associations. Investigations. Secret maps. The painting hasn't surfaced.* Words he had heard and tried to ignore now pounded against his reasoning and began pointing in one direction.

"What if the painting was stolen to keep it hidden, with no intention to sell?" he said.

"Hidden for what reason?"

"That's what I don't know."

Charlie's face lightened. "If a painting were stolen to keep it hidden, then it wouldn't surface again. Lorenzo would never catch wind of it."

"Right."

Charlie dropped his head. "Then the phone records are all we've got."

"Unless Lorenzo hears about the Pollock some other way."

"I don't know how long it will take. It's going to be work."

"But the switchboard operators will do the heavy lifting. All you need to do is ask for the initiating number to those incoming transfers."

At that, Charlie brightened and headed back inside.

Will climbed out of the trench on his hands and knees, out of the mud and over the roots. A muffled cry for help came from out in the field, retreating into the distance. Will screamed over and again, "Where are you?" But his voice wouldn't travel. The air was still and dead, his own scream echoing in his head.

Will's eyes snapped open, and he sat up. He dropped his legs over the edge of the bed and soothed himself with the soft threads of the carpet between his toes. He closed his eyes, but instead of Monet's blue-green sea rolling out before him, the red-orange sun rising above the harbor, he thought of Liz. He pictured the painter again dabbing at the canvas, blending the pigments to create the smooth pinkish-apricot hue of her skin, the coral color of her cheeks below the eyes that faded as it crested off her cheekbone. Her eyes were not deep-set. They had an almond shape with a slight rise at the top. Will could see her long neckline and round chin, the small pores around her nose. Her dimple showed only with a particular smile she gave. But at rest, her mouth turned down slightly and could cast an attitude when necessary. Will could picture each detail of her appearance, but her beauty came not from her physical features but from her whole being, from an inner strength. A painter would be challenged to depict her character vibrantly. Will was glad to know her, to understand the beauty that couldn't be captured by the painter's stroke.

The soldiers' screams drifted away into the back of his mind with the thought of Liz, and Will replayed walking together along the streets of Manhattan, dining at the Monkey Bar. He opened his eyes and laid back on his pillow, staring at the ceiling. The vision of her face stayed before him, and a sense of peace washed over him. The nightmares were coming much less frequently now, replaced more often by visions of Liz. He closed his eyes and drifted back to sleep.

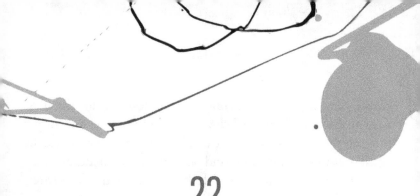

22

THE DAY OF THE ANDREI ROSCHIN TRIAL had arrived. Will decided to join Liz on the train to Washington because he still had no logbooks from the other central offices. Charlie had made the request, but the operator said she needed to place several other phone calls, and the girls would have to sift through the records, so it would be several weeks before they could provide him with the information.

Will stepped down the polished concrete steps of Penn Station and into the main steel-vaulted atrium. The morning sun broke through the arched windows of the cathedral-like space, its yellow ribbons stretching to the floor. The commuters rushed in and crisscrossed the travertine floor in a choreographed dance, off to Boston, New Haven, Philadelphia. Will stood in front of the departure board, searching for the Washington Express. The clap of the display flaps echoed against the high ceiling as they dropped and rotated with a rhythmic flutter like pigeons startled by the wind. The tiny squares scrolled rapidly, updating the board from top to bottom in a quick mechanical wave of movement. The man next to Will turned when the Philadelphia train status updated, remarking that he was late, and disappeared from the corner of Will's eye. Another like him took his place.

Will waited until the status of the Washington Express flipped to completion at the bottom of the board. *Platform 2. Departing.* Then he turned and rose on his toes to peer over the crowd. Scanning the main concourse, he searched for the stair-wells that led to the tracks below, a labyrinth of steel rail cutting through the Manhattan bedrock. After spotting the entrance, he raced over to the iron railing and peered down at platform two.

The great gleaming line of sleek silver cars and golden letter-ing stretched out as far as Will could see. A hulking and magnif-icent streamliner. Freshly washed, polished, and shined, the cars had been loaded with fresh linens and towels. Porters were lifting the step stools of the Washington Express, and the platform had already thinned out. Farther down, past the newsstand and kiosk selling pulp paperbacks, Liz stood at the platform's edge, talking with Dickie. Will assumed he must be covering the trial, but their conversation appeared contentious once again, and it caused Will to take pause. He wasn't jealous, but he had an unsettling sense that Liz was keeping something from him, downplaying the relationship.

Will took the steps two by two to catch them, but they had already boarded by the time he landed on the platform with a metallic thud. As the breaks released, hissing steam filled the ter-minal, and the train began to move out, imperceptible at first, then gradually increasing speed. Will ran to the first car, grabbed the smooth steel handrail, and pulled himself up.

"Ticket, please," the porter said as Will stepped into the inner corridor.

"I'll need to buy one," Will said. "I barely made it as it is." He smiled, offering his slightly crooked wink.

"Of course, sir. Washington?"

"And I need one for a roomette, number twenty-four. I'm joining someone."

The porter dug into his apron for tickets, pulled out two, and punched holes in both.

"This is your ticket for the trip," the porter said. "And this one is for the roomette." He handed Will his two ticket stubs.

"The roomette is the fourth car after the bar car. Number twenty-four will be on your right."

The train knocked along the steel rails as Will navigated through the gangway and walked into the observation car. Men were reading the morning newspaper at small round tables filled with coffee cups and ashtrays. A ribbon of windows wrapped around the sides of the oval car, and a wide skylight covered the top. Outside, the dark tunnel gave way to the bright day and the backside of New Jersey. Maintenance yards and track switches rushed by as the train rolled through the city. The Manhattan skyline slowly faded behind the Hudson River. Next he passed through the chair cars, which rocked back and forth, row after row of two-seater booths filled with men. Then he crossed into the bar car. Men in gray flannel suits stood two deep, talking, eating, and watching a small black-and-white television mounted in the corner. The smell of morning coffee and cigarettes filled the car, mixing with the sounds of clinking coffee spoons and laughter. Will guessed the men were mostly bank lobbyists and advertising men—lunch at the St. Regis, a cigar in the lobby of the Willard.

As he navigated the car, a familiar voice called his name from behind the row of men, and Will glanced over their heads. Dickie sat at the small counter that ran half the length of the train car, waving him over. Will squeezed through the shoulders and briefcases to join him.

"Headed to Washington, ol' boy?" Dickie said as Will edged an elbow onto the counter. A slice of toast and poached egg, half eaten, lay on a plate in front of Dickie.

"I'm joining Liz for the Roschin trial. You?"

"God, no. I wouldn't be caught dead in that circus. Dondero and those clowns in Congress wouldn't know a Communist if they bumped into one. I don't know how Liz stands it. Coffee?"

Will gave an accepting nod. "What's in Washington for you, then?" he said, curious about Dickie's purpose.

"I'm visiting my aunt before crossing the pond," he said, then signaled to the bartender.

"London?"

"Paris."

"Paris?" Will said with an arched brow. "I pictured you a Londoner. You know, fish and chips, that sort of thing."

"Hard to imagine I live anywhere. I travel back and forth quite a bit. I used to be in Berlin. God, that was a mess. Reconstruction. Jackhammers. All day breaking up the rubble. Then there were the dynamite explosions every morning during my shave; nearly cut myself to death more than once. Rubble everywhere, I tell you. A god-awful mess, ol' boy. God-awful."

Dickie buttered a corner of his toast, and it quickly disappeared into his mouth, followed by a swig of coffee. "What surprised me the most were the women," he continued. "They cleaned it all up. That's what was amazing. All the men were killed in the war. With no one left, the women went to work. I'd never seen anything like it. Thirty-year-old women stuffing dynamite into the side of a building, shoveling rock into wheelbarrows. But someone had to do it. General Clay manages our zone in Germany now since the war. It's the size of Michigan and costs us over two hundred million a year to run. He's got economic experts, educators, agriculturalists, magazines, newspapers—three hundred thousand people on the payroll, a specialist for everything. You name it—everything from fertilizer to culture."

"Culture?"

Dickie flashed a smile. "Sure. Get them playing baseball, and they'll love America. They took a while to catch on, but they got the hang of it. Everybody loves baseball."

"Who pays for all of it?"

"That's the best part. The Marshall Plan does. Reconstruction deposits. Each country that receives funds from the US for reconstruction must match the amount as a deposit into a central bank. Counterparty funds, they call it. It's a bunch of left-pocket–right-pocket stuff, but it allows countries to buy machines and equipment even though they have no money. But here's the kicker. We take five percent for fund management. They call it administration, but it is a total headache, I tell you." He rolled his eyes.

Will considered what Dickie had said. Payment for reconstruction, money flowing from bank account to bank account. There were negotiations and contracts to sign. And everything took money. Money that had to come from somewhere. Interparty funds, counterparty funds. It could all get lost in a series of transactions. How could anyone keep track?

"Our side is not the problem," Dickie continued. "The problem's the Russians. You know they've nationalized their zone in Germany and turned it into a Communist state. Now we've got two Germanys, East and West. And I tell you what, if we're not careful, the Russians will try to take the whole goddamn city. And it's not isolated to Berlin. It's everywhere in Europe. The war left a vacuum, ol' boy. And if we don't fill that vacuum, it's left to the goddamn Russian Communists."

"So get them to play baseball."

Dickie laughed. "Now you're catching on. Exactly. Baseball. It's about getting them to love American culture."

"And what did you get paid for?"

"Me? Newspaper articles and essays, that sort of thing. All pretty highbrow. The paper was German, of course. *Der Wöchen*." Dickie took a large sip of coffee, then translated. "*The Weekly*. Not part of Clay's program, but we all got along pretty well."

"Similar work in Paris? Is that where you met Liz?" Will asked, trying to probe the relationship tactfully.

Dickie laughed. "No and yes. We met here, stateside. Ivy League literary club. Not members at the same time, of course. But some of us alums got together every so often. Scotch and cigars, that sort of thing."

Dickie pulled on his cigarette, then stripped the end in the ashtray. "When I transferred from Berlin to Paris, she came over with a few others to help start the paper. We put out some great stuff. Threw it right over the Seine to those Left Bankers."

"Left Bankers?"

"That's right. The intellectuals, the Marxists, that whole crowd. Berlin was full of them. Paris too. Fantastic articles, real letters, not the garbage the government puts out. T. S. Eliot, George Orwell. They all wrote for the paper. Not to mention the symphonies, operas, and ballets we organized. Last year's festival alone had the New York City Ballet and the Boston Symphony Orchestra. We bombarded them, by God. The barrage was fantastic. They didn't know what hit them."

"More baseball."

"Exactly. Everything we've got." Dickie began to make sounds like bombs dropping. *Boom. Boom.*

Will caught on. "And now MoMA. The artists, the paintings—that's more baseball too."

"Blanket bombing, I call it." Dickie laughed.

Will pushed back his coffee. Out the bar car window, the train raced along the rails.

"I should find Liz," he said, standing.

"But I haven't asked." Dickie caught Will by the elbow. "How's your search going? The painting? Tell me what you've got. I'm interested in all the details."

Will hesitated at Dickie's questions. The case lay on his desk, stalled, but he didn't want to tell that to Dickie. Clyde Barnett was a means to an end, the theft a made-to-order job. He had the phone books, a call from outside Manhattan, but no telling where that would lead. And the more Will deliberated the case in his head and the longer the painting stayed off the market, the more he convinced himself it had been stolen to stay hidden. But why? That was what Will couldn't figure out.

"I found the thief up in Harlem, a driver for Schneller & Schneller," he said finally, disclosing no other details.

Dickie did not seem surprised. "But he didn't have the painting. So where is it?"

"How did you know?" Will asked.

"You said you found the thief. You didn't say you found the painting. And I know that until you find the painting, the case isn't wrapped up. You can't just arrest the fellow and close the case, then sit back in the office."

"You're right. Trouble with my job is I'm not searching for the thief. I keep going until I find the painting. But he's a good lead."

"Are you certain you can find it? I was never any good at hide and seek."

"I won't stop until I do."

"That's the spirit, ol' boy!" Dickie said, slapping him on the back. "I have faith in you."

"Do you know the painting?" Will asked, wondering what drove Dickie's interest in the case.

Dickie mopped up the rest of his egg yolk with a piece of toast before answering. "Of course. I gave the picture to Liz, and she hung it in the office. I used to see it all the time. She let me work out of there, freelance and all. You know how that goes. Wonderful painting, though. Groundbreaking. Nothing like that in Paris at the time, or now."

Will's brows furrowed. Dickie had given the painting to Liz. Maybe that detail didn't matter, but the new information caused a piece of the puzzle so squarely set in Will's head to turn on its side.

"You gave her the Pollock?"

"Of course, an office-warming gift, I think. I guess I liked to look at it. I was in and out of the office so much."

What Dickie said disturbed Will, maybe because he didn't trust him. But Will considered this new fact more than a coincidence. He dropped fifteen cents on the counter for his coffee and nodded his goodbye.

By the time Will reached the roomette, New Jersey had slipped behind them, and a silver sun gleamed off the rippling edge of the Delaware River. The train had crossed into Pennsylvania's deep red pine woods and past Manor Lake, surrounded by modest Victorian homes tucked into the landscape. The low whistle of the horn echoed through the countryside as it passed the few road crossings.

Will pulled open the sliding door to the roomette and found Liz reclining against the booth, reading a magazine. She smiled as he walked in, taking her foot off the front edge of the booth opposite her, and laid her magazine down.

"You made it. I thought I'd lost you."

"You almost did." He kissed her on the cheek.

The roomette stood half the size of his office but twice as elegant. The two booths flanked a large picture window, through which tall pines flashed a picturesque woodscape. Delicate hand towels hung from a silver rack on the wall near the pull-down washbasin. A textured ebony wood trim finished the walls from the bathroom to the booths.

Will took off his suit coat and hung it in the small wardrobe. He tossed his hat on the overhead luggage rack of polished metal and picked up the menu the porter had left on the side table: consommé, poached salmon *au vin blanc*, and fresh strawberry shortcake.

"We can have lunch in the dining car before we get in," he said.

They rode for a long time, reading and enjoying each other's company. He rubbed her feet as she told a story of sitting at *Café Deux Magots* on Saint-Germain in Paris when a friend invited Picasso to join them for lunch. Picasso never left the city during the war, she told him, even during the occupation. While everyone else packed their cars to the rooftops and left, Picasso spent his time in his apartment, painting. And when the Nazis outlawed his work, he wrote instead.

At the Philadelphia stop, Will stepped out of the roomette and leaned out of the train door. Businessmen in suits and overcoats hopped on and off the train, tapping their hats down tight as they darted off. The platform swarmed with brakemen checking underneath the carriage. Cleaning crews, dining car stewards, waiters, and cooks all busied about their work.

Farther down the platform, a woman struggled with three small kids and her luggage, pulling them all along in her high heels until a porter stopped to help, picking up the smallest child and her suitcase. They pushed through the crowd along the streamlined train of stainless steel, past the dining car and lounge car and onto the chair cars. Several cars past them, Dickie stepped out onto the platform, smoking a cigarette. Will offered a nod when Dickie noticed him. With Dickie, Will got the sense he was hiding something behind the stories of Berlin and Yale, behind the newspapers and magazines, as if none of it were true. His demeanor seemed phony, as though he were acting a part in a play, and it unnerved Will. When he finished his cigarette, Dickie gave a mock salute to Will, and then stepped back inside the train.

Once the platform cleared and the porters raised the step stools, the conductor called for all to board, and the train glided out along the steel rails, three hundred passengers tucked inside.

Will stepped back into the roomette and sat opposite Liz, who had returned to her magazine.

"Dickie's on the train."

"Yes. I saw him earlier," she said matter-of-factly. Will didn't probe, but he felt Liz had held back. He couldn't help but be suspicious of Dickie.

"I visited with him in the bar car. He said he was visiting his Aunt before he goes over to Paris."

A look of surprise crossed her face, then she smiled. "Yes, of course."

For lunch, they moved into the dining car, which was crowded with men in suits and thick with cigarette smoke and conversation. Silverware and finger bowls topped the little square tables. Will would have mistaken it for a Manhattan restaurant had it not been for the clinking of the white porcelain coffee cups against their saucers as the train rocked. Will selected a table at the far end of the car and ordered them both a glass of wine.

"Why throw yourself into this fire? Why support Roschin?" he asked when the waiter brought their consommé and wine.

"Because he has the right to paint." Her answer came quick and easy, as if there was no other obvious choice. "They all have that right."

"People picket Roschin's work, and he's going up in front of HUAC. But de Kooning and Pollock spend the summer in the Hamptons."

"Pollock and de Kooning chose to divorce their art from politics, not because they were protesting in some way, but because they wanted their art to be solely about painting. They needed to focus their energy and did not want outside influences. Rochin should have the same choice. He should be able to create freely; all artists should. It's what our country is about."

"And that's what the MoMA exhibit is about?"

"More or less. It's a message."

"Get them playing baseball."

Liz rested her spoon from her consommé, confusion in her eyes. "What do you mean?"

"Something Dickie said. Get them playing baseball, and they'll love America."

She laughed. "I guess that's right."

"How did you end up with him?" The question came out almost unintentionally, but he was relieved when it did.

Liz pulled back at his directness. "Paris," she said. "We worked together. The days were long, with working dinners. Eventually it happens. But you must understand. We never socialized with other people. We couldn't live normal lives. None of us could."

The answer surprised Will. "Why not? It's the magazine business."

"You don't understand."

"Try me."

"I can't. There are things I can't say, things I can't tell you."

"Things you *can't* say or things you *won't* say?"

She shook her head. "Will, don't."

He remembered the night at de Kooning's. Her voice was clear in his head. *Don't hate me, whatever happens.* Will knew he shouldn't push, that the conversation needed time, but the urge to do so pressed upon him. Instead, he discussed the Roschin hearing while they ate poached salmon and asparagus.

After lunch, they ground out their cigarettes and returned to the roomette. Liz unlatched the top portion of the window, lowering the pane slightly to let in a light breeze. The wisps of her hair floated in the air as the train rushed along the rails toward Washington. Her work had not changed since moving from Paris to New York, Will thought. The Bower Foundation did similar work to what the magazine had done, supporting and promoting artists like Pollock, staging them through Europe like they were at war themselves, advancing their paintings forward like soldiers on the battlefield.

Will shifted on the booth opposite her, uncomfortable with questions he wanted to ask about her past, uncomfortable with both her possible answers and her reaction. Then, finally, he spoke. "I know we should be past this," he said, treading with care. "The simple questions that get covered on those get-to-know-you first dates, like 'Where did you grow up?' 'What are you interested in?' But there seem to be a few pieces still missing."

"Does it matter?"

"Maybe not." Will reflected on his answer, not knowing if he believed himself. Maybe it depends on the past or what the present hides. He knew he shouldn't care; everyone had a past.

"I'd like to think it doesn't," she said.

The comment came with a sense of yearning, as if she were asking him the one pivotal question that had held her back from having relationships with other men, as if she were saying that if Will answered this one question right, then she could see herself with him. If he told her he could live with her secrets, not ask about the past or whatever still lingered in the present, then she could open herself in every other way. She could love him.

"The past is the past, that sort of thing?" he said.

"Yes, I suppose." She straightened herself on the booth and focused directly on him. "And if it weren't in the past, should you walk away? Not give our relationship a chance?"

"Depends on what *it* is, I guess. But then, I wouldn't know, right? You can't question what's not there. Puts me in a tough position."

"Maybe I'm guarded."

"It's what you're guarded about that's starting to make me nervous."

Liz raised her brows. "Afraid you're going to get hurt?"

"Someone always gets hurt."

She shook her head and spoke with a gentle tone. "It doesn't have to be that way if there's trust."

"Trust without telling each other everything?"

"You trust your instincts, don't you, when you're searching for a painting? Maybe you don't know the answer, who's stolen the piece, but you get an idea, a hunch, and you follow it until you get the next one."

"Or until it turns out wrong."

"Do they? Do your instincts turn out wrong for you?"

Will knew the answer, but he reflected on the decisions he had made—starting his business, following his hunches, even choices he'd made during the war, like when to get out of the trench, when to jump the hedgerow, and when to wait. He shook his head. "No, not usually."

"Can't it be the same with me?"

"But in those cases, I'm trusting myself. Here I'm trusting you."

"Isn't that the point? You're trusting your feelings for me."

Will smiled at the distinction, then leaned his head back. A comfort filled him, satisfying his urge. "Maybe," he said. But he knew he meant yes.

The rocking of the train soothed him as they glided through the woods. The iron trusses creaked as they crossed a bridge over a small tributary; the couplings at each connecting section answered with their rhythmic clicking. Liz sat across from him, magazine in hand, a promise between them.

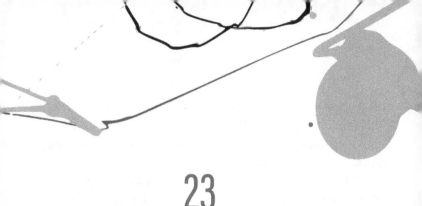

23

AT 1:00 P.M., the streamliner pulled into Washington, DC. Will helped Liz into a taxi, and they traveled down Independence Avenue, south of the Capitol to the front of the Longworth Building, a block-long edifice with an unyielding row of Corinthian columns that stretched down a sloped street.

Picketers paraded in clumsy unison along the wide concrete walk, shouting discordantly and holding signs that read *Roschin Is a Red Rattlesnake*. News cameras swiveled on their tripods as the picketers circled.

Will and Liz pushed through the crowd, then climbed the granite staircase to the building's entrance. Inside the front hall, journalists from every newspaper rushed from one interview to another. Other journalists were leaning against the wall or standing in groups, flipping papers and checking their watches. Several representatives from the museums had congregated together on the far end, and Liz explained they had put together a petition citing the historical accuracy of the murals and planned to present the argument to the committee.

When the hearing room doors opened, the crowd herded inside. A hundred voices filled the room as people rushed to secure a seat with a prime view. Newsreel cameras lined the back wall, and magnesium flashbulbs popped from all directions, their thin trails of smoke rising to the ceiling. More news reporters lined themselves against the side windows, winding their small film cameras by hand. Two grand chandeliers hung from thirty-foot ceilings, and heavy purple drapery covered the long windows, blocking the early afternoon sunlight.

Center front, Roschin had been placed at a large mahogany table crowded with microphones. White-hot floodlights illuminated the arena, all pointing accusingly toward him. He wore his paint-splattered boots and a crumpled brown suit. Entirely out of place and miles away from the Cedar Bar, he had been plucked from his easel and put on display.

"It's a circus, isn't it?" Liz said as they squeezed between rows of wooden chairs, looking for seats. She nodded toward the front tables. "Most of those are government officials, from what I can tell."

On either side of Roschin were two additional massive tables covered with microphones, glass ashtrays, and water glasses. Men in official-looking suits crowded both tables, twisting and turning in their chairs to gape at their audience behind them. Will and Liz found seats four rows behind Roschin, who sat organizing his papers and mouthing silent words to himself as he prepared for the hearing. How alone he must feel, Will thought, sitting by himself with a room full of accusers surrounding him.

Past Roschin, at the front of the hearing room, a row of committee members with pressed suits and pocket squares organized themselves behind a long courtroom bench elevated on a dais, with the Speaker of the committee strategically positioned in the center. More water glasses, microphones, and papers were strewn across the top of the bench. Behind the committee members, staffers sat two deep, shifting and shifting again in their folding chairs, crossing their legs as they tried to get comfortable in the tight space against the wall. Next to the Speaker sat Congressman George Dondero, chairman of the House Committee on Public Works, whom Will recognized from photos in the paper. The two men whispered together, and then the Speaker wielded the gavel.

"The committee will come to order. Quiet, please. Quiet."

The slam of the gavel shattered through the room, breaking the noise of the crowd. Blinding flashbulbs popped and sizzled from all directions.

"The committee will be in order."

The Speaker paused to gain control of the room. The crowd hushed in unison, leaving only the shrill sound of wooden chairs scraping across the slate floor as people moved them into place for a better view.

"The committee begins its hearings on the vital issue of the Roschin murals at the New York Post Office Annex. We will begin by questioning Mr. Andrei Roschin." The speaker leaned forward into his microphone as if inches from Roschin's face. "Mr. Roschin, could you tell the committee when and where were you born?"

Roschin placed his forearms against the table, bracing his slight body as he leaned forward. He shifted his head back and forth between the three microphones as if trying to decide which to speak into. Flashbulbs blinded and popped, cutting through the silent anticipation in the room.

What it must be like to sit in that chair, Will thought to himself, knowing no matter what answers you gave, they would be wrong. HUAC trials on subversive activity had been going on for a year or two, and the scene always escalated to the dreaded question: Are you or have you ever been a member of the Communist Party? If the answer was no, the interrogators pressed harder, dismissive of any explanation until proceedings knotted into a stalemate. And most often the accused returned home like all the others before him, fired from his job by a nervous employer. A rare few answered yes, only to be asked for additional names, for incriminating evidence on acquaintances with whom they associated, or be charged with contempt of court.

As Roschin began to speak, feedback from the microphone pierced the room, the crowd jolted back, and everyone started talking over each other again.

"Quiet, please." The Speaker rapped his gavel. "Quiet. Will someone adjust the level of the microphones? Quiet, please."

The crowd settled down and waited, suppressing their whispers behind protective hands and the occasional hat brim.

After a moment, the Speaker started again. "Mr. Roschin, I will ask again—when and where were you born?"

Roschin leaned forward again, with his back straight, acting more confident. "March 20, 1905, in Moscow, Russia."

The crowd gasped in unison, and the room burst with the sound of rustling notepads and whispers of shock. More flashbulbs popped in everyone's eyes. The Speaker slammed the gavel down again with rapid succession. "Quiet. Quiet. Mr. Roschin, what is your profession or occupation?"

"I have worked at many things, at many jobs, but for the most part I'm an artist, a muralist." He stammered at first but gained strength with each word.

"Well, which is it? An artist or a muralist?"

"I guess I'd consider them the same."

The Speaker again leaned toward Congressman Dondero, conferring about Roschin's answer. Then he returned to the microphone. "And most of your work has been in New York?"

"Yes, for the most part."

"And when did you move to New York?"

"I left Russia when I was fifteen. I moved to Paris and then came to New York in 1923."

"And you practiced your profession when you came here?"

"It's hard to call it a profession. I painted, if that's what you mean, but not for many people. Nobody wants murals. They want the cheap interior decorations like I expect you have in your home—paintings that go with your furniture and the color of your walls and make your wife happy."

A few abrupt laughs broke out of the crowd, and Roschin's expression brightened at the response.

The Speaker's voice grew stern. "Mr. Roschin, answer the question, please."

"But I want to make it clear that my painting wasn't a profession."

The Speaker put down his reading glasses and, with a fiery face, peered down directly at Roschin. "I'll ask again. Did you practice your profession while in New York?"

"I painted, if that is what you're asking."

"Thank you." He put his reading glasses back on and nodded to the men around him, grinning.

The panel of men shifted back and forth, conferring with each other, and Will realized why Liz called it a circus. The panel was misinformed and uneducated about the topic. As they flipped their papers and consulted with each other, they seemed confused, ill-informed about terminology and additional pertinent information. The young men behind the panel continuously whispered in their ears and handed them slips of paper.

"And where did you live?" the Speaker asked while flipping through his papers.

"In upstate New York, in Croton-on-Hudson's Mount Airy section."

"That is an artist's colony, am I right?"

"There are artists who live there, yes," Roschin said, his voice strengthening with sarcasm and his answers coming at a quicker pace. He had grown agitated and lively like he was back at the Cedar Bar arguing for argument's sake. His eyes brightened, and Will pictured him sunk in the cushions with a beer in hand, ready to pick a fight.

"And are the residents in Mount Airy members of the Communist Party?"

"Sir, I have no idea about the political affiliations of all the residents of Mount Airy. In fact, I refuse to answer such a ridiculous question. I have no knowledge of other people's intentions."

"But you have talked to them about their intentions?"

"I have talked to them about any number of things. I can't for the life of me remember all the topics we discuss."

Will laughed to himself about the absurdity of the conversation, the line of questioning, the witch hunts and side agendas, all tangential to the topic at hand.

The Speaker leaned back in his chair and waved over a young man, who jumped at the signal. He squeezed between the double row of chairs and dropped a thin stack of papers at the Speaker's side. The Speaker held up the papers for the room to see. "Mr. Roschin, I have before me photostats of the twenty-nine mural panels in the New York Post Office Annex. You were chosen to decorate the new annex in 1940, is that correct?"

"Yes. By the Treasury Department's Section of Fine Art."

"You were paid twenty-six thousand dollars to design and paint a chronological history of the city. Is that correct?"

"Yes, I believe that was the sum."

"And you had been asked by the Public Building Administration to alter those panels on two separate occasions. Is that correct? I believe once in 1949 and again last year."

"Yes."

"And you refused in both instances?"

"I didn't refuse. In fact, I made the changes requested and—"

"I also have in my hand an ungodly number of complaints," the Speaker said, interrupting and raising another set of papers. "My office has been flooded with complaints from the American Legion, Daughters of the American Revolution, Veterans of Foreign Wars, and others claiming your panels are, and I quote, 'little short of treason,' and that they 'unfairly depict what is believed to be the true history of our State.' That they 'cast a derogatory and improper reflection upon the character of the settlers,' and that other panels are 'subversive and designed to spread Communistic propaganda.' Mr. Roschin, I ask you, do you believe it is the right of taxpayers not to be insulted by radicals such as yourself and bombarded by your images?"

"Sir, I intended to paint the past not as a romantic backdrop but as the way the stories unfolded, with all the trauma, the depression, the strikes. The good and the bad of our state's history."

"Would you consider these paintings modern?"

"Modern? I would like to know what is modern," Roschin asked.

"Answer the question, will you, Mr. Roschin?"

"Again, I would like to know what is modern."

Congressman Dondero broke in. "I will tell you what it is not, Mr. Roschin," he said, speaking loudly into his microphone, his face flushed. "It is *not* academic. It is *not* traditional. It is *not* of beautiful images. Your images are distorted and ugly. Look at these lanky figures, the angles." He waved the copies in the air for emphasis, like an actor on stage, a seemingly impromptu reaction that Will knew had been well-rehearsed in a mirror.

"I, for one, can't get over the distortion of the people. It pains me to think of my wife and children seeing these images. Think of the schoolchildren who tour the post office. It pains me to think of all the true Americans having to see these images."

The Speaker let Dondero's words hang in the air like a noose. The crowd stood in silent anticipation until the Speaker began again. "Mr. Roschin, I'll ask you to answer the question. Do you consider these paintings modern?"

"With all due respect, Mr. Speaker, I refuse to answer the question for lack of a definition of what modern is."

Dondero jumped in again. "Mr. Speaker, the witness said he wouldn't answer because of a lack of definition, which I have already given. I ask you to direct the witness to answer the question."

"Yes, I agree. Mr. Roschin, I direct you to answer."

Roschin leaned into his microphone, his words deliberate and slow. Each person involved now on show. "Sir, I find this whole line of questioning absurd. It is complete nonsense."

"It is legal, Mr. Roschin," the Speaker shouted, his voice echoing from the walls. "Not only is it only legal, but the vice president himself, Mr. Richard M. Nixon, instructed this committee to make a thorough investigation of modern art, *subversive art*, in government buildings for the protection of the taxpayer. Therefore, I ask you again, what is your answer?"

"I have given my answer."

"And what is it?"

"I have no intention of repeating myself. The stenographer can read it back if you wish."

"Mr. Roschin, it is my duty to inform you that we don't accept your answer. I'll give you one last opportunity to answer the question at hand."

"My answer remains the same. I can't answer a question about a topic with no definition."

"Have you finished your answer?"

"Yes. In fact, sir, I have."

The Speaker lurched backward and threw his reading glasses down. The crowd let out a collective breath, but the tension in the room remained. The double row of men flipped papers back and forth in a whir of excitement.

Will leaned over to Liz. "What's the point?"

"There is none. It's grandstanding."

Congressmen George Dondero made an exaggerated effort at filling his water glass from his carafe, then turned to the microphones. "Mr. Roschin, I assume you have heard me say that modern art is a Communist menace?"

"I have. And I'll say I don't believe you have any education in art whatsoever."

Dondero ignored the comment, but the crowd shifted nervously in their seats. "So you understand that we believe the Communist Party is using modern art as a weapon of the Kremlin. I will go so far as to say that some of the paintings are quite possibly communicating Soviet messages and strategic maps pinpointing American military defenses. It is my opinion"—he angled toward the audience—"that any exhibition showing works by Communists should be condemned and shut down." A roar of applause came from the crowd.

Roschin laughed out loud. "I don't see how such a preposterous thing could be possible, Mr. Speaker."

"It is possible, Mr. Roschin, because modern art is ugly. It is distorted. It is designed to create disorder for the purpose of Communist subversion. It aims to destroy through disorder, ridicule, and denial of reason, Mr. Roschin."

"Are you suggesting we censor our art, deny the artist the right to paint of his own free will?"

Dondero slammed his hand down. "I will ask the questions in these proceedings, Mr. Roschin. This administration is not on trial."

"I didn't think I was on trial either, Mr. Congressman." Roschin's voice reverberated through the speakers and felt like a slap across the congressman's face.

The audience both gasped and laughed. Congressman Dondero's ears reddened, and a small vein in his forehead bulged. "Mr. Roschin, I ask you: What number of people do you think would agree that these paintings are sympathetic to Communistic ideas?"

"I would think none at all, Mr. Congressman."

"I, for one, don't consider it art, but I am no artist."

"I think a great number of people would agree with you on that."

Dondero glared. The crowd scooted to the edges of their seats. "Mr. Roschin, I'll ask you one simple question. Are you now, or have you ever been, a Communist?"

Roschin sat back, reached for his cigarette resting on the ashtray, and gave it a long pull, making them wait.

After the lunch break, the hearing continued, with one congressman after another describing in detail what he disliked about the mural, panel by panel. And when another congressman began reading the dossiers of other artists associated with Roschin, Will stepped out for a break, exhausted by the circus act. He wandered down the great hall, passing photographs of men from the past who had served on government committees, who were passionate about American ideals.

Liz was passionate about art in a way the panel did not understand, almost in the way they were against it. She was passionate about art because it represented the freedom of the artist to paint of his own will. Roschin could paint with red paint, with *Red* intentions, if he wanted. Pollock could splatter paint simply to express the act of painting. The artist was free to choose. The men hanging on the walls had served their country to give them that freedom, fought for it in their own way. He had fought for the same freedom, as had everyone who fought in the war.

Will smelled the cigarette before he saw the man leaning against the wall, blocking his way. The man stood in front of Will with a disdainful look across his face, pulling on his cigarette. Will stared into the man's eyes. They were the same beady eyes he had seen outside the Stable Gallery, the same eyes he had chased on the streets.

"It's you," Will said. "Are you following me? I ought to have you arrested right here." Will finished the sentence with an angry tone.

The man sloughed off the threat with a chuckle. "You're just a cog in the wheel."

"Why are you here?"

"I wouldn't miss watching these rats squirm. Let's just say I have information when they need it up on stage. I collect information on everybody."

"Who are you with?" Will said, almost yelling.

"Doesn't matter," the man said, taking a long pull from his cigarette, letting the smoke float into the empty hall. "What matters is who *you're* with."

"Who the hell are you?" Will demanded again, out of patience. His voice echoed in the hall.

"I wouldn't worry about who I am." The man's words were cold. "I'd worry about who *she* is. There's always a lead operative, someone with a direct link to Moscow. Someone like that could get you on the wrong list."

Will grabbed the man's collar and shook him. "You got something to say, say it. Otherwise, fuck off," he said through clenched teeth.

The man knocked Will's hand off, and his face reddened. "Are you sure you know her?" His voice came out low and slow, like he was waiting for a reason to explode. "What did she do in Paris? What about here? Why is she here?"

"What do you think you know? What do you have? My bet is nothing, like the rest of them. You're like the men inside, full of fear and misinformation."

The man looked Will up and down. "Maybe you're part of it too. Why not?"

His words hit Will hard, and he stepped back to recover. "Part of what? What the hell are you talking about?"

"You plan your schemes together at night, don't you? In bed together like those Rosenbergs." A smirk stretched across the man's face. "Do you plan before or after you finish?"

Will's fist landed first, sinking into the man's stomach, which was soft and unprepared for the punch. The man doubled over, coughing, only to recover more quickly than Will wanted. He coughed again as he straightened himself back up and shook off the punch. "Maybe you were there too, in the beginning," he said.

Will's stomach sickened, and he braced against the wall. What was the man talking about? What did he have on Liz?

"The weekend they all showed up at the Waldorf," the man continued. "I should have checked the registry for your name too." He dropped his cigarette on the marble floor and let it burn. "Doesn't matter; you're sleeping with one. That's enough for me. And it'll be enough for them," he said, pointing toward the hearing room. Then he turned and sauntered down the corridor.

The accusations repeated in Will's head, hitting him over and again, almost paralyzing him in the moment. Will knew what the man meant, but the accusation did not make sense. With adrenaline still pumping through his body, he tried to work through the fragments of information, but they began to meld together in a confusing blur. Had he let the case get too personal? Had he ignored something that stared him in the face? Liz—her work with the paintings, the artists—none of what this man said made sense.

On the train ride back, Will stared out the window, numb, not wanting the accusations to register in his mind. Liz talked about the hearing, but her voice played like a radio in the background, white noise to his thoughts, fragments of sentences and a collage of words. She mentioned historical references, how clear the support had been. But Will struggled to hold on to any thought but flashes of his interaction with the beady-eyed man.

He wanted to ask her about what the man had said, talk to her about the accusations, but he was afraid of what the answer might be, where it would lead him, and the choices he would have to make. Like the artists, everyone was free to choose, but choices had consequences. He wondered if he could live with the consequences of his own choices. Could he leave Liz to her secrets like she had asked of him, knowing now what they might entail?

After Philadelphia, they moved into the dining car and ordered vodka gimlets. The soft radiance of her face under the candlelight disarmed him. When they leaned into each other on the white tablecloths and whispered together, the weight lifted, and the alcohol lifted the weight even more. Maybe it would be easier than he thought. Maybe he could do it, not ask any questions.

By the time they finished another gimlet, the scene in the corridor had faded like a bad dream, an incident that had happened to someone else. They held hands as they strolled through the train cars and had another drink at the bar. Sitting on the vinyl stools, they shared delicate touches, their knees tenderly close, until the Manhattan skyline crested over the horizon.

24

DE KOONING'S SHOW OPENED the following week. *Time* magazine called the woman paintings "Big City Dames," but the *New York Times* and *New Yorker* refused to accept them as art. The power shifted with nothing new from Pollock, placing de Kooning on top. Not confident he could restrain himself from questioning Liz about the accusations, Will declined her invitation to attend the opening together. That whole week, he gazed out his office window at the Gothic spires of Trinity Church, and every day he replayed the conversation from the courthouse corridor. *Someone like that could get you on the wrong list. . . . Maybe you're part of it too. . . . Waldorf registry . . .*

With an absent mind, he waited for the switchboard log-books and listened to Charlie complain about how he didn't expect the logs to provide any leads. He called both Mid-Orange and Auburn State Prisons, hoping Clyde had miraculously appeared now that the prisons had had time to sort out their paperwork. But the records were still a mess.

To stop ruminating on what the beady-eyed man had said, Will turned his focus on the office. He moved the old newspapers he rarely referenced from the shelves and placed them in the open-topped cardboard boxes. He moved the books onto the shelves with the *ARTnews* magazines, maintaining the organization, and left the stills of paintings with them. After devising a new filing system, he organized the police reports, auction records, and notarized appraisals together by case. But the distractions didn't help.

He stared at the stack of paperwork on his desk all the rest of the week until Charlie would not let him stew any longer.

"What aren't you telling me?" Charlie asked. "What happened in Washington?"

Will hesitated, rubbing his hands against his face. He had to acknowledge there might be a connection: the painting stolen to hide something, the beady-eyed man's accusations, and Liz. There was no avoiding the possibility. And did Dickie fit into it at all? He wanted to go to the Waldorf Astoria and ask questions, but doing so would betray his promise to Liz. Or maybe not. He was not certain what he would find or what it would mean, but he had to know for himself. If he left the question unanswered, the suspicion might fester like a small splinter in his finger, worsening over time. A distance would grow between them, and he feared the void might be one he couldn't close. On the other hand, if he knew what the accusations were, maybe he could help. Will straightened himself and cleared his mind the best he could.

"What do you know about the Waldorf?" he asked Charlie.

"The Waldorf? Jesus, Will, what's that got to do with anything? If the answer isn't in the logbooks or doesn't help find the Pollock, you'd better drop it. Pritchett's been in here twice this week asking why the hell you had to go to Washington for the goddamn hearing and where the hell you are on the Pollock case, and it sounds like you've got nothing." Charlie moved forward in his chair and placed his arms on the desk. He spoke in a quiet voice. "Hell, sometimes things don't work out the way you want."

Charlie was right. Plans could unravel. Even if you painted by number, the image could come out different than expected. But the gnawing uncertainty wouldn't let go. He couldn't leave the beady-eyed man's accusations unanswered. Will pushed his chair back and stood up. Without another word, he put on his suit coat and walked out.

———————————————

Will pushed through the revolving door of the Waldorf Astoria and climbed the broad flight of plush red-carpeted stairs to the expansive lobby. He reached the top of the stairs and stopped directly underneath the crystal chandelier. Fragments of big band swing reverberated through the doors of the Empire Room as band members prepared for the evening.

He needed to find a registry of some nature, but he had no other information. Without a better plan, he crossed through the brightly lit lobby and elevator bank to the central reservation desk. A girl with winged eyeliner and doe-like eyes greeted him with a cheerful face.

After Will provided a vague explanation, the girl suggested he take a seat in the waiting area while she fetched her manager. Will crossed the floor and dropped into a plush wingback chair. In the muted light, the guests ebbed and flowed through the elegant lobby and around the nine-foot bronze clock that rose from the middle of the floor. Eagles guarded each of the gold and white pearl faces of the clock. The bas-relief busts of American presidents adorned the octagonal tower: Lincoln, Jackson, Harrison. The second hand turned, and Will's thoughts began to circle in his head. Like the Waldorfs and Astors, the Bowers and the Rockefellers were prominent New York families, as were the Whitneys and everyone in Liz's social circle. They were the American elite. These were venture capitalists and industrialists whose money built and drove the economy. They had political connections and economic power, access to vital information. As Will turned these thoughts in his head, a fear presented itself. If that circle was infiltrated and compromised by a Communist, or if one of them had turned, secrets could be stolen, control of the infrastructure could be taken, and newspapers could be manipulated.

A quick voice came from behind, startling him.

"Can I help you, sir?"

Will turned to see a thin man dressed in a hotel uniform. "Are you the manager?"

"One of them." He offered his hand. "Donald Pennifield. How can I help you?"

"A colleague of mine came in earlier looking for a registry," Will said, pretending to be associated with whoever had come before him.

With a start, the thin man glanced around, crouched down to Will's level, and continued in a low whisper. "Didn't we provide what you needed? Everything seemed to be in order when your partner left."

Will slid into the role of partner and suggested they go somewhere quieter to discuss a few follow-up questions. Pennifield straightened up and his face brightened. With a light gesture, he directed Will to follow him and crossed the lobby. Behind the concierge desk, he pressed against a panel in the mahogany wood wall, which released and opened like a door. Once behind the front lobby, they walked through an open office, brightly lit and filled with rows of desks manned by young girls in fitted sweaters, typing and answering phones.

"These are our reservationists," Pennifield said at a quick pace and with childlike excitement. "We take reservations from all over the country. They also fulfill room service requests. We're the one hotel in the country to provide room service." He lifted his chest with the boast and continued to walk through the typist alley, saying hello to each girl as he passed, displaying pride in his managerial skills. Pennifield led Will into a small office in the back and shut the door behind them.

"I'm sorry, Mr. …"

"Oxley."

"Yes, of course. Mr. Oxley." Pennifield smiled and leaned back on the front edge of his desk. "Like I told your partner, as a Legion member, I'm proud to help with ALERT's efforts."

"You know ALERT?" he asked, unaware of the name yet searching for an explanation.

"Of course. The American Legion, the Chamber of Commerce, we all buy your information—the background on potential targets, the lists of subversives. The Legion feeds it up to the Senate Internal Security Subcommittee." He adjusted his position on the edge of the desk. "That's above my pay grade, though. But we're all working together to flush out these Communists." He grinned, waiting for Will to give a response. Receiving none, Pennifield continued like a windup toy.

"Have you been on a black bag job?" His words came out at a giddy pace. "When I was on one with boys from the Legion, we waited outside this guy's house. He was a labor leader or something, small townhouse out in Brooklyn. We hid on the corner of the street for two hours, waiting for him to leave. That was in November, mind you. Two hours in the cold. But once he left, Hoover's guy placed the wiretaps while we dug through his trash and grabbed his mail."

A fresh image of his overturned apartment flashed in Will's mind, his own experience with a "black bag job." His face tightened with anger. "Isn't that illegal?"

Pennifield laughed. "Sure, I guess. But would you rather have the Communists take over? A small price to pay in my view. Anyway, it's never used in court. They feed it to employers, get rid of the Communists that way. The information helps with the questioning in hearings too, I guess. And you know those aren't legal proceedings, either." He rubbed him palms together. "Now, what is it you need today?"

"The registry," Will said, hoping Pennifield would complete his thought and fill in what information Will did not know.

"Right, the Scientific and Cultural Conference for World Peace. Like I told your partner, the conference was nothing of the sort. I remember the event because I started working here that day. March 25, 1949. I'll never forget it." He stood and walked behind the wood desk to a large metal file cabinet, then began flipping through files, talking all the while. "Nothing seemed right. Artists and writers and scientists filled the lobby, but they were all Soviets. I'm certain of that fact."

"Soviets?"

"Sure. I mean, that's why all the riots and picketers, right? The police blockades. Don't you remember?" He didn't wait for an answer. "Soviets meeting in our own country with every goddamn liberal that lived here. Imagine the magnitude. Soviets building a network right in the open, right here in the U-S-of-A. And how did it happen? That's what boggles my mind. The sponsor of the event, The National Council of Arts, Sciences, and Professions, was a Communist front. We never knew. They kept everything hidden. I mean, how are we supposed to catch these guys? They're so goddamn sneaky."

Pennifield pulled out a large manila folder and leafed through the papers, handing them to Will. "Here are the sponsors of the event. They're all connected with Communist front organizations, nonprofit cover-ups. I've researched all of these. Over twenty people are connected to forty different front organizations. It goes on and on. God knows how many sleeper spies are out there now. And we let them do it. We let them right into our country."

"What about the registry? The one my partner was interested in?"

"Right. He asked about the Americans in attendance. That was difficult." Pennifield flipped furiously through his list, eager to display the fruits of his research. "They were mixed in with everyone else, of course. But we knew if the Americans stayed at the hotel, the room reservations would provide a record. But if they didn't, any record of their attendance would have to come from signing an attendance list, which was unlikely."

Pennifield returned to his file cabinet, searching again, and continued his account of the day's events, a flood of words strung together without end. "That was one hectic day. Because of all the protesters, the delegates had to arrive through the back entrance on Lexington. They wore those dark heavy coats and fur ush-ankas, and they milled around the lobby speaking God knows what languages. Most of them seemed to be writers and agents for cultural committees, 'cultural attachés,' so to speak."

He continued to flip through files, chuckling to himself. "Here it is," he said, pulling out one file and tossing it on the desk in front of Will. "That's the attendee list." He pointed to the file. "That's where you'll find the official organizations and some individuals. Many of those have already been deemed sub-versive by HUAC. You can read through that if you're inter-ested." Pennifield turned with excitement. "I'll find the room reservations. Like I said, I've done a lot of this research already, so I have things pretty well organized." He pulled out another drawer of his file cabinet. "The funny thing is, I remember the day like yesterday because I spent most of my time running around the hotel and setting up additional phone lines in guest rooms."

"Phone lines?"

"Two or three rooms kept requesting additional phone lines. That stuck out in my mind. I had cords running throughout the halls on multiple floors. Then they asked for more table lamps, more notepads, more hamburgers, more everything. The pace was chaotic. People were running around everywhere, yelling at each other. Bellhops brought up telegraphs all throughout the day. And the accents, everyone had accents except the Americans.

"Thinking back on it, I figure the FBI was keeping track of the Soviets. That's obvious. And the Soviets were keeping track of the FBI, but who knows who else? KGB? CIA? Everyone was watching everyone." He shook his head with baffled concern. "I mean, spooks everywhere, right? The FBI guys were all so obvious. All you needed to do was spot the briefcase; they all carried them. But no telling the others." He turned back to Will. "Anything interesting?"

Will ran down the list of attendees and sponsors, non-profit organizations and foundations, surprised at the number of names Pennifield had checked as Communist fronts. The names were unassuming and innocuous. The Physicians Forum, next to which Pennifield had written, *Contributed a feature column in the Daily Worker*. The Voice of Freedom Committee. Theatre Arts Committee. American Artists and Writers Committee. Will's eyes continued down the page. The New York Conference for Alienable Rights. Pennifield's notation: *Cited as subversive by HUAC*.

"What were the names again?" Pennifield asked.

"Bower. Wasn't that the name my partner gave you?"

"That's right. Bower. That was easy enough. Nothing hard like Dimitri Gorchakov or some name like that." He looked up with additional consideration. "Well, Bower sounds a bit German to me. You never know anymore. Maybe a derivation of Bauer. God, they all started flooding over here after the war, right? Who knows if that's a real name, either? They're all liars and cheats with fake names and fake passports. Those Reds try to be so damn secretive. Here we are." He slapped the papers. "The room reservations."

He scanned down the pages. "Bower, Bower, Bower." He repeated the name as he flipped through the list, then turned the pages toward Will with an amused smile. "Here we are—room reservation for E. Bower. I told you I can find anything in these records. I've got it all organized."

"E. Bower?"

"That's right. E. Bower. I found it right there on the list. It was easy, took a little digging, that's all. Same as I told your partner."

"Elizabeth. Liz." Will spoke aloud but more to himself than to Pennifield.

"That's right. March 25, 26, and 27. All three days of the conference. It's all right here. We keep track of all the reservations. You saw my girls out front. They're diligent to a tee. I make certain of that."

Will struggled to wrap his mind around what lay in front of him: a list of attendees at a conference full of Soviets. Precisely what the beady-eyed man had said. Will wanted to grab the list and run. Protect Liz. But he realized the futility of such an act. They had already seen her name, researched her background, and put her on their own list. He handed the papers to Pennifield, deflated. He had seen more than he wanted.

After thanking Pennifield, he stepped back into the typist alley, forgetting whether he was coming or going. The girls smiled at him as he walked through the room, but he moved past them without a response, and before he knew where he was going, he found himself standing before the clock again.

Could she be working for the Party, hiding behind the artists and their paintings? But why? Then, like a deluge, everything he had heard on the radio and in the hearings, what he had read in the newspapers, flooded into his mind, somehow connecting to the Pollock. Hidden messages. Secret maps. Infiltrating Americans' minds. Exporting secrets to Europe.

He traced through the last few months in his mind. How did it all begin? His relationship with Liz. Who began it? The night at her apartment, on the balcony, did he pursue her, or did she pursue him? Was she using him, protecting the Pollock, protecting whatever was hidden on the canvas, and deliberately keeping him from finding it?

At that moment, Will no longer trusted his instincts. Unlike paintings, his investigation presented no clear lines, no distinct colors. Everything had become different shades of gray, blurring together with no beginning or end.

He stood outside the Waldorf Astoria, underneath the gold porte cochere. Darkness had covered the city, and the lights of Manhattan flooded streets that were quiet but not empty. He stood lost, not knowing where to go or what to do next. He walked up Park Avenue past St. Basil's church, staring dully at the cracks in the pavement, watching them pass underneath his feet. Each time he reached a corner, he stared out into the street, his eyes fixed on the foreground but not focused on any particular object. And when nothing blurred past him, no cab, no car, he stepped out and crossed the street, trying to solidify his thoughts.

He could not imagine that what he had learned was true. The connection had to be a mistake. The wrong name. The wrong list. But the pieces fit. Bauer, German descent, an intellectual, Left Bank in Paris, writers and artists. That was the kind of profile the Communists could influence. That was who the Soviets would prey on and recruit.

He tried to shake off the implication. The profile seemed right, but not the person. Not the Liz he knew. She worked too hard promoting the abstract expressionists, supporting them, trying to extend their reach into Europe. And not as subversives but as Americans. Her words resonated in his head, how she had spoken of the power of art and how it could shape a culture. He knew the accusations had to be wrong or a terrible mistake.

Confusion set in, and he felt like he had been played with like a child's toy. And he realized as a pang of guilt settled in his stomach that he would not ask her about the connections. He wouldn't confront her, and the reason was that he still wanted to be with her. He wanted to feel her next to him, to be in her world.

And that he loved her.

When he stopped walking, he found himself in front of her building, not remembering how he got there. He started inside, then took a step back, afraid of what he might find inside. Then the image of Liz on the train to Washington—with her soft smile and warm glow, asking him to trust her—came to mind. A sense of ease washed over him, and he stepped inside. With a wave from the doorman he entered the elevator.

When the door to her apartment opened, Liz stood before him barefoot and in a short bathrobe. Without saying a word, she gave him a smile of acceptance. He reached around her waist and pulled her close. With his whole body he kissed her.

"Whatever it is, I don't care," he said. "I don't care about any of it."

She smiled like he had given her the answer she had been waiting for her whole life, and she stared into his eyes like she was reaching deep into his soul. "Trust me," she said.

Then she led him through the hallway and into her bedroom, turning off the lights as they went. The darkness heightened his sense of touch as he explored her body like he was touching her for the first time. He slid his hand up the inside of her thigh until his fingers brushed against her hair and the soft mound. Excited by her moan, he pressed hard against her. She let the bathrobe drop, standing there exposed, naked, for him to take in with his eyes. He undressed and gently moved her to the bed, cradling her in his arms. They twined in a comfortable embrace, locked together, moving in rhythm. He wrapped himself in the moment, its perfection, not desiring anything else, and the rest of the world fell away. Her bare skin felt water smooth, and he made love to her slowly, breathing in the subtle mix of shampoo and lotion.

But afterward, behind the soft touches, the Pollock lingered on the edge of his mind where secrets are pushed down deep. Eventually, he would have to find the painting. And what then?

The days at the office grew longer, and for several weeks the Pollock files lay on Will's desk untouched. The photo of the Pollock remained tacked on the wall, and Will studied the picture—the lines, the images they created, the whips of paint—but he couldn't find any part of the canvas that resembled a message or a map. The accusations were ridiculous. Pollock was too much of a drunk to orchestrate a bicycle ride, much less an effort of Communist subversion.

Will spent time with Liz as if nothing had happened. He tried to convince himself the connections did not mean anything and he could ignore the fact that his case and Liz's secrets were colliding. They drank at the Cedar Bar, listening to Kline and de Kooning discuss their work. They would delve into discussions on Freud and Jung, psychoanalysis, and the intricacies of existentialism that blurred Will's vision but kept him from conjecturing about implications of the Waldorf registry.

One night, Pollock tore through the bar in his cowboy boots and tried to pick a fight, as he usually did. When no one paid attention, he joined de Kooning, who tempered his anger and drank with him through the night. They argued and laughed together, the years of friendly rivalry showing through their unfinished sentences. When the bar closed, Will and Liz left the two artists sitting on the curb, sharing a bottle of bourbon and slapping each other's backs, talking about de Kooning's show and arguing about who was the better painter.

Some nights, Will visited the bar alone and listened to the artists talk with one another as they floated in and out of the bar. One night, sitting on the curb, Ellis turned to Will after they'd had several beers together. "How's your case coming?" he asked.

Will hesitated. The Pollock file still lay untouched on his desk. But more than that, he felt paralyzed, torn between finding the painting, exposing whatever secrets the canvas hid, and protecting Liz. "A lot of dead ends," Will said.

"Kind of like painting, trying to find the elusive answer. Get an idea, experiment, then follow a hunch even though a painting may never emerge. And sometimes one does, and the picture doesn't turn out the way you expected, but it's right anyway."

Will pulled on his beer.

"We have to trust what we're doing," Ellis continued. "That what we're putting on the canvas is right. You have to do the same. You have to trust your instincts."

De Kooning staggered out the door, and Ellis shouted, "Bill, why do you paint the way you do?"

"Because I have to. It's how I find truth. Painting isn't confined to what you can see. It's what's behind it, what's in it—the emotion, the anger, the pain, the love." The door slammed shut behind him, and he stumbled down the street toward his flat.

Ellis smiled and turned back to Will. "Our work is in our heads and on the canvases. Your work is out on the street." He took another pull from his beer. "For what it's worth, I like my canvases better. I trust them. They're more direct. We make them flat to destroy illusion and reveal the truth. I don't know that you can say the same about your streets and your cases, can you? No illusions, just the truth?

"That's the thing about hunches," Ellis continued, "They're spontaneous gestures. That's how we paint. We release our creativity on the canvas. But I can still make a choice. I can choose a different action." He studied Will with piercing eyes as if he knew Will struggled with hard choices. "Do you have that choice? Can you choose to reject where your investigation is leading you?"

Will let the question hang, not wanting to answer. The painting hid a secret, maybe one that could expose Liz. He wanted to protect her, whatever happened. At the same time, he wanted to abandon the case, the whole mess, and be with Liz as if the turmoil never existed. But he recognized that he did not have that option.

"No, I can't. Not if I want to get to the end. Not if I want to do the job right," he said, knowing there was one path forward.

"That's your challenge. You have a specific end, a painting to find. My work is different. I don't know where my painting will end until I stop and step back to see what's on the canvas."

Kline joined them at the curb, and they passed the hours drinking and talking until the blue neon sign that read *Bar* flickered above them, then clicked off.

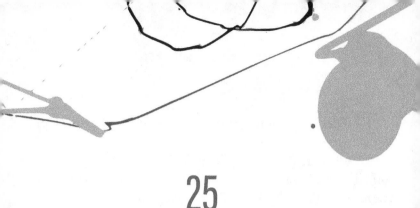

25

WILL DID NOT HAVE THE SAME CHOICE as the artists. He could not reject where the investigation would take him. He could not scratch the paint off or choose a different color and cover up what he did not want seen. And it hurt to know that he might have to confront Liz, to know what he might have to ask her. He did not know what he would say. There were no proper words to break someone's trust, to break their heart. And once you did, they would never consider you the same way again. But he could not ignore that the connection existed. And maybe if he made the admission in his own office, to a friend like Charlie, it would soften the impact.

"Tell me you've got something else, Will," Charlie said from the other side of the desk. His voice was low and serious. "These calls seem like a waste of time, even if we ever do receive the information." Then he paused a moment, as if afraid to say what came next. "To tell you the truth, I'd stop screwing around with that woman and get to work. She's bad news, Will."

"It's her painting I'm trying to find, Charlie."

"Are you?"

Will did not answer. He was scared to voice his thoughts, as if once he said them aloud to another person, they would become real. They would be out in the open and take on a life of their own. "They're related."

"Who?"

"*What*. The painting and Liz, the beady-eyed man, all of it. It's all related."

"What are you talking about, Will? Jesus, red flags are going off all over the place. Give me something to make me feel like we're doing the right thing. What's going on?"

"I don't know yet; that's what I'm trying to figure out. But I don't think the theft is as it appears."

"Tell me something, at least."

"I need time."

"Will, this isn't a game anymore. No more fucking puzzle pieces. You're being investigated; you know that, right? Your girlfriend is being investigated, and maybe rightfully so. And if Pritchett gets word, you're out. No one knows how deep the Communist Party runs, where the spies are. People are scared shitless about everything. For Christ's sake, three weeks ago the government sent bolts of electricity through the Rosenbergs. I'd keep my head down and my mouth shut if I were you. Buy yourself a washing machine. Get a nice white picket fence and a Chevy in the driveway. That's what McCarthy and Congress want to see. If you're buying the American dream, the Communists can't get to you. They can't get in your head. But instead, you're fucking around with everyone on the goddamn watch list. And believe me, they're all on the watch list."

"But it doesn't make sense, Charlie."

"What doesn't make sense? That she lived in Paris with half the Left Bank liberals? Or that she runs around with half the ex-Communist artists here in New York? Or that she spent three days at a Communist convention in the Waldorf? Which is it, Will? Which one of those doesn't make sense to you?"

Will jumped out of his chair and grabbed his coat and hat.

"Where the hell are you going?"

"To see Liz."

But when Will turned to go, Pritchett's squat frame stood in the middle of the doorway. "Will, can I see you in my office?" he said, bleary-eyed. The words came out almost as an apology, and the lines on his face revealed hours of worry. A hot flash of panic hit Will, and suddenly he knew Charlie was right.

The blood throbbing in Will's ears pounded out any other sound. Charlie mouthed the words "I didn't know," and his sad eyes apologized for whatever might happen next. Will turned slowly, sluggish, like a boxer dazed from a hard punch. Every emotion boiled inside him, and his head began to spin. To keep himself present, he focused on the Catskill painting that hung on the wall. The dark purples and deep grays of the storm clouds popped from the image. The painting seemed different now—sad, with looming darkness and isolation. Will remembered what de Kooning had said that night at the Cedar Bar about drama and pain and love and how painting was not about what he could see but what was behind it and how they created the images, the emotion. De Kooning and Pollock had stripped out every figure, leaving nothing more than creative emotion on the canvas, the sheer act of their painting. He pictured the stolen Pollock's splatters and twisted ropes of black and yellow, the violence and turmoil built into the painting, right there in front of you, emotions jumping out at you. As he imagined the Pollock, he began to understand what the New York painters were trying to do. And suddenly, Will understood. In the middle of all the shit breaking around him, he got what the paintings were about. Pollock, de Kooning, Kline, and the others were trying to put the act of painting, the emotion of it, right on the canvas. Nothing else but the sheer act of painting. He shook his head at the timing of the revelation. Then he collected himself, stripped his cigarette, and stepped out of his office.

As he walked down the hall through the main office, he tried to smile at the younger agents at their desks. Most had their heads down in actuary tables, figuring their risk on the newest clients, reminding Will of the days with his dad. He'd spent hours at the desk with his dad, learning the tables and calculations, going over the sales pitch. Since returning from the war, Will had tried to make him proud. But this was not where he wanted to end up, all dead ends and headed into Pritchett's office for what he knew were bullshit accusations.

Charlie was right. Why didn't he walk the same path as all the other agents? The white picket fence and a washing machine in the suburbs? The pressed gray flannel suit? But as soon as Will asked himself the question, he knew the answer. That life did not fit him. Those pieces belonged to someone else's life, fitting together for someone else. Maybe his dad's life, maybe Charlie's, but not his. That life had never felt right, and he'd always known it. And it fit even less now that he'd returned from the war. He had come back different and could not settle back in. He couldn't pretend to be someone he was not—the awkward conversations at business lunches, trying to fit in with the right words, the right stories, the same as everyone else around the table—knowing it was all an act. He could not pretend anymore, and he didn't want to. If Pritchett pushed him out of the firm, he could deal with the consequences.

As Will walked past Pritchett's secretary, he tapped on her desk lightly. She gave him an awkward smile, and he eased open the door to the corner office.

Pritchett stood behind his desk, holding a piece of paper. "I don't know what to do here, Will," he said, dropping into his chair. He slid the paper across to Will, who remained standing in defiance. "I found this under my door this morning. I don't know how it got here, but you and I both know what it is and where it came from."

Will picked up the paper and studied it. Plain white, no watermark. At the top it read *Confidential Memorandum*.

A blind memorandum, unmarked and untraceable. But everyone knew they were sent from the FBI, from Hoover and his Responsibilities Program. Will began to read the words that outlined a loose association with Roschin, the Artists Union, the Stable Gallery. There was a mention of the Bowers, something about the Cultural and Scientific Conference for World Peace, suspicions, his attendance at the Roschin trial, even that he was sleeping with Liz. "Intent for Communist subversion" was what the memorandum claimed. Nothing substantial, nothing tangible, but enough to make Pritchett nervous.

Will gripped the back of the chair, holding back his anger. He wanted to punch someone, anyone. How long had they been watching? Was it more than the weekend break-in? His apartment, her apartment? His pulse raced through his body and pounded against his chest. Who? ALERT, the beady-eyed man, the FBI, others. Had they been in his mail too? His trash? He threw the memorandum back on Pritchett's desk.

"Lou." His voice came out sterner than he'd intended. "You know me. You know this is bullshit."

Pritchett threw up his hands. "What do you want me to do, Will? I'm in a tough spot here. You know where this is coming from. And I've got to think of the firm. Help me. Give me some explanation."

Will believed him. What could he do? A blind memorandum was no less than a notice from the government, the FBI telling a business owner to fire a person.

"I've got a goddamn memo on my desk, Will, and I don't know who else got a copy."

"You've got to be fucking kidding me. Are you listening to yourself, Lou?"

"My God, Will, it's never been right in front of me before. I mean, it's not in my backyard. It's right here in my goddamn living room—your name linked to Communist front organizations, to subversion. I told you to be careful. Jesus Christ. Did you have to go to the Roschin hearings? I can't have something like this bring down the firm. Listen, I respect what you're doing. I do. I worked with your dad for twenty years, for Christ's sake. But my hands are tied on this."

"It's a mistake, Lou. There's something else going on here. I don't know what, but there is. It's all lies. Give me time to work through this mess." Will clenched his jaw to steady himself and keep his emotions level. He needed time. He needed to understand the connections between the Pollock, the artists, and the MoMA exhibit. And he needed to figure out how Liz fit into it all. "Give me some time, Lou."

Pritchett dropped his head. "How much longer do you have on this case?"

"I'm close."

"How close?"

"You know how these things go. What do you want me to say?"

Pritchett slowly shook his head, downshifting, and for Will the moment moved slow and quiet, like the end of a funeral. "Your dad and I practically built this business together," Pritchett said, gesturing toward the rooms beyond the door, where agents were busy making calls. "There were five of us out on the floor when we started. He was a lot like you, Will. He wasn't just selling—he genuinely cared. He wanted to do it right, but he would do it his way, the way he felt the job needed to be done. And sometimes that meant going against the grain." Pritchett pulled the memorandum back and folded it in half, cinching it between his fingers.

The weight in the room pressed down on Will. He needed Pritchett to trust him.

"I can suspend you; that's the best I can do, for a while at least. I can't have you in the office. There are too many eyes, too much misinformation."

"Jesus, Lou."

"I hate to do it. Get this thing cleared up and away from the firm, or I've got to make it permanent."

Will grabbed the memorandum out of Pritchett's hand and shook it in front of him.

"It's all wrong, all of it. And what they say about her too."

"I hope so," Pritchett replied. "Show me. Get this cleared up. Prove them all wrong."

Will turned to the door.

"I'm with you on this, Will. I am. I'm just too old to fight. I have too much to lose."

Will slammed the door behind him, but he wanted to run back in and grab Pritchett by the collar and shout, "Everyone has something to lose. What makes you any different? Stand up for what's right."

Pritchett's secretary mouthed "I'm sorry" as he passed by her. Silence filled the office, and Will surveyed the room as he crossed. He could feel the agents' eyes peering at him from behind their records. The heat of the office lights pressed down on him like a spotlight, and the low whispers made his face flush.

He walked straight to the bathroom, his heart pounding against his sternum. He slammed his hands on the cold porcelain sink and leaned over. In the mirror, his dad stared back at him through the furrow in his own brow and his deep eyes. Yelling "I'm sorry" didn't feel right. What had he done? His job. He had to fight his way out of the corner. Like attacking Saint-Lô in the war, he needed to jump the hedgerow and storm the hill. He needed to stop the barrage of bullets, get on the offensive. He wanted to find whoever dropped the memo, shake the ignorance out of him, and punish him for violating his life. He inhaled and held the air tight inside his chest until the pressure pounded at him from inside. He wanted the hurt to match his anger. Then he let it rush out. His chest heaved, rising and falling in the mirror.

He had to find the painting, but he feared doing so would expose Liz. He had to find the way out.

Then, while staring at the mirror, beyond his own image, a realization formed before him. Maybe he did have a choice. Maybe he could paint the picture he wanted to create, scrape off just the right amount of paint to get the image right. Maybe he could follow the case, find the painting, *and* protect Liz. Will stepped back from the sink, wiped his hands with a paper towel, and walked out into the hall and down to his office.

With Charlie gone for lunch, Will lit a cigarette and stood alone in the office, wondering if he should pack a box or abandon it all and walk out—desert the work to show his anger. He wanted to pull the shelving down and throw the books out the door. Not knowing how long the suspension would last, Will grabbed the Pollock file and a few phone numbers. He could call Charlie for everything else. He needed to call Lorenzo. He needed to chase every lead he had. Would the police know anything more? Who had he not called? What favors had he not pulled in?

The ring of the phone interrupted his thoughts, and he grabbed the receiver on instinct. "This is Oxley." He answered hot, still aggravated and angry.

"This is Jeanette from the Philadelphia central office. Is Charlie Beam there? I have the information he wants about the calls in question."

"Yes. I need those calls. Where did they come from?"

Will sensed hesitation on the other end of the line. "He said the issue was a private insurance matter. I really should speak with him."

"We're partners. We work on the same cases together," Will said, trying to convince the operator of his connection with

Charlie. A rustling came through the line, and Will pictured her hesitating, searching for some protocol in the random papers on her desk. "It's okay. I know the case," he said. "The calls came through the Philadelphia office to a Manhattan warehouse. Two calls, two weeks apart, asking for a Clyde Barnett."

He could sense her give in. "Okay, I guess it's fine. Well, both calls came in from the same number."

"Yes, but from where?"

"Washington, DC."

Will stood in the middle of the office, stunned, unsure which question to ask next. Clyde got a made-to-order job from Washington?

"Which number?" he asked.

"It wouldn't matter. It's been disconnected."

Will thanked her and hung up. The moment stood still; his thoughts were detached from his hand, which was still on the receiver. Will did not know how much time had passed when Charlie stepped back into the office holding two sandwich bags.

"Reuben or roast beef?" he said with apologies in his eyes. "I heard on the way back in."

"Washington."

"What?"

"The calls came from Washington," Will said, reaching from one spot on the desk to the next, searching for a pen, trying to capture the thoughts flashing through his head.

"I was talking about the blind memorandum, FBI, Hoover. All that."

Will waved him off. "Forget about the memo. The calls to Clyde Barnett came through Philadelphia from the Washington central office."

"Washington?" Charlie dropped into his desk chair and placed the sandwich bags on his desk, forgetting about them. "What does that mean?"

"It means something about that painting makes someone in Washington nervous. Nervous enough to get it out of the public and hide it away. That's why Clyde got the made-to-order job."

"So who's in Washington?"

Will asked himself the same question all the way to the ALERT offices, but he could not hold on to a complete thought. Words from the memorandum kept piercing through, fragmenting his mind. They had crossed the line, and he felt ambushed, like he had been punched from behind in an unfair fight.

The taxi dropped Will off at the corner of Forty-Fourth and Broadway, which was the address he had found in the telephone book. He scanned the office directory in the small unmanned lobby, struggling to focus on a complete company name. Instead, he scanned down the list, reading the first few letters of each line. Halfway down he found it: ALERT. Second floor. Suites 205 and 206.

He stepped into the elevator, which cranked upward, knocking as it climbed. When the doors opened, Will stepped out into the thick, stale air of the narrow hallway. A naked light bulb cast dim yellow light from the drop ceiling across a disagreeable olive wallpaper. Stamped in white on the first door to his left was the number 201, which meant the ALERT offices were at the far end.

As Will approached, the sound of muffled shouting worked its way out from behind the door. Will's anger built at the sound of the two voices. He jammed the brass door handle down, almost breaking the lever, and barged in. The door slammed against the wall, and the two men turned to Will, stunned. A beefy man stood behind an oversized tanker desk in the small desolate room, hunched over like a bulldog on watch. Closer to Will was the beady-eyed man, sitting on a folding chair.

"What kind of assholes are you?" Will shouted.

The heavyset man lunged forward, hands on his desk. "Who the hell are you?"

"This is him," the beady-eyed man said, poking his finger at Will. His response was subdued compared to the man behind the desk, as if he had been expecting the intrusion.

"Him who?"

"Oxley."

The big man dropped his military-issue glasses onto the desk and studied Will. His face contorted with disgust. "I don't like snakes in my office." He turned to the beady-eyed man. "Get him out of here."

Will shot the beady-eyed man a glare that held him still. "It's all lies. Don't you understand that? You're wrong."

"Lies?" the bulldog of a man said, spittle on his lip. "Is it a lie you're sleeping with that Communist slut? Is it a lie that she's supporting Communist artists and organizations, funding subversive propaganda, depraved and destructive images, the MoMA exhibit?"

The big man gave a slow smile as if a devious thought had worked its way to the front of his mind. "Are you that naïve? Did you think the other relationship was over? The old boyfriend, Dickie Lang? He flies in and out—Paris, Berlin, Washington. Do you think he's never in town, never in her office, over at her apartment? Do you think that he's not on our list too?"

Will lunged at the fat man, but the beady-eyed man blocked him with a hand against his chest. Will grabbed his wrist, twisted it downward, and then threw a hard punch. The cartilage of the man's nose cracked under Will's knuckle, and he crumpled into his chair. He shook off a heavy daze, and a trickle of blood formed at his nostril. Will kicked the front edge of the chair, and it toppled over like a tin can, spilling the man out on the floor.

Will glared down at him so that he cowered under his own arms, then turned to the fat man behind the tanker desk. "It's my life. Don't fuck with it." He shoved the contents of the man's desk on the floor and stormed out.

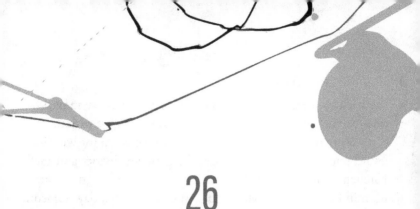

26

WILL SLAMMED THROUGH THE REVOLVING DOOR of the ALERT build-ing. He could have punched the man twenty times, and his anger would still be seething. In his mind, he popped the beady-eyed man in the nose again, but this time, when the chair spilled over, he kicked him in the ribs twice. He replayed the scene repeatedly before slowly shifting his focus back to the street in front of him and to a man leaning against a black Mercury idling at the curb. Will shielded his eyes from the late afternoon sun gleaming off the fender, shining like wet paint. The image of his fight with the beady-eyed man faded as Will recognized Lorenzo Marzano stand-ing before him. Will took a moment and focused on Lorenzo, his familiar face out of context on a Manhattan street, away from the Fulton Fish Market.

"What are you doing here?"

"Why don't we go for a ride?" Lorenzo gestured toward the open suicide doors of the car. It wasn't a question but a command. Will's options were limited anyway. He had no other place to go, no more phone calls to make. Without a next move, he bent low and peered into the Mercury, making sure nothing unexpected waited for him, and then stepped in.

"You haven't answered my calls," Will said with impatience when Lorenzo slid in next to him.

Ignoring the comment, Lorenzo shut the door and tapped

the back of the driver's seat. The long black Mercury moved out onto Sixth Avenue, the seats vibrating as the engine roared.

Will dropped his head back. They drove down the wide boulevard and through the city, past the garment district and Hell's Kitchen. Content with the silence, Will pushed the fight out of his mind and replayed what he'd learned earlier that day. Someone from Washington had placed the calls. He could have used the information before Pritchett kicked him out of the office. But now he had it, although he didn't yet know what it meant.

The Mercury crossed over to Mulberry Street and into Little Italy. Red, white, and green flags hung in the still air. Restaurant signs hung from the brick facades, and a group of boys darted across the street playing stickball. None of the memorandum made sense to Will as he replayed the sentences he had read. There was no truth to what they had written about him, and he did not believe what they'd implied about Liz either. And even if the memorandum were valid, if she was a Communist, did he care? He had fought hard in the war. He had risked his life for his country so people like Charlie could have the white picket fence and a Chevrolet in the driveway, so that Pollock could paint as he wanted. And if he didn't care whether Liz was a Communist, what did that mean? Had he become what he had fought against? Would he be no better than the German soldier on the other side of the hedgerow with a gun? And yet, if he loved a Communist, maybe they weren't all bad? But none of that mattered because he believed the accusations were false. The situation couldn't be as the memorandum made it appear. It was like selecting the wrong key for a lock; the pieces seemed to fit together, but they didn't.

The long black Mercury moved its way through the narrow streets of Little Italy, past the pushcarts and grocers, and stopped outside D'Angelo's restaurant on Mott Street.

Lorenzo waited a minute, then nodded toward the restaurant. "Sal wants to see you."

Will's stomach tightened, and he did not move to get out of the taxi. Instead, he stared out the window toward the restaurant, wondering if he'd made a mistake. He shouldn't have gotten in the car. Salvador Sciacca—Sal or Fat Sally— had been in the papers several times over the years. Palmer would know every one of his bureau file numbers: 092 Racketeering, 058 Bribery, 009 Extortion and Blackmail, 292 Money Laundering. Maybe he shouldn't have been coercing Lorenzo.

Lorenzo gestured again for Will to exit the car, and with no plausible alternative, Will stepped out onto the curb. The restaurant appeared empty from the street, giving Will even less comfort. Once inside, Lorenzo led him along the dark wood bar to the back of the restaurant. The pungent smell of garlic hung against the wood-paneled walls. In the far back corner, an obese man sat hunched over a plate of fettuccini. He looked up when they approached.

"Sit down," Sal said, opening a hand to the chairs across the table. Then he waved over a petite waitress, who brought a bottle of table wine. She filled their glasses, then left the bottle on the table. Fat Sally rolled fettuccini around his fork tines then stuffed the large bite into his mouth. He chewed while he surveyed his plate, carefully moving the pasta around to select his next bite.

Will swallowed half his glass of wine then shifted in his chair. There were no friends at this table. He had squeezed Lorenzo long enough, ignoring the possible consequences. Where did he get off continuing to use Lorenzo? He had paid his debts long ago. Will's mind bounced around the room. Should he talk first? What was Fat Sally waiting for? Why drag Will all the way here and not get to the point? They went through another glass of wine while everyone pretended nothing weighed on their minds. Will waited through the minutes that stretched long like hours as Fat Sally tended to his pasta. Will had begun to wonder if Sal was going to say anything when, after finishing a bite, he laid down his fork and turned his attention to Will.

"Lorenzo appreciates what you did for him some time back. The problem is your work interferes with his work, which interferes with my work."

Feeling pressured to explain, Will began to interject, but Sal raised his hand to stop him.

"I'm going to offer you a way we can clear his debt."

Will sat back, relieved. He did not need to scramble for an explanation. He took a slow sip of his wine with purpose, waiting to respond. The dynamics of the conversation had shifted.

"Okay. What do you have in mind?"

"I have a lot of business in this town," Fat Sally continued. "My business provides me with information that is sometimes helpful to different people." He nodded to Lorenzo, who slid a small object wrapped in a slip of paper across the table. Will unfolded the paper to find a bronze key.

"Some of the people who work for me also work at banks, some of them near the safety deposit boxes." He pointed at the key. "That's a copy of an owner's key to a safety deposit box."

Will studied the handwritten three-digit number on the paper: 602C.

"About a month after that Negro boy pulled off his job, a Negro comes into the bank with your painting rolled up in butcher paper, the ends sticking out."

"How do you know it was my Pollock?"

Sal was quick to answer. "How many fucking paintings do you know get deposited in a bank after a robbery by a Negro?"

Will conceded, feeling like he had asked the one dumb question Sal would tolerate. But he did not want to appear too gullible, so he pressed. "How'd he get a safety deposit box? Like you said, not too many Negros are walking into banks."

"Our guy says he had a janitor friend at the bank, which is probably where he got the idea. He was in a real nice suit, so other than some raised eyebrows, no one got alarmed." Sal stood up. "Chase National. You'll meet one of my associates inside, Anthony Myers. I expect that should be the end of it."

"Eighth Avenue?"

Sal threw his napkin over his empty plate. "Have the spumoni," he said and walked past Will without another word.

Lorenzo stood and patted Will on the back in a graceful goodbye, and the two men walked out, leaving Will sitting in the empty restaurant, the brightness of the afternoon receding out the front windows.

The waitress returned with a square slice of chocolate, pistachio, and strawberry ice cream on a small plate. Maybe his instinct had been right, Will thought as he forked a bite of ice cream. Clyde had kept the painting, and because he was in jail, the canvas remained in the bank. As Will realized he was close to recovering the Pollock, a surge of excitement raced through him like coffee in his veins. He wanted to run down to the bank at that moment, but there wasn't time to reach the branch before closing. He would have to wait for morning.

He imagined the moment when he turned the key. What he would find in the safety deposit box meant everything. He hated to ask himself what would happen if he found more than the Pollock painting. Could he cover up the evidence if there was some proof of Liz's communist ties? He wanted to, but he didn't know if he could live with that decision. Then again, maybe the beady-eyed man was wrong. Who knew who the spies were? Informants were collecting information on anyone they met. Hoover was investigating the government, the military, and the CIA. Dickie had said that Hoover was making everyone in Washington nervous, investigating everyone.

And at that moment, the answer developed in his mind like the pins dropping in a lock.

The calls came from Washington. At once, separate conversations converged together, and a singular individual began to solidify in his mind, someone who lived in Paris and Berlin and Washington, someone whose transient lifestyle as a journalist could be a cover allowing him to come and go without explanation, someone ALERT was watching.

Dickie was the missing piece that allowed all the other parts to click into place.

ALERT was watching Dickie. *Dickie made the phone calls.*

Will's instinct told him his hunch was correct. He had everything but the why. He rushed to the back of the restaurant, pulled open the sliding door to the wooden phone booth, and grabbed the receiver.

"Local call," he said to the operator and then gave her the number. After a moment, a familiar voice came on the other end of the line.

"Yes?"

"Can we meet? … No, somewhere out of the way."

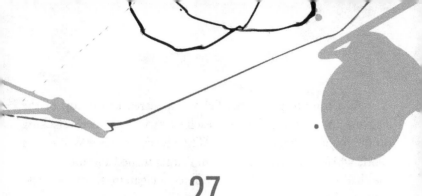

27

THAT NIGHT WILL CROSSED INTO CENTRAL PARK at Seventy-Second Street and took the lower pathway lined by giant American elms toward the Bethesda Arcade. Tall black lampposts stood like sentinels along the path. Their glowing orbs shed cones of white light across the black shadows of tree trunks, creating angular forms deep into the park.

He reached the top of the arcade and gazed over the stone railing. The plaza stood empty and quiet. The hot summer air hung still around the angel and cherub fountain, empty of water for the evening. Will's watch read five minutes before nine. He turned to the stairwell flanked by two large Gothic posts and descended the stone staircase. The smell of damp air greeted him as he entered the subterranean walkway. The evening lights from the fountain plaza were too weak to penetrate the darkness and cast strange shadows into the mouth of the arcade. Halfway down, he ducked into a small side corridor and leaned against a column to wait in the shadows for Palmer.

All his cases had been straightforward: steal a painting and make money. But Dickie's motive was different. What was he hiding? He always seemed to be telling half-truths. What really concerned Will, though, was how Liz was connected. He could not protect her without knowing Dickie's purpose and what secrets the painting hid.

At a minute past nine, Palmer appeared at the top of the staircase and descended, taking each step with care, heels clacking on the brick herringbone floor. When he came close, Will gave a gentle whistle to call his attention. Palmer turned and moved into the shadows next to Will, then offered a cigarette from his pack. "What's this about?"

Will did not know where to start. So much had happened in the last twenty-four hours—the memorandum, the phone calls to Washington, ALERT, the Pollock painting in the security box. "I need information on someone."

Palmer frowned and waited for Will to continue.

"The painting is in a safety deposit box in Chase Bank."

"Not where you usually find them."

Will nodded in agreement. "I need to know what I'm walking into."

"You think this someone stole the painting?"

"I think he had it stolen to hide something, and I need to know what. If I open that door, I need to know what's behind it."

Palmer pulled on his cigarette and gazed out into the dark arcade. Will waited for his response. Asking Palmer to investigate another citizen was against protocol. But the two of them had been through the war together. They had spent nights in the Gremecey Forest, ready to drag each other's bodies to a medic if necessary. Will hoped that mattered. He told Palmer about Dickie and how ALERT was watching him, about how he needed to know if Dickie was on any of the FBI watch lists.

Palmer looked down at the pavement, shaking his head slowly. Will waited, his chest tightening with anticipation. He needed Palmer's help. Then Palmer looked up. "I don't know, Will. Things are changing. Hoover's manic, and he doesn't trust anybody. He's investigating everyone, even his own people."

"As a country, we don't even trust ourselves?"

"No, we don't. The FBI is crossing too many lines. We're in the business of trust, and if anyone knew we were breaking that trust …" Palmer turned away and stared out into the darkness like he was disappointed in himself for taking part in the betrayal. When he turned back, his face was long with concern. "Americans trust us, Will. They don't know we're inside their living rooms, breaking the laws we're trying to protect, and Hoover wants to keep it that way."

"I have to know if Lang is in your files. Who is he? What he's doing here? What he's been doing in Paris, Berlin, Washington?" Will broke off, second-guessing his whole direction. What did he care? He had the painting; wasn't that where the job ended? What he needed to do was save himself. Charlie had told him as much. But if he were honest with himself, he wasn't investigating Dickie because of the painting. He was investigating Dickie because he was trying to protect Liz, to keep her off a list, off the grandstand in Washington with the cameras and lightbulbs flashing in her face as she froze at the center table. Will needed to know what Liz had been doing in Paris and what she was doing in New York. Why she had been at the Waldorf and how it all connected.

"Poking around like that makes me nervous. I don't know who I'm investigating or who's watching me do it. I'm worried about what we might find."

"You're all I've got." Will's plea was as close to begging as he could get.

Palmer shifted his feet, then peered back through the darkness at the staircase, checking for movement or sound. Then he turned around and remained fixed on Will for a long time. "Maybe some things are better left alone," he said.

They stood there for a moment, silent. Will had planned to leave Liz out of the conversation, but he needed to be honest with Palmer. He would expect as much if Palmer were in his position. "I need to protect someone."

"You need to protect yourself. You've gotten too involved, haven't you?" Palmer's voice held genuine concern, and he reached out, placing his hand on Will's shoulder. "You and I have been through a lot, Will. This could go south. I hope she's worth it."

Before Will could respond, a female laugh bounced off the acoustic tiles of the arcade and reverberated through the tunnel. Will and Palmer turned toward the stairwell to see two sets of shoes appear, descending the staircase. They dropped their cigarettes to the floor, ground them out, and moved back into the shadows.

Will and Palmer eyed the young couple as they walked through the arcade laughing, with their arms around each other, oblivious to the world around them and enveloped by a haze of youthful love. The girl was no more than twenty, and the boy as young. Palmer scrutinized the young man as if determining whether he was someone other than who he seemed—searching for the wrong shoes, wrong watch, tracking his eyes to see if they diverted to the corners to search for someone in particular. They listened to the young lovers' words as they rounded the turn toward the park's east side and strolled out of view.

"I should be going," Palmer said.

"It's a couple of kids."

Palmer shook his head. "There are too many different sides, Will. Too many people conducting surveillance. Now you want to investigate this guy, Lang. Who knows how many eyes are on him? Who knows which side he's on?"

It became clear to Will that no one stood outside the reach of the FBI and their network of informants, even those inside the organization. All it took was a wrong turn, the wrong friend, the wrong association. Whisper the wrong word at dinner and maybe the waiter turns you in. At this point, anyone could get on a list, even with no credible accusations. Whatever Liz's secret was, he would hear her out. He would listen to her side of the story.

Palmer pulled out another cigarette, lit it, and took in a long, slow pull, the glow casting warm tones over his face in the darkness. "Richard Lang," he said, almost to himself. He straightened his hat and turned. He moved out of the shadows and into the central corridor toward the angel fountain, then disappeared down the pathways of Central Park.

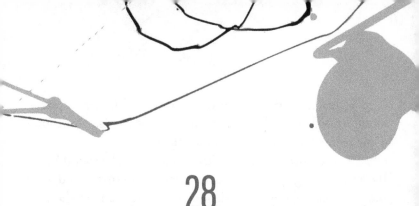

28

WILL STUDIED THE BANK from the front window of the cramped deli across the street. He sipped his coffee and turned his spoon on a white paper napkin while waiting for the bank to open. In other cases, in this moment shortly before recovering a painting, he'd always known what he was going to find. Each case had been about the painting and nothing more. This moment was different. He replayed the night when he'd stood in Liz's doorway trusting her, telling her he didn't care if there was a life she needed to hide. He hoped he could keep that promise no matter what he found.

At nine o'clock, a doorman in a maroon uniform unlocked the bank's glass doors. Will stood up and prepared to cross the street, steeling himself as if his Higgins boat ramp had just dropped and he was about to wade onto the Omaha beachhead. He took the last sip of his coffee and stepped out of the deli.

All along the sidewalk, people rushed about their ordinary daily routines. No one appeared to be watching him at the corner—ALERT, Communists, or FBI. Will had lost track of who might be following him. Anyone could be at this point. Will no longer understood which side anyone was on, including himself. He loved Liz and was fighting for her—of that he was certain.

Seeing no signs of alarm, Will crossed the street, pulled open the heavy door, and stepped into the white-marble lobby of Chase Bank. As Will adjusted to his new surroundings, his pulse beat hard against his chest. The measured ticking of the center podium clock echoed through the expansive and otherwise silent lobby. Time seemed to move slowly inside the bank.

Will reached into his pocket and fingered the round head of the key, rubbing against the small, jagged teeth that would release the tumblers of the safety deposit lock. He scanned the lobby again, searching the employees' faces and trying to identify Fat Sally's man, as if he had a marker. Finally, Will decided to ask for the man like he was conducting a regular bank transaction. He crossed the lobby with determination until he reached a gray-haired man with his nose buried in a ledger. Will placed his hat on the man's desk. "I'm here to see Anthony Myers."

The man squinted at Will, his eyes adjusting from the rows and columns of small numbers, and then nodded to a series of desks behind him. "Further back with the other account managers," he said. And as indifferently as he'd answered, he returned to his work, placing his ruler back on his ledger and moving his finger across the page as if Will had never interrupted.

In the last row of desks against the far wall, a man peered over his account book, watching Will with intent. When their eyes met, the man stood up, and his lanky legs made awkward motions as he crossed the carpeted floor to meet Will.

"Myers. You Oxley?"

"That's right."

"Follow me." He gestured over his shoulder with his head. Myers moved along the back wall and pulled out a small photostat of a note card, slipping it to Will without drawing attention. "Study that," he said in a quiet voice. "It's a signature card. To access the safety deposit box, you will need to sign in with the right signature. Study the card." He said it all matter-of-factly. "You have the key, right?"

Will nodded and studied the signature: Clyde Barnett. Will had half expected to find a fake name or an anonymous safety deposit box, but Clyde had not been that clever. He had not been given instructions beyond dropping off the painting in the trunk of the car. The moment Clyde had decided not to leave the Pollock in the trunk, he was on his own. There was no plan or cover-up protocol to follow. The signature was written in print—a large *C* with a straight angled *y*, a missing *e* at the end of *Clyde*. There was a heavy angle to the *B* at the beginning of *Barnett*, which was missing the last *t*.

Myers led Will down the lobby's back wall, past more polished brass and a massive round vault door. He made no attempt to hide himself. As they walked, Will surveyed the lobby. Myers might not be the only person in the bank working for someone else. There could be other informants. Hoover may have men in the bank. Tellers and doormen. Will's imagination began to run, and he studied each account manager with suspicion. Who could be tracking him? Every eye seemed to be watching him, peering in his direction, and he thought he saw a teller jot down a note? Or was that his imagination? He couldn't be certain.

He shook his head to slow his panic and bring his focus back to the moment. Several steps ahead, Myers led him into a smaller carpeted room that resembled a living room, with deep colors melting into the mahogany furniture. A dark painting of an English horse hung on one wall. A young man sat behind a small desk accessorized with a black phone and a green lamp. He fidgeted with the pen and papers on his desk as Will and Myers approached.

"602C," Myers said.

The clerk opened a desk drawer and pulled out a large black leather registry book with a long placeholder ribbon. He pulled up slightly on the ribbon to separate the pages and opened the book with a delicate flip of his hand. He pointed to a blank line. "Signature, please."

A row of signatures filled the page, each different from the others, some legible, others not. Will lifted the small black pen with the gold tip off its stand, concerned he would not be able to replicate the signature. He pictured the card—large *C* and missing *e*, heavy angled *B*—then he wrote on the empty line in the book with his best effort. The signature rolled out more naturally than expected. He studied it, comparing it to the image in his mind.

The clerk opened a side drawer and flipped through a series of index cards. He plucked out a single card and placed it next to Will's signature on the registry book. His two index fingers ran along the signatures in tandem. He paused at the *B* and bent forward, lowering his eyes close to the page. Will eyed him, wondering where he'd made a mistake. Was it the wrong angle? Had he pressed down too hard?

The clock's slow tick in the lobby counted the seconds as they passed. After what seemed like an hour, the young man raised his head. "Thank you, Mr. Barnett." He replaced the card squarely in sequence and stood. "It's always nice to have new customers." He spoke as though they were good friends, as if his connection to Will as a customer equated to years of shared experiences. The clerk smiled at Myers, a collegial handoff.

As Myers led Will through another door and a security gate, he welcomed him to Chase National with a salesman's tone, spouting the history of the bank and its proud relationship with the Rockefellers as their largest shareholders. Inside the next room, the tiny silver doors of the safety deposit boxes covered the walls from ceiling to midway down, glistening brightly. Each small box was an exact square, six inches by six inches. Directly below those were larger safety deposit boxes, each half the size of a school locker. A long mahogany table stood in the middle, with two green lamps on either end.

"Let's see … 602C," the clerk said as he walked along the far wall with a finger poised in the air, tracking the numbers. He stopped at a larger safety deposit box whose silver plate shined in the light from the ceiling. "Here we are," he said and pulled out his keys. "Ready?"

Will pulled the bronze key from his pocket and stopped midmotion. Once he opened the box, he could not go back. He fidgeted with the key and read the numbers on the door, focusing on the six, uncertain if he wanted to uncover Liz's secret. But whatever it was—hidden messages or secret maps—he had promised her that it did not matter. He had made love to her with that promise between them. He still had the chance to walk away, to leave the secrets locked inside. He could go back to dinners under candlelight, unaware, forever searching for the stolen Pollock. But to protect her, he knew he had to find the truth. He had to know if he could cover up the accusations. Then again, maybe there were no treasonous secrets, and he had let his imagination run too far. Perhaps he would find the painting and nothing more. But to know for sure, he had to turn the key—no illusions, only the truth. He had to know what the painting meant.

Will slid his key into the keyhole, and the clerk did the same. They turned in unison, and the door loosened at the latch, free to open.

"I'll leave you alone," the young man said then turned, shutting the gate behind him.

He had left the safety deposit door slightly ajar, a thin piece of metal between Will and what lay inside. Will flipped the door open then dropped to one knee to peer in. Leaning against the back corner was a rolled canvas wrapped in brown butcher paper, the ends sticking out and covered with paint splatters. He reached in and pulled out the canvas, then turned to the mahogany table behind him and spread the lamps farther apart to give himself more room. With careful fingers he tore off the butcher paper, and the canvas roll sprang open wider.

As he unfurled the painting across the tabletop, he recognized the thick and thin strokes swirled across an unprepared canvas—red, yellow, a muted green-blue, black, and white. Will leaned over the canvas and studied every inch, the corners, the edges. He followed the patterns of the splatters from up close and then stepped further back, studying them again from a distance. The picture in front of him was a Pollock painting and nothing more. He rotated the painting ninety degrees multiple times, scrutinizing each bit of paint from every direction. He examined the design for patterns. He ran his fingers over each inch of the canvas, discerning no map or Soviet code. It was simply a painting.

He let out a long, slow breath. The air came freely, and he felt light again, the worry washing away. His imagination had got the better of him. He could return the painting to Liz, and their lives could move forward. He hesitated to imagine how it would unfold, Saturday's in the park, a drive upstate to Sugar Loaf for the weekend, maybe a trip to Paris.

Will turned the painting over to roll it back up, and at that moment he spotted a small black rectangle no larger than a business card taped to the right corner. He leaned toward the painting and studied the object. He reached out and gently pulled the card from the canvas. He pinched the paper-thin translucent Mylar film between his fingers at the corner, careful not to leave prints, and raised it to the lamplight. A ghostly image of data appeared like a photographic negative. A microfiche. At the sight of it, Will's stomach sank and hollowed out. He felt sick. What was this? All the accusations and fears came rushing back, filling the void that had opened inside him. What shone through the translucent film were rows and columns organized in a table. But without a microfiche reader, the small image was utterly unreadable.

Will ran through his options. He could not access the reader at the office anymore. A law office would have a machine, but he would not be able to gain access to it, either. He closed his eyes to focus his thoughts, and in a matter of seconds the answer came to him: the New York Public Library. He tucked the microfiche into the pocket of his suit jacket, rolled up the Pollock, and walked back to the registry room.

Everything was the same—quiet and still—no alarm bells, no one waiting for him as Will had half expected. But when he rounded the front desk, Myers dipped his head toward the clerk, who appeared busy with his logbook, studiously taking no notice of Will's return. They stepped back into the lobby, and Myers leaned into Will. "Be careful. You can bet I'm not the only one working for someone else here. Come this way."

Myers led Will through a back door and then through a corridor with cardboard boxes stacked along the concrete wall, past the service elevators to the back entrance. "Go out the delivery entrance. It'll put you out on Fourteenth. At least you'll be going out a door they won't expect."

"Keep this." Will handed him the rolled Pollock. "Don't give it to anyone. I'll be back for the painting later." He had no other choice. Besides, the Pollock would be safe. The painting was not what anybody wanted. He placed a hand on Myers's shoulder. "No one but me. Got it?"

Myers's eyes widened. He shifted on his feet but nodded in agreement.

Will pushed through the exit door and stepped out onto Fourteenth Street. He wanted to run, but that would draw more attention. Then again, maybe no one was watching. At that moment, getting to the library was all that mattered.

He turned and bolted down the street, cut across Fourteenth, passed St. Barnard's rectory and a series of apartment stoops, then pushed into a deli on Ninth Avenue. He stood at the window and scanned the street, the shop windows on the far side, the office building at the corner. Nothing unusual. Nobody following him. No strange movements. Five minutes passed. Ten. When the deli owner began to ask his purpose, Will stepped back out onto the street. He remained sensitive to his surroundings, studying for anything out of the ordinary—a man holding a newspaper he was not reading or a city worker lingering over a covered manhole. Or maybe they would come at him directly, jumping him in an alley. But none of that occurred. The day seemed ordinary. The early lunch hour had begun, and people were filling the streets, scurrying to run their afternoon errands, detouring around him as he stood on the sidewalk like a post. The moment unfolded before Will like a surreal movie spinning around him, nobody aware of anything but themselves.

Removed from the real world now, Will was hiding in the shadows. He began to get a sense of what it must be like to live in secret, where everything had significance, where every slight movement could be a signal—an apartment light turning on, a man tipping his hat, a coffee cup turned at a certain angle. The tiniest details could mean something, a message, or nothing at all. How could anyone tell? He felt alone, out against the enemy on his own. In the Thirty-Fifth Infantry, they never went out alone. They never left their bunker, never dug a latrine without a partner.

At the corner, Will picked up the pay phone and called Charlie, asking him to meet him at the library in twenty minutes. The case had become too personal. He needed Charlie to help sort out his thoughts, to help understand his options with a clear head. Will wasn't certain he could trust his own thinking. He needed to find out what he had on the film, what the truth was, and then make a choice. As quickly as his hand went up, a cab pulled over, and Will took his first full breath in more than an hour. He pulled the door open and hopped in. "Fortieth and Fifth Avenue," Will said.

The cab jolted forward, and Will peered out the back window, scanning for any car that might be following them. Pedestrians darted across the street between gaps in the traffic. His cab circled back on Fourteenth and shot up Eighth Avenue, and the bank disappeared behind the tall buildings. Will dropped his head back, and the cab rolled along the avenue toward the New York Public Library.

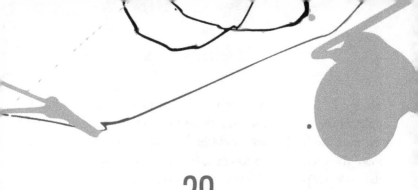

29

THE CAB ZIGZAGGED through the Garment District. Rolls of brilliant-colored fabric decorated the windows. Along the street, men pushed racks of clothing from cutting shops to seamstress shops, avoiding the crowded sidewalks full of fabric cutters, pattern makers, and tailors out for lunch. Will flipped the microfiche between his fingers and angled it toward the light, studying the matrix of micro images he could not decipher. The right next move was to turn the microfiche over to Palmer, but Will could not allow himself to do that—not without knowing what information it contained or giving Liz a chance to explain her side of the accusations. He owed that to her. He had to learn how she was involved and if he could protect her.

The long, finger-like windows of the New York Public Library came into view as they passed along the southern promenade of Bryant Park. Men in suits and others in hard hats rested on the ledge of the granite fountain, eating their lunches out of brown paper bags. When the cab crossed Fifth Avenue instead of stopping, Will leaned forward and knocked on the plastic partition. The driver gave no acknowledgment but continued down the street.

"Hey!" Will said, hitting the plastic partition rapidly.

The cab picked up speed, and the driver stared straight ahead. Panic rose within Will; his face flushed with heat. He searched the cab as if he would find a sign telling him what was happening. He replayed the moments leading up to this one, standing outside the deli near the bank. How could he have been so careless? Flagging down the cab had been too easy, but he hadn't given it a thought. Half a dozen possibilities ran through Will's head in a split second.

He jerked at the door handle, but the door didn't budge. He pulled up the lock, and it clicked back down. Will pulled again and simultaneously yanked on the handle. The door flew open, and Will fell forward, gaping at the street rushing beneath him, the yellow line repetitively flashing past. The cab slowed then jolted forward, as if the driver were trying to close the door with the force of forward motion, but Will held tight to the door handle as the pavement rushed past his face. He looked down the street, hoping for a red light, but green lights dotted as far as he could see. The cab had slowed to a cruising speed as if about to brake for a light. He had no time.

Without thinking about the pain, Will pushed himself out the door before his mind could stop him. A piercing pain flashed up his forearm like fire when he hit the ground. He tumbled on the pavement until he crashed into a parked car, pinning his cheek against the tire. Throbbing pain moved from his shoulder to his palms, both scraped raw. He pushed himself up and slid over the car's hood and onto the sidewalk. As he staggered forward, the cab screeched to a stop at the corner.

Will doubled back down Fortieth Street with a hundred questions popping off in his head. They knew where he was going, of that he was certain. The cab driver could have told a contact by now. But how? How fast did information pass in their network? And who was chasing him? Where would they be next? Which street corner, which door entrance?

Will shot across Fifth Avenue and up the grand marble staircase of the library flanked by stone lions. A woman with a child in tow stared at him as he climbed. His suit coat was torn at the forearm. His hands were scraped at the palms and sides, but he was able to wipe away the blood. It resurfaced, but he dabbed at his suit to contain the bleeding. When he reached the top, he surveyed the street one last time, trying to spot anyone following him. He did not know how long he had before someone would be on him again. Ten minutes, maybe fifteen. He mentally listed off who might be following him as he pushed through the revolving door to the library. ALERT, Dickie's men, his Communist spies. The people following him could be any of them, but it did not matter. He needed to find the answers first; he needed to know what information the microfiche contained before facing them.

The vast, open space of the entry hall echoed with hushed voices against the cold marble. Two massive staircases flanked the lobby and led to the second-floor balcony. Will darted left and underneath the staircase, dropping back to remain unnoticed. His shoulder ached and palms burned from the open scrapes. He tried to shake off the pain, but it held. People flowed in and out of the hall, and Will studied them for any suspicious signs. Each person appeared like the others, oblivious to him as they headed toward their destinations in the library.

By the time Charlie pulled open the heavy brass door to the library, Will's nerves had calmed. Three people had lingered in the main hall, but Will considered none of them suspicious. He stepped out from under the staircase and flagged Charlie over. Charlie gave Will a hard stare and winced when he approached.

"Don't ask." Will was eager to move past explanations.

"I won't. But are they still around?" Charlie said, handing Will a handkerchief.

Will wiped his face and cleaned his hands the best he could. The bleeding had stopped. The suit he couldn't fix, but the tear on the back side of his arm wasn't terribly noticeable if he was careful to conceal it. "If not, they're close behind."

"Jesus, Will. I was joking. Thanks for getting me involved," Charlie said with sarcasm and shook his head. "You've got yourself into a real shit storm, haven't you?" He paused, then added, "Palmer called the office."

Will grabbed Charlie's arm. "What did he say?"

"That guy, Dickie. Palmer confirmed he's on Hoover's list. The FBI is watching him, but he doesn't know why. He said the surveillance didn't seem like the other investigations. They were watching him but nothing more—no collecting of information, no phone taps, no black bag jobs. Will, what's this all about?"

"This way."

Charlie followed Will, peppering him with questions, underneath the second-story balcony and down a series of marble corridors. They found a wooden door marked Government Information and Microforms and stepped in.

The room, while not small, had a low ceiling. Mid-rise shelving filled with magazines, newspapers, and government periodicals crowded the front entrance, and two large reading desks stood behind those. They approached the back wall and stopped in front of three microfiche machines with large gray screens resting on a long table. Will reached into his suit pocket and pulled out the microfiche. "I found this taped to the back of the Pollock."

"You found the Pollock?" Charlie spun Will around by the shoulder. "Where the hell is it?"

"Safe. That's not the point. Whatever is on this film is the point."

"What are you talking about? Jesus, Will. Turn the painting in. You're done, right? What are you thinking? You did the job. Turn it in."

"To whom?"

"To the police, to whoever is chasing you. I don't care."

"I do," Will shot back. "I don't know what's on this film," he said, trying to maintain a whisper. "I don't know whose lives it could ruin."

"Yours if you don't turn it in, that's for damn sure. Do you think this is a game? Do you think people aren't locked up for this kind of shit? Locked up and questioned and tortured for all I know."

Charlie stood there, breathing heavily from his outburst, waiting for Will to answer. Then his shoulders dropped, and Will detected a flash of understanding cross his face. "It's because of her, isn't it?" he said, stepping away from Will as if distance would separate him from any consequences Will faced. "You're protecting her, aren't you? You'd risk it all for her?"

Will looked him dead in the eye. The years they had worked together, the years knocking on doors, the phone calls, the lunches together complaining about the firm—all those experiences hung in front of him, rolled up into this one moment. He needed Charlie to believe him. He needed Charlie to be with him. Will did not want to jump over the hedgerows alone. Without Charlie, it would be too hard to admit he had taken the wrong path. "Trust me," he said. The words came out a question and a promise in one. Unable to watch if Charlie walked away and abandoned him, Will turned his back.

Charlie let out a heavy sigh. "You're like a brother to me, Will. I'll do this, but I hope she's worth the sacrifice."

At the sound of Charlie's voice, a calm washed over Will. Charlie had chosen to stay. Will turned back and gave Charlie a nod of gratitude, a nod which said how much staying with him meant, that he knew what Charlie was sacrificing, and that he would be forever grateful.

Will oriented himself in front of the microfiche reader. The gray reading screen, slightly larger than notebook paper, gave off a cloudy reflection blurred by the translucent plastic. Positioned below were the controls, dials, and wheels. Will flipped up the on switch and an interior lamp turned on, then the machine hummed as the motor warmed. He placed the microfiche on a square tray under the raised glass plate and moved the tray around until an image came into view, enlarged by the internal magnifying glass.

At first, Will did not understand. Rows of names and numbers covered the screen, some that repeated; dates accompanied each row. He moved the tray up and down, left and right, trying to make sense of what appeared before him. Then he recognized a name: Bower Foundation. Next to the name was a number—125,000— preceded by a plus sign. Will realized it was a dollar amount. Next to the dollar amount was another name—Fairlane Foundation—then the same amount, but this time in parentheses to indicate a withdrawal. The line of text was dated October 5, 1952.

"Look at this." Will pointed at the screen and leaned to the side to let Charlie get a better view.

"What am I looking at?" Charlie asked.

"It's a record of transactions, a type of accounting ledger. Ins and outs, credits and debits. This is the flow of money between accounts." He pointed to the screen. "This is Liz's foundation, and this is a different foundation. One's funding the other."

"Okay," Charlie said, frowning at the banality of the discovery.

Will scrolled up and down the image, reading the account names; he did not recognize most. Weston Group, Lilly Endowment, Johnson Fund. Then he found several he did know, including the Ford Foundation, the Rockefeller Foundation, and Jock Whitney's trust.

The list of names continued. Will counted nearly one hundred and twenty, all foundations of one kind or another, and almost all receiving funds from a single source. Other transactions occurred between foundations—into one, then out to another—with the monies deposited into different accounts.

He turned to Charlie. "It's a list of foundations, account names, account numbers, and transfer amounts. But they're all funded by the same source. That foundation is acting as a central bank. The others appear to be pass-throughs, conduits. The central foundation is depositing funds into each of the other foundations, which are in turn funding different entities."

Charlie pushed up close behind Will. "Okay, so the foundations are funding other foundations, and some of it goes to MoMA, to different magazines, to newspapers. Isn't that what foundations do?" Charlie glanced up at the ceiling as if answering the question in his head, then added, "But why is it all funded by a single source? And why bother transferring between different funds and different foundations? It's as though they are trying to hide the funding and source."

"Right. This isn't fundraising activity," Will added. Then Pennifield's words at the Waldorf echoed in his head. *We never knew. Everything hidden.* Will closed his eyes, trying to visually piece the puzzle together. *They're all connected with Communist front organizations, nonprofit cover-ups.*

And in a snap, the picture emerged. On the surface, because the money flowed from one foundation to another, then to various entities, no one could identify the true, singular source of funding. There were too many transactions and too many shell accounts. Maybe the recipient knew—they were involved—but needed the cover-up. But for Will, this nuance did not fit. The Rockefeller Fund, the Ford Foundation, and the Whitney Trust were all American institutions. Their involvement did not make sense, not unless they were unaware. Will struggled to believe they were Communist fronts, knowingly or unknowingly. He leaned back, considering what lay before him. If Dickie was the originating funding source, he could be funding a network of Communist fronts hidden behind layers of foundations, exactly as Pennifield had said.

Will studied the transactions again. The last one was dated one month before Clyde stole the Pollock. The central foundation had transferred funds to three different foundations, including the Bower Foundation, which in turn transferred that amount into the Museum of Modern Art. "What does MoMA have to do with the transactions?" Will asked aloud.

"Is it what everyone is afraid of? Communists infiltrating our country, our infrastructure, controlling our newspapers? Art with secret maps to our defenses and subversive propaganda?"

Will shook his head. "I don't think so. Look." He pointed to the screen. "By the account names, I'd guess most of these entities are overseas. Even the MoMA exhibit is going overseas." Will stood up, pausing a moment, trying to compartmentalize his thoughts. There was a network of foundations, each with different account numbers and a series of regular money transfers. But one foundation in particular acted as a central bank. He needed to find out who the controlling stockholders were. How was Dickie connected? He led Charlie back to the front and asked the librarian where to start if he wanted to find controlling members of foundations?

She pursed her lips and tapped her glasses against them before answering. "At first, I was going to suggest you go to the Records Bureau downtown because foundations all have to file with the state. They must file articles of incorporation or a charter document. Those will provide the date of incorporation and the names of the president and directors. I'm not sure about board members, though." Then she added, "But this library has the *U.S. List of Foundations* in the reference collection. Those would show newly formed nonprofits for each year and provide you with several types of information. You could check if there is information on the initial boards."

She beamed as she described the workings of the library, her eyes wide, and Will could tell she enjoyed the problem, mentally weaving in and out of the library, triangulating a specific piece of information with mental cross-checks and multiple references. "Of course, you'd have to search by year until you found the foundation you were looking for," she said.

"It'll be within the last few years. Around 1949," Will said, remembering when Liz started her foundation.

The librarian's voice brightened. "Everything's upstairs in the Rose Main Reading Room. The reference collection is on the balcony against the east wall of the room. But if you need a different type of book, you'll have to start in the catalog room, find the call number, and then fill out a call slip. You can give the slip to a librarian behind the circulation desk, who will then drop it down to the stacks."

"Stacks?" Will said.

"The seven floors below the Rose Main Reading Room are called the stacks, and that's where we house all the books. But it's not open to the public. The call slips are taken below by pneumatic tubes, and a librarian will place the books on a conveyor system to send them up."

Despite living in New York most of his life, Will had never been in the library. He assumed the layout was like every other library, with floors, shelving, and books you pulled off as you found them.

Will thanked the librarian and led Charlie back down the corridor to the front hall and up the grand staircase. A map fixed to the wall guided him at each landing as he climbed: *Current Periodical Room*, *Library Offices*, *General Research*, *Circulation*, and *Catalog Room*. On the second floor, they had to switch staircases to one that led them farther up into the rotunda of the third floor, its ceiling bathed in gold light as if freshly painted. They crossed through the card catalog room with its small drawers and slips of paper and eventually made their way into the main reading room.

Two separate rows of long oak library tables filled the room, as long as a city block. Nearly fifty people were scattered throughout the room, sitting two and three at a table to study. A small balcony with an iron railing wrapped around the top of the reading room, creating a second story of bookshelves. Sunlight streamed in through the massive arched windows at the ceiling. Will searched the faces dotting the library tables, canvassing for piercing eyes or sudden movement toward him.

Seeing neither, he focused his attention on the massive bookshelves along the walls, which stretched fifteen feet high to the balcony. With Charlie close behind, Will crossed the marble floor toward the balcony, staying vigilant. No heads lifted from their books. No one paid him any mind. They climbed the wood and iron steps to the balcony.

Once on top, Will walked along the wall of bookshelves, running his fingers over the canvas coverings, bumping along the ridges as he walked. Each reference series contained thirty or fifty books. They appeared as a field of blurring colors, one series ending where another began, creating large blocks of muted greens, rust red, and yellows. The white lettering of the reference titles repeated from one spine to the next like a long white zipper ready to peel open, exposing the information within.

Will fingered the spines until he reached the *U.S. List of Foundations* and pulled the volume *1948 to 1952* off the shelf, the single book almost two inches thick. Charlie crowded in closer as Will cracked open the book to search for the B section. Will's eyes scanned the page until he stopped on the name Bower. "Bower Foundation," he read aloud, "incorporated in January 1950."

"Three years ago," Charlie said, anxious to make connections.

"Yes. And Elizabeth Bower is the Foundation President." Will read two additional names he did not recognize, then stopped. Richard Lang. *Dickie*. Exactly as he had feared.

"What?" Charlie asked. "What do you see?"

"They're both part of the Bower Foundation. Both of them." Will shook his head. "Lang. He's on her board."

Charlie leaned over to read the names. "The same Dickie that Palmer mentioned?"

Yes, Will thought.

He shut the book and turned to Charlie to explain. But beyond him, at the far end of the balcony, a man in a dark gray suit was walking toward them. Every thought in Will's mind cleared out. He turned to race down the other side on instinct, but he stopped short in panic. Another gray suit had reached the top step of the balcony, blocking the opposite end.

Charlie followed Will's gaze. "Jesus," he said, his voice shaking.

"Hang on, Charlie. Don't panic. They'll follow me, not you."

"What are you talking about? Will, turn the microfiche in, turn the painting in. To Hoover, to Palmer, to whomever. I don't care. Turn it all in."

"I have to talk to her before I do. I owe her that." Will didn't care about protecting Dickie, but Liz was connected. He needed to protect her. He needed to hear her side.

"After all this, you still trust her?" Charlie asked, his voice quivering.

The thought had been in Will's mind ever since the night at de Kooning's when she'd asked him the same question, a question he should have answered truthfully for himself long ago. And once he realized the answer, the burden lifted, he became certain of himself, more certain than he had ever been. He did trust her and he always had. "Yes," he said with ease and clarity. When he said the answer aloud, his priorities and focus crystallized, his resolve strengthened. He knew what he had to do. He peered over the balcony railing to the floor—eight, maybe ten feet below.

"You can't protect her, Will. Whatever it is, you can't protect her."

"They're going to follow me, Charlie, and when they do, I want you to run."

Will grabbed the railing and leaped over, landing hard on a wooden library table below. The sound echoed throughout the room, and all heads turned. The pain in his ankles shot up through his body to his head, and his stomach went hollow. Then as quickly as it came, the pain shrank back down into his ankles, narrowing deep into the bone, sharp and burning. He leaped off the table and ran. As he did, he tracked the movement of the gray suits by the sound of their heels—down the balcony stairs, two of them, across the marble floor. They had left Charlie alone. He'd be okay.

Between the main reading room and the card catalog room, Will spotted a door labeled *No exit* and threw it open to find a metal staircase leading to the floor below. He grabbed the cold metal railing and slid down the stairs, holding himself up by his arms. He landed with a metallic thud. Then he pushed through another heavy door to find himself in a massive room with no interior walls, only rows of metal shelving filled with books. Lead pipes crisscrossed the ceiling overhead. The dusty smell of books filled his nose, and his eyes adjusted to the murky light, which was muted by the shelves of books stacked against the dirty windows. The dull hum of a conveyer belt tremored somewhere on the floor. He had entered the stacks.

Not until Will had darted down one row of bookshelves and through another did he hear the sound of a door slamming shut one floor up. Then heels on metal stairs. Will counted the best he could, maybe one set, not two, which he hoped indicated only one man was following him. Will remained still, pressing himself flat against a bookshelf as if he were against the hedgerows again. He cocked his head and listened for movement. Moments later a door slammed open, then footsteps running to the left down the rows of bookshelves. Now they slowed, walking. Will pictured the gray suit creeping a few rows behind him, peering down each stack. Quiet. Senses alert. Will knew the gray suit eventually would peer down his aisle. He had to move.

He slipped down the side corridor, trying to avoid notice, but the gray suit's heeled footsteps began after him, the echo dissolving into books and paper. Will found another door in the back corner and threw it open. More metal stairs. He jumped down them two at a time, down one floor and then a second before he shot back into the library stacks. The room appeared the same as the first—rows of metal shelving filled with more books, more pipes running along the ceiling. Will darted in and out of the rows along the dark spines and metal shelving.

Then he stopped. Adrenaline pumped through his veins, and his heart beat hard against his chest. He struggled to suck in air that came in slow and thick, blocked as if a hand covered his mouth, suffocating him. He could not keep running. He had to consider his options. The man would keep coming. Another floor down, maybe the one after that. But he would not stop. They would inevitably meet. And when they did, Will might not have the edge. He might not be ready. The confrontation needed to be on Will's terms. If he had learned anything from the war, the lesson was to ambush your enemy rather than be ambushed yourself. He turned and walked back to the stairwell while listening for wooden heels against the concrete.

When he reached the door to the stairwell, Will flattened himself against the wall next to the entrance, his chest heaving. What he needed to happen would take a strong punch, fast and quick and precise. He would aim for the temple, right between the hairline and the eyebrow, or the nerves right behind the ear. Either would work, but he had to strike hard. He waited and listened. He could hear the man one floor up, circling like a vulture around the aisles of books, then the metallic sound of the door as it yawned open, wide and heavy. Will imagined the gray suit sticking his head into the stairwell, listening for Will to make a move—both men frozen, calculating, listening.

The man descended another flight. Will remained still, almost not breathing. He cocked his ear to catch the sound as it floated down the stairwell and onto his floor: slow steps, one at a time. No doubt the man was listening too. Will froze in place against the wall; the sound of his blood throbbed in his ears, loud and heavy.

When the gray suit stepped through the doorway, Will focused on the shape of his skull, on the soft tissue that filled the indention at the temple beneath the brown hair. Calculated and precise, his shoulder and hip thrust forward and his arm shot out. His knuckle hit hard bone that was slick with sweat. The man's head snapped hard and fast to the left, and Will imagined the brain hitting the side of the skull, the coils compressing together, the impact turning off a switch inside. The man turned like he was floating in water and, with dazed eyes, tried to focus on Will. He struggled to lift an arm, trying to reach for Will. But Will knew the man was lost, feeling as if his brain was bleeding down his body. Then he dropped to the cold concrete floor.

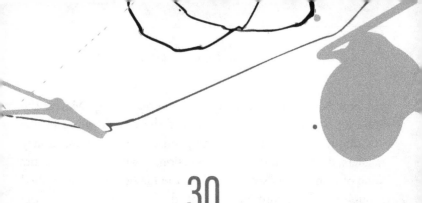

30

WILL RAN MOST OF THE WAY to Liz's apartment on Park Avenue—twenty-four blocks. He ran past the doorman, who shouted after him as he stepped into the elevator. The lights of the floor counter illuminated as he passed each floor. The blood vessels pounded in the backs of his legs, and he wanted to collapse.

When the doors opened, he shuffled into the empty hall. He was dizzy from exhaustion, but the pain in his arms and legs kept him in the moment. He lumbered toward Liz's apartment, and when he reached it, his knocks landed soft and weary on her door. He waited, wondering where the conversation would go and what explanations she would be able to give him. He hoped they would be enough. When Liz opened the door, she stepped back upon seeing his condition.

Will stood before her, scraped and in a full sweat. He was at her mercy for the second time, needing answers to questions he was desperate to ignore. He wanted this moment to be like last time he'd stood at her doorstep. He wanted to say he didn't care, that whatever the microfiche meant, wherever it led them, he trusted her. He wanted to be able to tell her they would fix the situation together, scrape off the paint and start a different picture.

But he needed to know the truth first. He needed to know about the choice he was making. Then they could deal with the problem. Maybe the beady-eyed man was wrong. Maybe she didn't know about Dickie. Or maybe she did. Maybe she was a Communist. But what was the plan? Account names, money transfers, the foundations, the subversion … what was it all about? None of it made any sense based on the Liz he knew. He pushed through the door, stumbled in, and dropped into a chair in the small study, surrounded by photos of her life.

"My God. Are you okay?" she asked. She reached for his arm, but Will pulled back.

There could be no more secrets. He pulled the microfiche out of his pocket and presented it to Liz. "What's this?" he said, waving the film in front of him. "What is the Bower Foundation?"

Liz stilled, and Will realized that he had never seen her surprised. She had always been in control as if she knew the plans before they laid themselves out. Now, though, she was off her guard. She shut her eyes for a moment as if mentally connecting dots, and then composed herself. "It's not what you think, whatever that is," she said.

"What do I think, Liz? What could I possibly think?" He flipped the microfiche onto the table next to her, surrendering. "What haven't you told me?"

Before she could reply, the front door slammed open and crashed against the entry table, shattering the moment. A voice yelled out. "Liz?"

Will jumped out of the chair and turned to see Dickie storming around the corner and into the study. One of the gray suits from the library followed close behind. Or another gray suit—Will couldn't be sure. But the vision twisted inside his head. They were all there together. Dickie. Liz. The gray suits. The chase had ended in her apartment. Their voices clouded his thoughts as he tried to draw lines and understand the connection.

Dickie stood in the middle of the room with lumbering breath, staring at Will and then at Liz. "He ran," Dickie said, catching another breath before continuing. "We figured he was headed here. Caught sight of him five blocks down." Then he turned to Will. "You gave us a bit of a run there, ol' boy. No harm, no foul, though. All part of it. I can't say as much for my guy you knocked out back there. Gave him quite a headache."

"What the hell is going on?" Will shouted. "These are your goons?" He grabbed one of the gray suits by the shoulder and shoved him away. "They nearly killed me in the cab, and then they chased me through the library."

Dickie's face tightened, and his words came out quick. "You didn't give us a chance," he said, holding Will back from throwing a punch at the gray suit. "You ran. We were bringing you in to explain everything. I sure as hell didn't imagine you'd jump out of a moving cab."

Liz whipped her head toward Dickie. "What are you talking about? Jumping out of a cab?"

"That's what I'm trying to say," Dickie yelled back. But no one was listening; everyone was shouting back and forth. Then Dickie turned to Will. "We started to wonder which side you were on."

"Which side?" Will continued to shout. "Liz," he said, glaring, feeling betrayed. "What the hell's going on? Did you know? Did you know about Dickie? The foundations?"

Liz started slowly, and when she spoke, her quiet words calmed the situation. Her eyes were apologetic. "Yes and no. I didn't know—"

"Didn't know what? That I'd find it? That they'd shanghai me into the back of a cab? That I'd get blacklisted?"

She shook her head as if trying to keep Will with her, trying not to lose him to the kind of anger that would make him say something he could not take back. "I didn't know he put the microfiche behind the painting. I didn't know there was a microfiche, for Christ's sake. And then they lost it, or never got it in the first place." She stopped talking and inhaled a long, shaky breath. "You have to trust me, Will. I thought we had that understanding."

"Liz, why didn't you tell me?" Will asked.

Liz turned to Dickie. "It's finished now. Leave us alone, please."

"Don't give up on her, ol' boy," Dickie said. "She meant well. I knew you'd find the painting, though. You're a better detective than I am. When the painting wasn't in the trunk and Clyde disappeared, you were our best bet." He stuck his hand out with a sportive smile. "But you can hand me the microfiche now. Sorry. I know all you bargained for was a painting."

Will glared, wanting to punch Dickie in the throat. Stealing the Pollock had never been about the painting or selling it on the black market. The theft was about the microfiche hidden behind it—the secrets, the trail of accounts, the transferring of funds. Will dropped into his chair, surrendering. He flipped his hand toward the microfiche on the table.

Dickie thanked him, gave him another "ol' boy," said something about grabbing a scotch together, adding one more "no harm no foul," and walked out the door.

With his legs stretched out, Will laid his head against the chair's cushion. The shadows of the gray suits followed Dickie out the door, and Will collected himself as best he could. "Why didn't you tell me, Liz? What's this all about?"

She didn't answer at first, as if taking a moment to let the room settle. She turned to the small bar, and the ice clinked in the lowball glasses as she fixed them both a drink. She handed him a bourbon and sat on the corner of the ottoman. Her knees brushed against his, the delicate touch feeling like another apology, attempting to reconnect. "It wasn't until the fundraising party that I learned Dickie had the painting stolen," she said. "When I put the painting in Elaine's show, he was in London. I didn't know he had hidden a microfiche behind it until he returned from Europe and told me that night."

Will reflected on the argument he'd witnessed the night of the party. What he had seen wasn't a quarrel between old flames. She'd been angry with Dickie for hiding the microfiche without her knowing, then having the painting stolen when he was in Europe, for putting her at risk and getting her involved.

"Once I found out, they wouldn't let me tell you," she continued, her voice soft and kind as a kiss. "After the deal went wrong, once Dickie lost the painting, everyone was on the search. If you found it, we'd deal with it then, but I couldn't tell you. I wasn't allowed. They told me to let you do your work. The theft was more of a game to Dickie than anything else, another covert operation with midnight break-ins and drop spots. But it went wrong. Then you showed up, which made it more exciting for him. You found the painting, though, and the microfiche. I knew you would." She paused, searching his face for a sign she could mend the tear in their relationship. "Will, I'm sorry. It wasn't supposed to be like this."

He wanted to believe her. He wanted it to be okay. He angled toward her, fearing her answer to his next question and what it would mean. "The Bower Foundation," he said. "The Fairlane Foundation. All the others. The network, the transactions, all the funding. They're Communist fronts, aren't they?" He closed his eyes, not wanting to hear the answer he knew was coming, not wanting to face the decision before him.

Liz shook her head. "Not Communist. CIA."

Her answer hit like ice water across his face. CIA. Not Communist. Not the Kremlin or Soviet spies, but the CIA. He thought back to the event at the Waldorf. They were all there. Communists, yes. But also the FBI and the CIA. Liz had been at the Waldorf as CIA, not a Communist. The beady-eyed man was wrong. They were all wrong, ALERT and the FBI. Hoover was panicked, investigating everyone, even the CIA, and that was why Dickie and Liz were on ALERT's list.

The points started to connect in his head like dots on a map. The realization filtered down, releasing tension from his body, and he relaxed against the cushions. "CIA." He dropped his head back and laughed aloud. Relief washed over him, and the anxiety, the concern, all disappeared, popping like a balloon. He had trusted her, and his instinct had been right. The Bower Foundation was a CIA front. "The list held over a hundred and twenty foundation names," he said, trying to find explanations.

"Most of them are pass-throughs."

Will smiled. "Funding different entities, magazines, MoMA." He had figured that part out. "But the Rockefeller Foundation, the Ford Foundation, and the Whitney Trust are real."

"Yes. Willing participants. Nelson Rockefeller is an ardent supporter of what we're doing. Foundations provide a cover of limitless funds without any oversight. The various foundations initiate CIA projects without anyone knowing the source is us."

"CIA projects?" He repeated the words, hoping for more.

"There are many." Liz took a sip of her scotch then placed her glass down. "Pro-American magazines in Paris, magazines targeting the non-Communist left, the funding of universities here and abroad, foreign institutes promoting American arts, the funding of Russian publishing houses to promote Western ideas." She let the moment sit, giving him time for the information to sink in. "Then there's the MoMA exhibit, the *Twelve Modern American Painters and Sculptors*. The abstract expressionists."

The final piece clicked for Will. "Baseball," he said. "Get them playing baseball, and they'll love America."

A smile crossed Liz's face. "Right."

"You're funding the baseball of the intellectuals. MoMA, the exhibition, the artists, creative freedom."

"We're still fighting a war out there, Will. It's different from the one you fought, but it's a war nonetheless. It's a cultural war. It's psychological. We're fighting for the minds and wills of men. If we can win over the minds of the intellectuals, show them what they can do with freedom, then Communism has no place to go."

Like Charlie had said: a white picket fence and a Chevy in the driveway, a new washing machine. If you're buying the American dream, the Communists can't get to you. As his thoughts came together, the enormity of it crystalized. If the CIA had people in MoMA and behind the magazines, where else? Why not everywhere?

"How deep does it go?" he asked.

Liz let the moment draw long, and Will could see she was considering the question with the seriousness it deserved. Finally she said, "It's in our interests to control as much as possible, Will. We fund magazines and newspapers, banks and corporations. We fund the art exhibits abroad. We create propaganda without anyone even knowing it's propaganda. How could they? Consider Pollock. He's on the cover of *Life* magazine. He shot to the top." She leaned back. "That's no coincidence. Take the MoMA exhibit. On the surface, it's an exhibit from the Museum of Modern Art, not the US government and definitely not the CIA. It's Jackson Pollock, Franz Kline, and Willem de Kooning, not government agents. Yet what better group to send to Europe but ex-Communists who paint about their creative freedom? No political images, merely paint. The fact that they have the freedom to paint that way, that's our propaganda. They are our weapons. Their art—their creativity, their freedom—is our propaganda."

The points began to intersect and connect for Will as he considered everything Liz had said. The CIA had created a network of foundations, a crisscrossing web of pass-through entities to conceal the source of the money that funded covert projects, influenced magazines and newspapers, and built art exhibits, sending a wave of American culture throughout Europe.

Will shook his head, realizing how deep the covert efforts went. The CIA had partners on company boards and at magazines. He thought back to the fundraising party, to the venture capitalists, the heads of corporations, the industrialists, and the magazine moguls he had seen. They were all part of it. All were protecting their interests, providing channels for the CIA to fund a war, to stop Communism from taking over their corporations and bank accounts. Rockefeller, McCray, and Whitney were all connected. Everything was cross-pollinated—politics, money, MoMA. He wondered if it went all the way down.

Will took a sip of his bourbon, remembering the night he met Liz; her message had always been the same. How art is a powerful way to communicate. How patrons give people the art they want them to have. The pictures of her life hanging on the wall were like dots in a paint-by-number picture, everything leading to this exact moment. School at Wellesley, the literary club. Will imagined her in Paris working with the magazines, and then returning home to manage the CIA front, funding the art exhibits, the artists, American culture. The approach had always been planned, calculated, hidden.

ALERT and the HUAC trials were distractions, meaningless roadblocks that she and the rest of the CIA had to circumvent to fight their cold war. Their war was abroad, a fight for a different kind of territory. The territory of the mind, the psyche. A fight for the ability to make a choice. The ability to live a life of freedom, to be an individual with opportunity.

Will dropped his head into his hands. The silence hung as still as the pictures on the wall. He did not know what to say or where to go next. He stared into her eyes, trying to see past everything he knew, past other secrets she might harbor. He lifted himself out of the chair, his body thick and heavy. "I don't know what to say, Liz. I don't even know where to begin."

He started gathering himself, checking his pockets. Maybe he was reaching for his thoughts, too, trying to hold them together. He would have to create an alternate story, a false truth, some variation of Clyde Barnett. He didn't know if his relationship with Liz would survive or if it would have to be painted over, too.

"Don't walk out on us."

He turned. "Was there ever an us?"

"Don't be like that. My feelings were true. This doesn't change anything. This is what I needed you to accept, to be able to live with. It's like a little club, and now you're on the inside. I couldn't tell you, but you found out. Don't you see? This is the best way. Now there are no secrets. There is no other history."

And that was all it took. They had reached the bottom with nowhere else to go. They had made silent promises to each other, putting everything on the table. He had fallen in love with her, and that kept him in, even now. Will lowered himself back into the chair, and she smiled when he did.

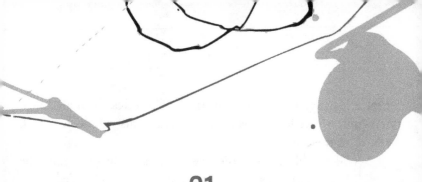

31

THE REPORT WILL WROTE FOR PRITCHETT did not mention the CIA or Dickie. In fact, on paper, Clyde Barnett had stolen the painting and hidden it in the bank safety deposit box, where Will recovered it. All still true. That was the same story he gave Charlie when he returned to the office.

"I still don't get it all," Charlie said, his feet propped on the desk. "You say they were Clyde Barnett's guys?"

"As far as I could tell."

Charlie grunted. "You don't want to tell me, that's fine. In fact, I'd rather not know. The last thing I need is those guys pursuing me. But they were professionals, and Clyde Barnett was no professional. And what about the microfiche?"

Will pulled on his cigarette and exhaled; the smoke floated across the long rays streaming in through the window. He had repainted the story for Charlie in wide brushstrokes and hoped that would be enough. "That's all there is."

"Jesus, Will. What about the phone records, the calls, Washington?"

"All dead ends. We wasted our time."

Charlie dropped his feet, a loud clap sounding when his heels hit the floor. "You're telling me." He made the comment like he did not want to bother with the suspicion any longer. Charlie was happy with a simple answer. "You know how much time I spent getting those records. I had to track them all down, remember?" He leaned back in his chair, arms behind his head, staring at the ceiling.

Will would miss Charlie. He would ask him to come if he could, but Charlie needed the sense of security. He needed the white picket fence in New Jersey, a two-car garage, and car tires filled with precisely the right amount of air. Charlie would not be able to handle the clandestine reality. He needed the stability, the safe story.

Will placed another book into his cardboard box and then gathered his manila folders. The art books needed to be packed separately because of their weight. He had collected more paperwork through the years than he had remembered. Some of the records were his dad's, but most of them were his by now, after ten years with All American. He would pack the important files and leave the rest behind. Seeing his hard work packed tight into a cardboard box somehow made it all seem less important, easy to discard. He knew the details of every case, and this one would be the hardest to pack away. The case had taken everything he had.

Before packing his typewriter, he sat down one last time at his desk and typed out the final page of his Pollock report. Then he stood and shook Charlie's hand.

He walked across the main room, and agents' heads turned as if they were tied to him by string. This time, Will read admiration and respect on their faces. He had fought back, and they knew it. He walked into Pritchett's office and slid the report across his desk.

"I just don't get it. It's not one I would have stolen," Pritchett said.

"No, I don't imagine so. The painting wouldn't have brought much on the black market."

"So why did the kid steal it?"

Will gave Pritchett the answer he had carefully constructed. This case was no different from any other, but this time Clyde couldn't figure out how to pawn the painting.

Pritchett shook his head and pulled out a photograph of the painting, turned it horizontal, then vertical, studying the image. "I don't understand this art. Never will." He flipped the photo into the folder and dropped it on his desk. "My wife hates it. My kid could do as good. But you've got Pollock on the cover of *Life*, and now MoMA is shipping them abroad. Rockefeller is hanging abstract expressionist paintings in every Chase Manhattan Bank." Pritchett threw up his hands. "Who the hell knows."

Will turned his head and gazed out the window, across to Trinity Church. He had grown to like the paintings, their rawness, their aggression, the action behind them. He understood them now. He understood that the paintings showed the pure act of painting, the creative work of the artists, their personalities splattered across the canvas. The paintings were about freedom, filled with spirit and character.

Will contemplated everything that had happened and smiled. He laughed to himself at the idea of the CIA, a clandestine government agency, acting as art critics. The galleries and art collectors drove the market, but Liz helped. She pushed what she believed to be American art to the world. How many more were involved? How many more CIA front foundations funded magazines, newspapers, and universities? And where did it stop? Or did it? What else were they manipulating? And if they were funding their psychological war today, why not tomorrow?

"I think you're right, Lou," Will said, standing. "We don't ever know. Nothing is as it seems, and I expect it never will be." He picked up his hat and headed for the door.

"Will," Pritchett said.

Will turned back. Pritchett's face was soft and fatherly.

"It's all cleared up, you know. The memo. The suspension. ALERT sent a retraction and is headed into a lawsuit for libel because of the damage they caused people. It's the beginning of the end, Will."

Will thought of the beady-eyed man tied up in lawsuits for the next several years, ruined. Will wished he'd seen his face when ALERT shut down, when he had to pack up the boxes, turn over any trial evidence.

"I hear McCarthy won't last much longer, either," Pritchett continued, "with his investigations into the secretary of the army. I hear he's losing support suspecting military leaders." Pritchett paused a minute then said, "What I'm saying is, you don't have to go."

"I know, Lou."

"You won't change your mind?"

"I need to do this."

Pritchett's gaze traveled past Will and toward the main room. "Your dad would be proud," he said softly.

The comment warmed Will, words his dad never got to say.

"I'm sorry he wasn't here when you returned from the war. But you've found peace, haven't you? He wanted you to be happy. That's all dads want."

"I will be, Lou. This is a good thing."

Pritchett eyed Will with a smirk. "Your own firm, huh? Fine Arts Recovery, is that it?"

Will stepped halfway through the door, then turned back. "I figure I can earn more off you this way. You can insure the paintings, and I'll charge you to find them."

Pritchett laughed as Will shut the door behind him. Will walked back through the main room, past the rows of under-writers filling out applications, and a feeling of weightlessness, of freedom, lifted him. Like the painters, he had made a choice. He was ready to set out on his own, and his spirits rose at the thought.

Will boarded the triple-tailed airplane, its streamlined silver body gleaming in the sunlight. Under the rhythmic sound of the four oversized propellers, the radio operator in the cockpit prepared for flight, calling out the checklist with the pilots. A young stewardess in a smart light-blue uniform greeted him with a smile and directed him down the aisle to his seat. She offered him a glass of champagne as he sat.

Will recollected everything that had happened over the last eight months, starting with the night he'd met Liz at Elaine's and how intently she discussed the paintings, how much she loved them. He knew now what was behind it all, behind everything. He had trusted her throughout and knew he could trust her forever. He eagerly awaited what lay ahead—an adventure—his life a blank canvas. The propellers roared as the plane accelerated down the runway. And as the view of Manhattan faded, Will looked toward Liz, who sat next to him. He slid his hand over hers, and her thin fingers intertwined with his. Her face radiated with the vivid colors he now saw each time he looked at her—the subtle hues of pink, white, and apricot, the myriad of blues in her eyes. He had found peace with Liz. Paris would be lovely together.

AFTERWORD

ON FEBRUARY 25, 1967, the *New York Times* exposed the Whitney Trust—a charity trust founded by Rockefeller appointee and chairman of MoMA's board of trustees, John "Jock" Whitney—as a CIA conduit.[1] The Whitney Trust is one of nearly one hundred and seventy foundations, including the Rockefeller Foundation and the Ford Foundation, through which the CIA filtered tens of millions of dollars to fund a cultural cold war.[2] They sought to influence the foreign intellectual community by releasing propaganda images of the United States as a free society in an effort to build a stronghold against growth of the Iron Curtain—Eisenhower's *psychological warfare.*

Through the intricate web of foundations, well-placed front men, and a front organization they called the Committee for Cultural Freedom, the CIA produced media and newspaper publications and sponsored numerous cultural events internationally, including international art exhibitions. Their aim was to educate, inspire, and promote American ideals.[2]

The CIA collaborated with MoMA on international art exhibitions first and foremost through Nelson Rockefeller, who was a former head of the government's wartime intelligence agency for

---

1   Eva Croft: "Abstract Expressionism, Weapon of the Cold War." In Francis Frascina ed., *Pollock and After: The Critical Debate* (Harper & Row 1985).

Latin America and acted as MoMA president during most of the 1940s and 1950s. Additionally, the CIA relied on strategic front men such as John "Jock" Whitney, a longtime friend of Nelson Rockefeller and former agent in the Office of Strategic Services (OSS, the predecessor to the CIA, which was not formed until 1947). Porter McCray, a former attaché in the US Foreign Service assigned to the cultural section of the Marshall Plan in Paris, was director of MoMA's circulating exhibitions. All of these men were in some way connected to fighting the CIA's covert cultural cold war.[2]

The CIA chose abstract expressionism and its artists— Jackson Pollock, Mark Rothko (both members of the Committee for Cultural Freedom), Willem de Kooning, Franz Kline, and Robert Motherwell—as their weapons. Their art represented what could be created in a free society. The movement was fresh, avant-garde, independent, creatively free, and, most importantly, nonpolitical—everything Moscow loved to hate. Abstract expressionism exemplified freedom of expression, spirit, character, and the true expression of national will.[2] And the artists who created it represented independence and freedom. They were rebels, cowboys, and Americans.

---

2   Saunders, Stonor. "The Cultural Cold War: The CIA and the World of Arts and Letters," the *New York Press*, 1999.

A NOTE ON THE ARTISTS

JACKSON POLLOCK'S PAINTING continued to deteriorate, as did his health. The four paintings he created in 1948 and 1949 were the pinnacle of his career and have held him in the status of an icon ever since. For the remainder of his career, he continually struggled with the public image of himself as the American hero and with the question of whether he was the greatest living painter in the United States. He largely alienated himself from the artistic community. In 1956, drunk behind the wheel of his car, he killed himself and a woman passenger. His 1948 *Number 17A* sold for $200 million in 2015, the fifth most expensive painting ever sold.[3]

Franz Kline continued to paint and achieve success, although he, too, drank himself to death by 1962, dying of a rheumatic heart condition. His 1957 untitled black-and-white painting sold for $40.4 million in 2012.[3]

Willem de Kooning arguably reached his prime in 1956, but he continued to live and paint until 1997. Over the next several decades he was regularly hospitalized due to complications from drinking and died an alcoholic with dementia. His 1953 *Woman III* sold for $137.5 million in 2006. His 1955 *Interchange* sold for $300 million in 2015, the second most expensive painting ever sold.[3]

Abstract expressionism, as part of the art historical narrative, largely ended by 1957.

---

3   As of December 2021.

AUTHOR'S NOTES

ON OCCASION, a reader may wonder what of this story is true. Although loosely inspired by the 1967 *New York Times* article and Frances Stonor Saunders' book *The Cultural Cold War: The CIA and the World of Arts and Letters*, this story is entirely fictitious. Several historical figures interact with fictional characters in the novel including Jackson Pollock, Willem de Kooning, Franz Kline, Nelson Rockefeller, Porter McCray, John "Jock" Whitney, and Congressman George Dondero; and, while my research formed the basis of their character and actions, their involvement in the story is a complete fabrication. This woven canvass of fact and fiction continues throughout the novel.

However, while the storyline and dialogue between well-known actual people were imagined, like all historical novelists, I tried to depict the world in which the story takes place with as much likeness and accuracy as I could, layering in strands of "historical truth" while still taking certain liberties to create a lively fiction.

First and foremost, I attempted to render the biographies and personalities of the artists, their art, and the art history to the best of my ability, particularly Jackson Pollock, Willem de Kooning, and Franz Kline. The Stable Gallery existed and was established in 1953 by Eleanor Ward, deriving its name from its first home, a former livery stable on Seventh Avenue at West 58th Street. The gallery focused primarily on modern and avant-garde art, particularly the abstract expressionists. Eleanor Ward held annual exhibitions of painting and sculpture; the 1st annual was held in 1953. Participating artists included Philip Guston, Hans Hoffman, Franz Kline, Willem de Kooning, Elaine de Kooning, Joan Mitchell, Robert Motherwell, Roy Newell, Robert Rauschenberg, and Jack Tworkov, among sixty-four others. Jackson Pollock did not show in the 1st Annual. The Club and Cedar bar both existed in close proximity to each other on Eighth and University and were important seedbeds of the Abstract Expressionist movement. Jackson Pollock did kick the payphone. While de Kooning's exhibition of his Woman series launched in 1953, the series first showed at the Sidney Janis gallery in March rather than the late summer as presented in the novel. And, he did not complete the paintings in his rented Hampton house. The MoMA exhibit "Twelve Modern American Painters and Sculptors" occurred, circulated to six countries in Europe (April 1953 to March 1954), and was primarily funded by a 1952 five-year grant from the Rockefeller Brothers Fund. There was no preview for the MoMA exhibit at the Stable Gallery. And, obviously, Elizabeth Bower and the Bower Foundation are complete fabrications with no involvement in the MoMA exhibit.

The painter Andrei Roschin and his HUAC trial are entirely fictitious yet modeled after a similar muralist painter and his mural *The History of California*, located in the Rincon Center Post Office in downtown San Francisco, California, which was the subject of a 1953 congressional hearing by the House Committee on Public Works chaired by Congressman George Dondero.

Congressman George Dondero was a Republican member of the U.S. House of Representatives from Michigan who did mount an attack on modern art. In 1949 and again in 1952, he delivered a now-famous speech in which he denounces the Artists Equity Association and American Artists' Congress as Communist fronts, museums as Soviet pawns broadcasting the Russian propaganda, and the art of the 'isms' as the weapon of the Russian Revolution—Cubism, Futurism, Dadaism, Expressionism, Abstractionism, and Surrealism. The Scientific And Cultural Conference For World Peace event did occur, was held at the Waldorf-Astoria for three days in March 1949, and was the subject of great political concern and protest.

And lastly, although the organization ALERT did not exist, it was modeled after similar organizations, such as the private interest group AWARE, which created blacklists for employers and 'special reports' like *Red Channels* listing names of purported communists. The libel lawsuit John Henry Faulk v. Aware, Inc., et al, which began in 1957 and concluded in 1962, resulted in a verdict that put an end to institutional blacklisting by private groups and individuals who claimed to be experts on Communism; and put an end to the organization itself.

To render this world, several books and articles were indispensable, as well as the obvious effort spent in libraries and on internet research. For the 1950s and McCarthyism, I am indebted to Ellen Schrecker's *Many Are the Crimes, McCarthyism in America*; and to the *Fifties* by David Halberstam. For the world of art, I leaned on several authors and their books including Irving Sandler's *The Triumph of American Painting*; to Steven Naifeh and Gregory White Smith's *Jackson Pollock: An American Saga*;

to Mark Stevens and Annalyn Swan's *de Kooning: An American Master*; and to *An Emotional Memoir of Franz Kline* by Fielding Dawson. The following essays were also helpful: Eva Cockroft's essay "Abstract Expressionism, Weapon of the Cold War" in Frances Frascina ed., *Pollock and After. The Critical Debate*, "The Suppression of Art in the McCarthy Decade" by William Hauptman; "American Painting During the Cold War" by Max Kozloff; "Art and Politics in Cold War America" by Jane De Hart Mathews; "The Philosophy and Politics of Abstract Expressionism 1940 – 1960" by Nancy Jachec with Cambridge University, and the "Review of the Scientific And Cultural Conference For World Peace" arranged by the National Council of the Arts, Sciences, and Professions.

ABOUT THE AUTHOR

JEFF LANIER earned bachelor's degrees in History and Art History at The University of Texas, Austin, with a focus on the History of American Culture through Art and Literature. He has a master's from Rice University, is a member of the American Society of Aesthetics, and currently lives in Houston with his wife and three kids.

To contact Jeff, download his book club kit, or view his media kit, use the QR code here or visit https://www.jeffdlanier.com/contact

Ira   investigate   ALERT / Anti-
                               Communist
                               GMEN

Will   Main character   Insurance / invest

9 781633 376106